The Voice on the Phone
Had Been Urgent

Come quickly, it said. *Your mother is dying.* But when I got to the hospital she was sleeping peacefully, her condition unchanged.

Numbly, I agreed that the nurses ought to report the prank call to the police.

They left me alone in the room.

It took me a slow-witted minute to comprehend that being alone was probably not a very smart idea, not smart at all. A thrill of fear propelled me quickly toward the comfort and safety of the hallway.

As I passed the closed door of the private bath in my mother's room, it opened quietly, swiftly.

"Shut the door," a voice said, "and turn off the lights."

A small handgun was pointed in the direction of my mother's head. I did as I was told. . . .

———

Books by Nancy Pickard

Bum Steer
Dead Crazy
Marriage Is Murder
No Body
Say No to Murder

Published by POCKET BOOKS

GENEROUS DEATH

Nancy Pickard

POCKET BOOKS

New York   London   Toronto   Sydney   Tokyo   Singapore

This book is a work of fiction. Names, characters, places and incidents are either the product of the author's imagination or are used fictitiously. Any resemblance to actual events or locales or persons, living or dead, is entirely coincidental.

The author sincerely hopes the Testered Bed With Alcove in the superlative Oriental Collection at the Nelson-Atkins Museum of Art in Kansas City, Missouri will never have to endure the rigors to which its fictional counterpart is put in this novel. On the other hand, who knows what mysteries it hides from centuries past . . . ?

POCKET BOOKS, a division of Simon & Schuster Inc.
1230 Avenue of the Americas, New York, NY 10020

Copyright © 1984 by Nancy Pickard
Cover art copyright © 1987 Richard Bober

Published by arrangement with the author
Library of Congress Catalog Card Number: 83-91197

ISBN: 0-671-70268-8

First Pocket Books printing December 1987

10 9 8 7 6 5 4 3

POCKET and colophon are registered trademarks of
Simon & Schuster Inc.

Printed in the U.S.A.

To Alice,
WHO TOLD ME SO.

Prologue

The Martha Paul Frederick Museum of Fine Art is housed in a, well, house. There's really no way around that bald and, to some locals, mortifying fact. You may call the house quaint and charming, or you may call it ugly and drafty, depending on your grasp of reality and your affection for truth. But adjectives, even when carefully chosen by our Chamber of Commerce, will never disguise the basic, humble nature of the Martha Paul Frederick Museum of Fine Art. It is no grand, granite edifice built by kings to honor avarice and art.

It's just a house—a rambling, crumbling four-story monster of a mansion of brick and wood, built in 1768 to shelter the piratical ambitions of the Paul family, those infamous builders of ships for smugglers and slavers. For the last thirty-five years, it has served as our municipal museum, the gift to the city from said Martha Paul, that legendary benefactress to the

1

arts—or, rather, art. With her death and no more Pauls to leave her fortune to, childless Martha managed in one fell swoop to buy her family's way back into respectability. Unfortunately, when she bequeathed all that money for the purchase of art, she also demanded that it be forever displayed in her home. So we've been stuck with it until time and nature tear it down. (The Town Council staged a successful and ironic fight a few years ago to keep the house from being included in the National Register of Historic Buildings. They knew if it ever got on *that* list, we'd *never* be able to get rid of it!)

Now it's all very well to point to other "museum houses," like the Phillips in Washington, D.C., and then demand to know what it is we're complaining about—as though to say that if a house is good enough for the Phillips, it should be good enough for little old Port Frederick, Massachusetts. But in so doing, the critic fails to consider that Washington has one or two other cultural landmarks to which it can point with chauvinistic pride. *They* can afford a little cold, drafty charm. In this town, however, the Martha Paul is all we've got. Culturally speaking—and not many of us do that very often—that's it. Philharmonics have we none, nor ballets do we see outside of touring companies; and the local Women's Theatre Guild for Tiny Tots has been, until recently, the closest we've come to repertory.

In other words, all our cultural marbles are rolling around the cavernous, dank hallways of Martha Paul's ancestral home. But what marbles! What astoundingly exquisite works of art we've cornered up here in Poor Fred, sufficient to inspire pilgrimages to these hinterlands by culture mavens from all over the world. "My God," they groan when they get their first glimpse of the building; and "my *God,*" they whisper when they see what's inside.

You might say the excellence of the art collection at the Martha Paul has been both our blessing and our curse: blessing because any museum would feel blessed to claim these masterworks as its own; curse because the collection is so good we've all become slaves to it. With few other outlets for cultural good works, the town pours most of its time, money, enthusiasm and volunteer efforts into our one claim to worldwide fame.

Port Frederick is definitely a one-horse town. But that one horse (though stabled in a miserable barn) is a thoroughbred Triple Crown winner if there ever was one.

All this is by way of explaining why Mrs. Francie Daniel, an otherwise intelligent woman, was spending Tuesday morning, February 12, conducting grade school children on a tour of the Martha Paul.

Chapter 1

Francie knew it was going to be a bad day as soon as she saw the skinny wrist. The little hand attached to it was just reaching out to stick used bubble gum inside the rim of the seventh-century Tang dynasty jar when Francie grabbed it in the nick of time. At the same instant, she spied the cherubic blond twins bringing up the rear of the grade school art procession.

"Girls!" she called out with a practiced blend of sugar and steel, "don't kick the legs of the tables, please. They've already survived five hundred years; I don't think we need to test their endurance further."

Francie cast an admonishing glare at the accompanying fourth grade teacher from the Greaves Country Day School. The teacher, a good twenty years younger than Francie, managed somehow always to be looking the other way.

One of the fourth graders flicked a dirty fingernail

against a priceless ivory Buddhist sculpture. He seemed pleased with the resulting soft thud.

At that point, Francie decided this was going to be one of those tours for which she'd better walk backward all the way if she wanted the revered Oriental galleries to resemble anything other than the path of a peculiarly sticky tornado.

"Children! Please don't pull the loose threads out of the silk wall hangings!"

Few of the grade school classes Francie guided through the museum were like this one. Most were sufficiently intimidated to be pleasingly docile. But now and then in her ten years as a volunteer docent at the museum, Francie encountered a classful of Holy Terrors. She remembered with horror one class in particular that she had shuffled through the Native American Wing (converted servants' quarters). Three years after the fact, the curator of Native American art still had not forgiven her for the missing eagle feathers in the eight-foot Sioux headdress.

Francie had a sinking feeling that this day's fourth grade class was going to be a legendary Holy Terror, perhaps even one that docents in years to come would speak of in hushed, almost reverent tones.

Backward, she rounded the corner of one gallery of Oriental treasures and led the way toward another. Her gum sole shoes—worn for comfort, not beauty—trod silently, but the old hardwood floors creaked and moaned piteously as if begging people to stop walking on them. Francie's eyes swept the children like those of a soldier searching for land mines. The analogy was not altogether farfetched.

"Now children," she announced in her best clear,

pleasant docent voice, "we are entering the gallery of Chinese furniture . . ."

"I wanna sit down," whined a little girl—a bad omen considering the tour had started only five minutes earlier. They didn't usually begin to droop until the tour reached the collection of Early American cooking utensils. Francie always considered that room one of the challenges of the tour since she not only had to revive small and weary spirits, but also somehow had to find a way to describe pots and pans without talking about food. At that point, the children were hungry and thirsty as well as pooped.

"You'll get a chance to sit on the floor in a moment," Francie said brightly, and prayed for the well-being of the exquisite, sturdily constructed but admittedly ancient chairs in the Chinese furniture collection.

She backed through the doorway.

The guard, knowing how to interpret the fearsome signal of a docent striding backward, stiffened into wary, watchful life. Despite his advanced years and creaky joints, he was fast enough to catch the class track and field star in mid-leap as she tried to hurdle the two-foot-high sculpted lions that graced the entrance to the gallery. Her tennis shoe nicked the edge of the porcelain and set it wobbling for a breathtaking moment. The lion and the old guard's heart settled back into place in the same instant.

"Most of the beautiful furniture in this room has been given to the museum in recent years by one of our great philanthropists," Francie was saying, while she stared in hypnotized horror at the offending tennis shoe. She jerked her eyes away but didn't blink. She was afraid to blink. Centuries could fall in ruin before a determined fourth grade class in the wink of an errant eye. She inquired doggedly, with no great hope, "Do any of you know what a philanthropist is?"

A fat little boy took his finger out of his nose, where he had been keeping it warm on this cold day. He paused in his business long enough to say, "It's somebody who gives things away to other people."

Francie said later that that was when she felt the first tickle of sheer terror tease her stomach. If there is anything more frightening than a classful of little monsters, it is a classful of intelligent ones.

"Yeah, so they can get a tax deduction." This from a budding CPA.

Francie remembered stroking the arm of a Pin-Yang chair and feeling as one with its fragile vulnerability. "I was," she said later, "only a middle-aged woman alone against the gathering storm." She and the old guard eyed each other like the officers in *Hamlet* having seen the Ghost. Horatio, she thought wildly, you tremble and look pale.

"Good now, sit down," she said aloud, unconsciously further quoting the Bard. "Sit around me in a half circle on the floor and I'll tell you about this magnificent Chinese bed behind me."

Giggles from the children.

"Well," she told us later, *"that* I was used to. Giggles I could handle." So she relaxed a bit, tucked a loose end of her blouse into her skirt and began her spiel about the most important, verily almost sacred, object in the Chinese collection.

"This is a Testered Bed With an Alcove," she told them, "and a very rare sight to see . . ."

More giggles and some pointing.

". . . the word *tester* refers to the canopy, or roof,

7

that shelters the bed and the alcove. If you had been born into a wealthy Chinese family many years ago, you could have entertained a friend in the alcove, or curled up for a little nap on the bed . . ."

Downright peals of laughter, and even the teacher was smiling.

". . . It's a beautiful piece of furniture, isn't it? And it looks comfortable, too, don't you agree?"

Absolute hysteria. Tears running down chubby little cheeks.

"Children, please!" Francie felt insulted and torn. Insulted because the bed was her favorite piece in the whole museum; she'd never heard anyone, not even previous Holy Terrors, actually laugh at it. And torn because she was afraid to turn around and see what could possibly be so funny. She wished the guard would look her way, but he was practically deaf and blind, and anyway, he was still busily shaking an arthritic finger at the erstwhile hurdler.

She frowned and raised her voice over the hilarity.

"This wonderful bed comes to us through the generosity of Mr. Arnold P. Culverson, one of our major benefactors. He has provided the funds to purchase most of the important pieces in our Chinese collection. But this is his favorite gift, as it is mine. In fact, Mr. Arnold Culverson loves this bed so much that he often stops by the museum just to see it." Francie smiled in prelude to Arnie Culverson's favorite jest. "He says he wishes he could bring over a pillow and sleep here!"

Pandemonium. Little fists pounding the floor, small bodies rolling about in helpless fits of giggles.

Francie could stand it no longer.

She turned to look at the Testered Bed With an Alcove.

It was occupied.

"Mr. Culverson!" Francie cried, and began to laugh too. She hadn't thought the famous philanthropist had a reputation as a practical joker, but one never knew.

Francie walked to the bed and stepped carefully up onto the lovely wood floor of the alcove so she could peer down at Arnold Culverson on the bed. He really did look quite funny lying there with his eyes closed and his mouth curved in a sweet little smile. A soft pillow cradled his bald head; a baby blue comforter, pulled up under his double chins, furthered the comical effect.

"Okay, Mr. Culverson," Francie said, good-humoredly going along with the rather eccentric joke. "It's time to get up now!"

She reached forward to give the old man a gentle shake, causing the children to scream with delight again. Her hand brushed the soft bluish skin of Mr. Culverson's face. It was deadly cold.

In the moment she stood there, frozen over the body in the ancient bed, Francie felt as if she had reached, horribly, through the present into a dead past. Her left hand reached out to grasp one of the wooden supports of the bed; her right hand rested heavily on its knuckles on the modern blue comforter. Steadied thus between two times and cultures, Francie Daniel smelled death.

Somehow, she managed to raise herself to a standing position again. She turned around and calmly smiled down at the children.

9

"Okay, kids." Her voice did not tremble. "Mr. Culverson says he wants to sleep a little longer." She paused for squeals and giggles. "So let's tiptoe out of here and go into the next gallery."

Caught up in what they perceived as fun and mischief, the Holy Terrors obeyed. When they were safely ensconced in the Persian Gallery, Francie abandoned them—for once in her career as a docent heedless of any harm they might wreak—and stumbled frantically down the long dim corridors to the office of the museum director.

It was a long time afterward before Francie could admit that she was rather grateful to Mr. Arnold P. Culverson for having brought an abrupt and early halt to the fearsome and rampaging march of the Greaves fourth graders.

Chapter 2

Arnie Culverson's death—and the peculiar manner of its discovery—caused quite a stir in our offices. For one thing, the coroner called it suicide and no one had expected that of Arnie. His body was loaded with a lethal combination of liquor and the pills he took for hypertension and migraines. It might have been an accidental overdose but for the rather eccentric fact of his having crawled up on that beloved bed to die. Two pill bottles were found on him—one of them empty, the other nearly so. There was absolutely no sign of foul play. Neither was there a suicide note, but we all expected one to show up.

His death also stirred the waters because he was one of the few truly wealthy people in town. And like many of that elite group, he filtered his philanthropy through our foundation. I say *our* not because any of the money is mine, but because I administer the

11

disposition of the millions of dollars of revenue it generates.

Everybody calls it The Foundation as if there were no other. In truth, of course, there are thousands of charitable foundations scattered across the country. But there's only one whose sole function is "to protect and promote the well-being; the cultural, spiritual and mental development and the superior achievement of all kinds of the citizens of Port Frederick, Massachusetts." That pretty well covers the waterfront, I'd say, which is exactly what the founders wanted. "If we state the objectives of The Foundation in bland and general terms, we can do whatever we damn well please with the money," they might also have said, and probably did behind closed doors.

Officially, legally, it's the Port Frederick, Massachusetts, Civic Foundation. It was established in 1968 by a family who, to paraphrase the rhyme about the old lady in the shoe, had so much money they didn't know what to do. So, having done well, they did good. Still more to their credit, they encouraged their rich friends to bequeath all or part of their estates to The Foundation, thus compounding not only its net worth and yearly income but also its potential for charitable grants.

Before Arnie Culverson died, the assets of The Foundation had a current market value of $12 million. That sounds like a lot of money, I know, but the $12 million itself wasn't ours to spend. That was the principal; we could only spend the income it generated from interest, dividends and rents.

Because of a sluggish economy, that yearly income had been declining every year for several years. And thanks to inflation, the money we earned didn't buy nearly as much as it used to. We could no longer support the town's charities in the style they deserved. And we weren't the sort of town to ask for more government help than necessary.

So we needed more private money for The Foundation—a lot of it, soon.

When I heard about Arnie's death, I knew The Foundation's net worth would jump to about $20 million because he was leaving all his money to us. Bless his heart. Under the terms of his bequest, most of the money would be channeled through The Foundation to the Martha Paul; the rest we could spread around to other charities that desperately needed help.

Arnie's money meant a lot more than nice little improvements to nice little do-gooders. To the museum and to some other nonprofit organizations, it meant survival.

But Arnold P. Culverson was not only a very rich man, he was also a nice old guy of whom I was quite fond. So I attended the visitation at the funeral home the night after he died as a friend as well as the representative of the beneficiary. It helped me feel less like a vulture hovering over the spoils, though I was sure I wasn't going to look less like one to Arnie's relatives. The truth is that The Foundation was getting all his money not only because he loved the town, but also because he hated his relatives. They, in turn, hated The Foundation, and I wasn't all too sure how they felt about me, its executive director. If I hadn't really liked Arnie, I don't think I would have gone.

That night as I crunched over the snow and gravel

in the parking lot at the Harbor Lights Funeral Home (an unfortunate name for a mortuary, if you consider the popular old song, "I see the harbor lights, they only tell me that you're leaving . . ."), I was thinking fondly of Arnie's shiny bald head. I'm fairly tall for a woman and Arnie kept getting shorter as he got older. He liked to ask me if I could see my reflection in his pate. "Your boyfriends only brush their hair so they'll look nice for you," he'd tease with that gentle smile that barely raised the corners of his wide mouth. "But me, I get a wax and polish. Did I miss any places, Jenny? Do you see any dull spots?"

There weren't any dull spots in Arnie's whole being. He vibrated with good humor and life. He never walked but always raced about with short little steps that made it appear as if his knees were perpetually bent and his feet in constant motion. "Aren't I a paradox?" he mused one time when we were discussing what The Foundation would do with the funds he was leaving us. "Here I am, this hyperactive old fart who can't sit still, and yet I have a passion for Chinese furniture. Me, I like something that represents all that is cool and calm and meditative! Can you beat human nature, Jenny?"

No, I couldn't beat it, but I was going to miss his highly individualistic and lovably human nature. I walked slowly up the wide stone steps to the front door of the funeral home, stamping snow off my boots as I went.

"Hi, Jenny." It was Stan Pittman, the son of the owner of Harbor Lights. He stood just inside the door to welcome visitors and help them with their coats and galoshes. "Coming to the Culverson visitation?"

he asked me, a little shyly, and I felt sorry for him. Stan's not really cut out for the funeral business, but that's just going to be his tough luck, I suppose, since he's the only heir to seven generations of undertakers. Like most New England towns, this one is lousy with descendants of "fine old" families. Most of them, however, have inherited only their distinguished names, and that won't pay the rent.

"Hello, Stanley." I patted down the collar of my acceptably conservative camel's hair coat. Like a banker or a funeral director, I have to dress to fit other people's image of my role. Given my druthers, I'd trade in all the beige and gray for red and purple. "Which room is it?"

"The Chapel of Quiet Blessings," he said and blushed furiously, as would I if I had to say things like that. He stuck out a friendly but awkward hand. I think we were both surprised to discover that the cold fingers I placed in his palm were trembling. He was too well trained and basically sweet to comment, but I'm sure he noticed the tears that had sprung to my eyes.

I wasn't crying over Stan's inherited problems. I was sentimentally hoping that in the years to come I would spend Arnie Culverson's money well, in ways that would have pleased and amused him when he was alive.

"Damn it," I said to Stan, making him acutely uncomfortable. "Why did he have to go and commit suicide? It makes me feel so sad, as if I didn't really know him at all."

"I know what you mean," said a whispery male voice behind me. It was Edwin Ottilini, senior surviving partner of Owens, Owens & Ottilini, and attorney to anybody who was anybody in Port Frederick. He reached out to help me with my coat. For a crazy moment, I thought he and Stan were going to fight for it; I felt like the rope in a tug-of-war.

"Thank you, gentlemen." I stepped safely away from them during an instant when they paused to regroup their combative forces. Quickly, defensively, I slipped out of my trusty camel's hair and draped it over my arm. Even then, a spirit of competitiveness reigned, as both men grabbed for it.

Stan, obviously desperate to maintain his firm's reputation for gracious hospitality, finally won the battle with a decisive jerk that tested the fabric and my shoulder socket.

"Sorry, Jenny," he said miserably, and trotted away with his prize to hang it up for me.

Edwin Ottilini, that ancient and tough old lawyer, winked at me and allowed as how there might be something to be said for women's liberation. We walked together toward the Chapel of Quiet Blessings.

"Are you going to open the door for me?" I asked him. He threw me a sharp, curious look.

"Of course. It's reflexive with my generation, like going to war and saving money. Why?"

"Because if you are, let's get it over with before Stan gets back and the two of you kill me with more courtesy."

He laughed quietly, appreciatively. Everything about him was quiet, from the dry, wry humor to the gray pinstripes on the fine black suits he habitually wore. He was a modulated man; if there was any Italian fire left in his thin blood, it did not often flame in public. His power, too, was quiet. Like many great

16

lawyers, he gave the impression of knowing everything, telling nothing.

Edwin Ottilini was, of course, Arnie's attorney.

We paused before the closed double doors of the Chapel of Q.B. He didn't say why he suddenly seemed loath to enter it, but I knew why I was. I didn't want to face that comforting room with its cheerful lamps shining in the gray, drained, made-up face of death. I didn't feel like smiling and being tactful; rather, I felt an atavistic urge to keen.

"I liked him, Mr. Ottilini."

"I liked him, too, Miss Cain."

"I suppose everybody's saying it, but I really *can't* believe he killed himself. I know his heart was bad; I know his doctors didn't give him long. But suicide? Arnie never took the easy way out of anything!"

"Maybe for him this was not the easy way."

"I suppose. But think of all his plans for the museum and The Foundation . . ."

The old lawyer cleared his throat.

"Mr. Ottilini," I said, "before we go in there, I want to ask you something." His silence was full of waiting. "Have you set the date for the reading of the will? I'll want to put it on my calendar."

He gazed at me for a long, steady and rather unfathomable moment. I thought, as I often do in my frequent dealings with lawyers, how cautious they are in all things.

"Miss Cain, there is no need for a representative of The Foundation to attend the reading of the will."

"It's no bother."

"You misunderstand, my dear," he said patiently. "There is, I'm afraid, a new will of which you are evidently not cognizant. Under the terms of this latest document, it is Mr. Culverson's daughter who will receive the entire bequest. There will be nothing for The Foundation."

"What!" He must have considered it a rhetorical question, because he didn't volunteer further information.

It was just as well that he opened the door for me. I no longer had the strength to open it for myself.

Chapter 3

Once within, Mr. Ottilini favored me with an inscrutable if rather sad smile and glided silently off across the plush carpet to greet the other mourners. The Chapel of Q.B.—which was really just a big sitting room—looked like a convention of his clients and my potential donors. The rich and powerful of Port Frederick always turn out in force to pay last respects to one of their own. Arnie lay—still for once—in an open and opulent casket at the far end of the room. I said a silent hello to him but didn't—couldn't—move that way yet.

I stood by the door, weak kneed and wishing I could fade into the tasteful floral wallpaper while I digested the horrid implications of the lawyer's bombshell. Instead, I was faced immediately with the two people I least wanted to see at that moment.

"Mother, it's Jennifer Cain." The forty-two-year-old son that Arnie called "that worthless-good-for-nothing" turned his mean little smile on me. It was hard to imagine short, squat Arnie as his father, but the resemblance to his elegantly thin mother was unmistakable, right down to their matching smiles. My assistant director claimed they could pass for brother and sister—with the face (and other) lifts that makes Mrs. Culverson look so much younger and with the general air of dissipation that makes Franklin look so much older, they meet in the middle somewhere around fifty-three.

"Ah, Jennifer, dear, so nice of you to come to the visitation," cooed Marvalene Culverson. "Could it be that you were truly fond of Arnold? Or maybe you don't know about the new will?"

Having already been struck dumb by Mr. Ottilini, I just looked at her. There's really no answer to that kind of nastiness anyway, except perhaps "up yours," and my position does not permit me such gratifying liberties.

"I think she knows, Mother. That's why she looks so pale and wan. Feeling pale and wan, Jenny? Really, I wouldn't if I were you; it *doesn't* go well with your makeup."

I gathered what little was left of my wits.

"I liked your father very much, Franklin. I'm sorry he's dead."

"Oh, so are we, dear." Mrs. Culverson reached out a sleek claw to pat my arm. "Particularly since he chose such an embarrassing way to do the deed. We're just awfully sorry he's dead. At least while he was alive we had *some* access to his money. You know, of course, who he left it to?"

"Your daughter, I understand."

"Then you understand more than I do." With which cryptic and angry remark she turned her back on me and stomped off to charm her other guests, leaving me alone with Franklin. Marvalene has family money of her own on which I knew she could probably support herself, Franklin and one or two top-name designers. My heart did not bleed for her.

"My sister's here," Franklin informed me. I couldn't tell if his cold tone was intended for her or me. Not even bothering with the pretense of courtesy, he pointed a long finger at a woman about my age seated near the open casket. Even though Ginger Culverson's head was lowered so I couldn't see her face, it was obvious that she'd been the child who had inherited Arnie's genes. I'd never seen her before. She'd been sent to boarding schools as a child and later she dropped out of Radcliffe to join a Marxist commune someplace in Idaho. Arnie rarely mentioned her, and then only with bitterness. He called her "the kid who ran away from everything."

But I was beginning to see that beneath that parental anger had been undying love. Or why else would he so impulsively have left all his money to her? It *was* impulsive, wasn't it? Surely he didn't string us along, knowing all the while he would leave it to her? I couldn't believe I was *that* wrong about him.

"I'd like to meet her."

"Really? My, you are the polite one, Jenny. But then I suppose you have to think of the future of The Foundation, don't you? Maybe if you insinuate yourself with her, my sister will leave you everything my father didn't." He glanced with malicious pleasure from my aghast expression to his sister's downcast head. "I don't know though, she looks goddamn

21

healthy to me. You may have to wait a while for her to kick off. We'll *all* have to wait a while longer, I fear."

He swiveled his thin face back to me.

"You think I'm despicable, don't you, darling, now tell the truth." He was playing the brittle sophisticate to a degree that set my teeth on edge. But Franklin didn't anger or shock me as his mother did; he only filled me with pity. I've known him all my life; there's a lot about Franklin to feel sorry for.

"My opinion of you is no lower than your opinion of yourself," I said.

He gave me a furious, terrified look before he quickly controlled his expression.

"I believe we've come to what is known as a conversational lull," he said stiffly. "I suppose it was nice of you to come," he added by way of farewell as he glided off after his mother.

I swallowed the bad taste left in my mouth by my own self-righteousness. Franklin might well be a mess, but who was I to tell him so?

My scowl lifted at the welcome sight of an approaching friend.

"Hi, Swede," said Michael Laurence, using the obvious nickname based on my ancestry and appearance. Sometimes he called me Sweedy—but only in private, thank God. He stood in front of me and said, "This may be a stupid question, considering the circumstances, but why the long face?"

We kissed, circumspectly.

"I was thinking about power, Michael."

"Its uses or abuses?"

"The way it abuses the person who holds it, if you let it. It seduces you into thinking you have the right—even the duty—to pronounce judgment on everything and everybody." His eyes said he was seriously listening, a great compliment from a man to a woman. Those eyes are so incongruous—sympathetic puppy dog brown irises set in that patrician face. My secretary says those eyes confuse her; she doesn't know whether to curtsey to Michael or to scratch behind his ears. I said, "Michael, do you think I'm smug or bossy?"

"No. I think you're relatively young to wield the power you do and you're not completely comfortable with it yet."

I must have grimaced.

"Don't grimace like that," he laughed. "You know you wield power in this town. With all that money at your disposal through The Foundation of course you do, everybody knows you do."

"Um," I said, meaning to be wry, "you may have noticed how many more friends I have since I took the job."

"Oh come on, Jen. That goes with the territory and you know it. Of course people cozy up to you! If The Foundation can do them some good, they'd be crazy not to. You may call it cynical, but I call it human nature and I don't see anything so terrible about it. You'd do the same if you were they, and so would I."

"You'd never use anybody, Michael."

"Oh, Swede." The gentle eyes were sad and serious. "I don't know where you got this notion of my sainthood, but I wish you'd drop it. I'm just an ordinary man who happens to be in love with an extraordinary woman."

"You only love me for my power," I teased, trying to keep the mood light and the topic away from that familiar, painful one.

"No." As usual, when it came to talking about his feelings for me, he refused to play games. "I love you because you're the smartest, nicest woman I know. Also the sexiest."

"Oh, Michael."

"Oh, Michael." Even his mocking was gentle. "Why don't you ever say, Oh Michael, yes I'll marry you. I'll throw away Port Frederick and The Foundation and run away to your little château in the Loire."

"I hate it when you make fun of yourself."

"Ah! You admit I have a fault! Well, that's progress, I guess." There was self-pity in his voice, an unattractive tone I'd only recently begun to hear. We'd dated off and on for a couple of years, always on my terms. Except for a briefly sexy interlude near the beginning, those terms had never got beyond the fondly platonic. The problem was not that I thought of him as saintly, but that he seemed more like a brother than a lover— and therefore untouchable. Still, he persevered with good humor and patience. My secretary thought I was crazy not to love him; she thought he was crazy to keep loving me.

"You favor the underdog, don't you, Jenny?" he said. "Well, has it ever occurred to you that I'm the underdog in the fight for your affection?"

He tried to make a joke of it, but the joke didn't come off. He only managed to sound melodramatic. I felt embarrassed for him, and uncomfortable. I hoped no one could hear us.

"*Look* at me, Jen! Just once, I wish you'd see the man I am instead of your sainted image of me!"

When he was done emoting, he looked as surprised as I. Suddenly, his grin was self-effacing, and real.

"Tune in tomorrow," he said, making me laugh.

"Will Jennifer love Michael? Will Michael make an ass of himself? Will Jennifer still go out with Michael on Friday night?"

"Of course." It had been a long day and I was suddenly exhausted. "You know, maybe I'm not so smart after all. And maybe I'm not such a great judge of character." I decided to share with him the news about the will. "I sure missed the boat with Arnie . . ."

But I never got to finish the thought.

We were abruptly interrupted by a small, noisy, elderly mob. Three of my favorite Foundation clients had converged upon us.

"Hello, children!" chirped Minnie "HaHa" Mimbs.

Hands were shaken, cheeks were kissed and greetings were exchanged all around. With Minnie were her old pals, Moshe Cohen and Mrs. Charles Withers Hatch. Not one of the three was younger than eighty and none of them stood any higher than Michael's shoulder or my chin.

The blue-gray of Minnie's hair perfectly matched the blue-gray of her Chanel suit, which I personally knew to have been designed by Coco herself—*many* years ago. Seeing her thus, I knew Minnie had dressed conservatively in deference to the solemnity of the occasion. Minnie likes to dye her hair to match her clothes, and since her favorite colors are orange and green, she looks pretty wonderful sometimes. She can get away with it, of course; the old can do as they damn well please if they have the money. Minnie had it in spades and real estate, and what she damn well pleased to do with it was give it away. I knew that when she died she'd be leaving half a million to her

Episcopal church and another half to The Foundation, mainly for the benefit of the Martha Paul.

She smiled gaily at us.

"Isn't this nice?" she said. "Arnie would be so pleased to see everybody here, give or take a wife, perhaps. I do just adore weddings and funerals."

"And christenings!" This from Mrs. Charles Withers Hatch, who was of the old school and always used her husband's name. Mrs. Hatch always told me that if I were a "good girl" she'd leave "a little something" to The Foundation, though I knew her first love was the Welcome Home for Girls. I had to promise, she said, to put the money to "good Christian use." Being of a handy ecumenical bent, I could easily agree to the terms. Just as I could agree to promise Moshe Cohen that most of the money *he* gave to The Foundation would be channeled to the Jewish causes he so passionately supported. He was also the financial force behind our sparkling new civic theater, due to open Friday night.

Moshe made himself known from beside Michael's left shoulder, or rather, below his shoulder. "Veddings, christenings," he said disdainfully to the ladies. "Give me a good bar mitzvah any time!" He'd never worked up the nerve for the big trip to Israel, so at eighty-two years of age, he had settled for an ersatz Yiddish accent. It drove his old friends crazy.

"What do you know from bar mitzvah, you old fool?" demanded Minnie. She and Moshe had dated back in the '20's and she felt she had a proprietary right to treat him with affectionate contempt. "You haven't seen the inside of a synagogue since the Six Day War."

"So maybe I pray at home and vear a skullcap to

26

bed, so how should you know about Jewish?" He winked at Michael and me. "They try to convert me, these two. For more years than I care to tell you, they try. They think maybe I should lead the local Jews for Jesus? I tell them, I say, Minnie HaHa and Mrs. Charles Vithers Hatch, vonce a Jew, always a Jew."

"Oy vey," said the very Protestant Mrs. Hatch. "Take us home, please, Moshe."

"Goodbye, children," chirped Minnie, with a wave of both of her gloved hands. "You look lovely, my dears."

And so, without Michael or me having contributed more than "hello" to their slightly hysterical conversation, off they went in search of Moshe's chauffeur.

Michael and I grinned at each other.

"Do you want to go to the cocktail party at the club before the opening?" he asked, speaking of the gala premiere of Moshe's new theater.

"Not particularly. You go without me if you want to, all right?"

"I think I will. Then I'll drive by and pick you up on the way to the theater."

"Fine, I'll see you Friday night then. Right now, I think I'd better go introduce myself to Arnie's daughter."

"I met her a few minutes ago."

"And?"

"She likes me."

I laughed—absently, probably—and turned toward the end of the room I'd been avoiding. There they waited: Arnie and the daughter for whom he had betrayed his promises to The Foundation and the Martha Paul.

As I worked my way along the edge of the quiet

27

crowd, I purposely avoided the eager glances that Simon Church directed my way. Simon, the director of the museum, would want to discuss Arnie's plans for the Chinese galleries. I couldn't bear to tell him there weren't going to *be* any plans.

Ginger Culverson glanced up when I offered my name to her. She looked as if it had rung a bell whose tune she couldn't quite recall.

"Who are you?" she said, but it wasn't rude, not like the same question would have sounded coming from her mother or brother, who would have italicized the *are*.

"I was a friend of your father's." The going was awkward from there. "I'm the director of The Port Frederick Civic Foundation, which is involved in some charitable activities that your dad was interested in. He and I worked together on some, uh, projects," I finished lamely. Did she know that her inheritance had scuttled those "projects" supposedly so dear to her daddy's heart?

The intelligent eyes she had inherited from him lit up her sad round face.

"Oh yes, The Foundation. Jennifer Cain. Yes, I've heard a lot about you." And then she giggled. The laughter escaped from her mouth like a burp and she put up a hand to cover it. But it was too late. Behind her hand, the wide mouth like her father's curled up in the familiar and sweet little smile.

I grinned back at her.

"I'll bet you have." I made a quick decision. "You wouldn't want to go get a drink with me, would you? Or a cup of coffee? It's been a long day and I don't know about you, but I've had it."

She gathered her purse and used tissues and stood.

The top of her head came just to the bottom of my nose, as her father's had.

"Let's get the hell out of Dodge," she said.

We settled into a cozy table at the Buoy and wrapped our hands around toasty glasses of hot buttered rum. As usual, the ancient bar was packed with a mixed crowd. In the darkest corner were the local fishermen, drinking late because the weather was too foul for work. Upright and chic at the long bar were the urban mariners in their immaculate pea coats and pipes, hustling the women who hustled them. I waved to a few local shopkeepers and smiled encouragingly at the few tourists who were bold enough to brave our February.

Like an English pub, the Buoy is everybody's favorite haunt, young and old, and has been for more than a century. The latest generation of owners stood behind the bar, mixing drinks and jokes and goodwill, just as their great-great-great-grandparents had.

Ginger had remembered the Buoy from her childhood and requested it. I was glad to oblige.

"I should have known I'd like you," she said and smiled, "just from all the nasty things my family had to say about you and that Foundation. I do remember that much about them—they're perfect judges of character in reverse."

"I didn't think I'd like you either."

"Because of how my father described me? I was the ungrateful brat, right? The kid who had everything and threw it all away."

"Is it true? Were you?"

"Sure. There was much to be ungrateful for and a lot of baggage to throw away. But I'll tell you some-

29

thing, Jenny, I'm a pack rat. I'd never throw away anything that was worth a damn."

Including your father? I didn't voice the question, but it hung in the air between us.

"My father . . ." The brown eyes like his did not fill with tears or regret. "My father just didn't have time to raise millions and kids, too."

"Evidently he loved you."

"Love or remorse, it looks that way, doesn't it? I'm told he was a lovable man, but I don't remember that quality about him. Actually, I don't remember much about him at all. He only seemed very important. Busy. Stern."

I could understand how he might have appeared thus to a child. His world revolved around profits and losses, taxes and capital gains. They taught his language at Pennsylvania where I got my M.B.A., but not at nursery school.

I ventured the hesitant opinion that she might have grown to like him once she became an adult.

"You think so? Have you ever known a child who forgave his parents for failing him? Children are an unforgiving lot, I think. I know I am." She said it with cold finality. "And no amount of money will change that. You probably won't believe this, but I don't even want it."

I didn't believe it. But I could see that Arnie's final "buy" was a loser. He wasn't going to get back a return of love on his investment of $8 million. I had a mean, irreverent moment of thinking how much he could have bought with that money if he'd left his original will alone: fabulous, rare pieces for the Chinese galleries; funds to exhibit and maintain them forever; an assistant museum director to relieve

Simon Church of too much responsibility; and more. Only a few of us knew just how much more had been promised under the old and now useless will.

I looked at Ginger Culverson and realized how incredibly rich she was very shortly going to be.

"Ginger," I said impulsively, "how do you feel about ancient Chinese furniture?"

She looked bewildered for a moment. Then the light dawned and she began to laugh that rich, infectious laugh of her father's.

"Oh, Jenny," she said, and finally there were tears, but tears of sympathetic laughter. "Oh God, Jenny, I'm just sorry as hell."

I was laughing too by that time. And damn near crying.

Chapter 4

I broke the news to my staff the next morning, the day of Arnie's funeral. They were not stoic.

"Arnie did *what?*" said Marv Lastelic, the controller.

"How could he promise us everything and give us nothing?" cried Faye Basil, my secretary.

"Well, I'll be damned," said Derek Jones, my assistant director. "What a lowdown miserable thing to do."

I let them get it out of their systems. After all, they'd been working hard on Arnie's plans; he'd led them down the same fantastical garden path that had ended in a brick wall for me. They were disappointed, flabbergasted, angry. It was important for them to say so, and to me.

"Didn't you have a clue?" they finally asked suspiciously.

"No." I threw it back at them. "Did you?"

They admitted to complete surprise.

"Although," Derek mused, "he was sure acting funny the last couple of days. Maybe he had a guilty conscience, huh? Maybe he didn't have the courage to give us the bad news."

"Well, you'd have thought he'd at least leave us a note!" Faye said indignantly. "Suicides are supposed to leave notes, for heaven's sake."

"My gosh, all those financial statements and meetings and . . ." Marvin was pale at the memory of the hours he'd devoted to Arnie's army of lawyers and accountants. "Jenny, do you realize what this does to our projections? Do you know what it will do to the museum budget? Do you realize how it will affect our net worth and earnings?"

"I know." Dear God, how well I knew.

"So when are you going to break the news to the trustees?" Derek murmured, going straight to the most intimidating point of all. "And *how?*"

"Today," I said weakly. "I've called an emergency meeting for lunch." But I didn't have an answer to Derek's second question. I didn't know how I would tell the five trustees of The Foundation that the $8 million feast over which they'd been licking their lips had just been cooked and served to another customer.

"Well." Derek gazed appraisingly at my conservative gray business suit. "I suggest a change of clothing for that meeting. Sackcloth and ashes."

My meeting an hour later at the museum with Simon Church was even worse than my staff meeting. I walked into his closet of an office unannounced.

33

He looked up impatiently from his overflowing desk, but his harried frown turned to leering welcome.

"Jenny, Jenny, Jenny!"

Simon puts the lie to the stereotype of the effete artist: He looks like a lumberjack, with the ribald personality of a truck driver.

"Jenny, my love," he said, "if I could get you alone in the European painting collection, I'd show you an Old Master! How are you this gorgeous morning, my darling? Come to sit on Simon's lap and tease him with visions of new galleries of Chinese furniture? My God, Jenny, I did like the old fart, but if he had to go, wasn't it nice of him to leave it all to us?"

I looked at him and felt rotten.

"Jenny?" He misunderstood my serious silence. "Oh shit, I'm sorry. I'm so damned tactless."

"We're not getting the money, Simon."

Sudden silence.

"Excuse me, Jenny. I thought you just said we're not getting the money."

"We're not. He changed his mind. I don't know when or why. There's a new will and we're not in it. He left all his money to his daughter."

"Did you say there's a new will that bequeaths all the money to his daughter?"

"That's what I said."

"You don't mean *all* of it."

"Yes, I do."

Simon rose and turned slowly away from me. His massive shoulders blocked the light from the small, single window. The cubicle was instantly dark and uncomfortable.

"I didn't know, Simon."

No answer.

"Please, Simon, I feel as terrible about this as you do."

No answer.

I left him staring at the death of his grandest dreams.

But the worst was yet to come—in the persons of five men, pillars of what passes for an establishment in Port Frederick, staunch defenders of the faith of capitalism, cautious and cagey doers of good.

They were my bosses, the trustees of The Foundation, appointed for life to oversee the accrual, investment and expenditure of the funds.

And they were waiting for me, twiddling their salad forks and swirling their martinis, at the Bosun Club downtown. After lunch, we'd all be adjourning to the Harbor Lights Funeral Home for one last meeting with Arnie.

From the tight smiles on their faces when they looked up to greet me, I guessed that Edwin Ottilini had already passed the bad word to his fellow trustees. He was one of the five.

"Good morning, Jennifer," said Jack Fenton, the seventy-seven-year-old chairman of the board of First City Bank. "Well, here we are in plenary session."

"I've saved you a chair by me." This command from Pete Falwell, retired president of Port Frederick Fisheries, the town's major employer.

"Good morning," I said in my most confident director's voice. Dealing with them on anywhere near an equal basis requires a bit of bluff at the best of times; this lunch was going to win me an Oscar. I took hold of the conversational lead before they could wrest it from me.

35

"It looks as if you already know about the Culverson bequest," I began cautiously, with a glance at Edwin Ottilini.

"*What* Culverson bequest?" Roy Leland, the rotund chairman emeritus of United Grocers, closed in quickly. "One day we've got $8 million, the next day we've got nothing."

Jack Fenton snorted. "Let that be a lesson to us," he said. "Never count your inheritances until they're hatched."

"Well, how did we screw up?" Roy demanded. He's stubborn and arrogant, but those qualities are mitigated by the good common sense that helped him rise from fish skinner to company president. "Did we offend the old buzzard? Did we make him mad at us? Disappoint him somehow? What the hell happened is what I want to know." He and Arnie were good friends; I sensed Roy was feeling personally betrayed.

"I'm not convinced we did anything wrong," I said. "It's just possible he had a simple change of heart."

"I think that's it," Pete Falwell said. "People do, you know, when mortality starts closing in. Why, my father didn't speak to his brothers for thirty-seven years and then on the day he died he insisted we call every one of 'em up so he could make amends."

"But we didn't have a clue," Roy insisted. "You'd of thought he'd of told somebody." That was a broad hint for Mr. Ottilini, whom they all knew to have been Arnie's attorney. He took it.

"He told me," he said and five faces, one of them mine, turned to stare accusingly at him. A wisp of a smile creased his wrinkles. "He called me the week before he died and told me what he planned to do about the will. And yes, it was a change of heart, simple as that. He loved his daughter very much when she was a child; lately, he said, he'd begun to feel an overwhelming guilt for having neglected her and possibly driven her away."

"You knew a whole week ago?" Roy expressed my own vexation. "And you didn't tell Jennifer or any of us?"

"Of course not," the lawyer said primly. "He was my client and he asked me not to. He very definitely said he would tell you himself. He meant to do so quite soon. He understood that anything less would be quite unfair."

"Well, why didn't he?" Roy again. Sometimes it's nice to have a buzzsaw in a group, to hack through the niceties to the brutal truth.

"He was having a hard time working up the courage." That wisp of a smile appeared again. "You know, he stopped by my office that last day to pick up his copy of the new will. He confessed then that he still hadn't found the nerve to tell Jennifer or Simon, or any of you, for that matter. He was quite in a dither."

"Well, I should hope," Jack said indignantly, but we were all relaxing a little now that some of it was beginning to make sense. Then he looked shocked. "You don't think, do you, that he killed himself just to get out of telling us?"

"Don't be ridiculous," Roy said, and that settled that.

"Why *did* he commit suicide, Mr. Ottilini?" I said. "And why didn't he leave us a note?"

But this time the wise old eyes held no smile or

wisdom for me. "I do not know," he said tiredly. "I simply do not know."

A few minutes of unhappy silence passed while we considered that mystery and the waitress delivered our salads.

"If it's any comfort," Mr. Ottilini said when the waitress was gone, "Arnie's plan was to work with us to see if he couldn't help us come up with alternate financing for the museum."

"Big of him," Roy said, but I thought he was somewhat mollified. His old friend had not totally let him down.

"Well, that's all very nice," Jack Fenton said, a shade irritably, "but that doesn't help much now, does it? I swear, if he weren't already dead, I could happily kill the son of a bitch, excuse me, Jenny."

I swallowed my smile. They're not quite used to equal opportunity employment. Sometimes they treat me like their generation's idea of a lady; sometimes I'm one of the boys. I don't care. I give them credit for hiring me at all.

I decided it was time to earn my keep.

"Jack's right," I said. "The point is, he did it. And now we have to pick up the pieces. I have already told Simon Church . . ."

"Oh lordy," Pete murmured.

". . . and this morning I put my staff to work on contingency plans and financial projections. In the meantime, you might wish to consider what this means, in the long and short run, for The Foundation and for the Martha Paul . . ."

Finally we heard from the fifth and youngest member of the board of trustees. As befits the lowest in seniority among such a group of powerhouses, he'd been thoughtfully quiet up to that point. But now he spoke up clearly.

"That's easy, Jenny," said my friend Michael Laurence, fifth generation president of the Laurence Construction Company. His spaniel eyes expressed sympathy and worry. "It means disaster."

Chapter 5

You were a big help," I said to Michael when he arrived the next night to take me to the theater opening. He was late. "The word *disaster* is one I could have lived without, thank you very much."

"You look gorgeous in that whateveritis color."

"Peach."

"Soft and fuzzy. Like that whatchamacallit material."

"Cashmere."

"Umm." He grinned goofily at me; I could smell a Scotch hint of the cocktail party. "You look so cuddly. The hell with the theater. Let's just stand here and nuzzle all night." He shook his head so drops of melting snow flew off his hair, completely my secretary's image of him as a soulful puppy. Puppy was sloshed.

"Don't come near me," I said irritably. "You're cold and wet and you've had too much to drink and

I'm ready to go and I can't stand people who arrive late at the theater."

That focused him.

"All in all," he said, enunciating carefully, "you're not very pleased with me."

And then, oddly enough, he smiled.

I slipped on my camel's hair and a peach beret to match my dress and then turned off the lights in the hallway of my parents' home. Or, rather, make that singular possessive, parent's—since it was Mother who got it in the divorce. I'd been living there by myself in the years since I'd moved back to Port Frederick. Keeping it clean and warm for Mom, you might say, until they let her out of the hospital.

Michael and I paced carefully down the front walk that I had not shoveled. I didn't take the elbow he offered; if I'm going to slip and fall I don't want to take anybody else down with me. Besides, I just feel more secure standing alone on my own two feet, which is an obvious metaphor for my whole personality.

"I said, Jennifer, that you're not happy with me." He was walking even more carefully than I.

"Sorry, I can't talk and walk on ice at the same time. I'll drive," I said firmly. I slid onto the cold leather seat of his Jaguar and waited for him to climb into the passenger's side. Damn it, I didn't want to drive.

"I *hate* to drive on ice," I said and started the engine.

"I'm sorry," he mumbled, but he didn't look very contrite.

I mercilessly ground the gears.

That got him.

"I'm *sorry*," he said clearly. I backed out of the drive. "Don't be so mad at me, Swede. I don't do this very often, you know."

"I know." I slid the gears smoothly from reverse to first and pulled into the street. My anger disappeared, but a knot of tension at the back of my neck did not. "Anyway, you only told the truth. It is a disaster, unless we contest the will and get some of the money back."

"Nasty proposition."

"Yes, it is." I thought of Ginger Culverson who had claimed she did not want the inheritance. Well, there was nothing like a contested will to test brave statements like that. But we had to do it; for the sake of the Martha Paul, we had to go after the money we had thought would be ours. Arnie had led us to count on that money for all sorts of things this town needed badly—including a brand new Martha Paul Frederick Museum of Fine Art. With his bequest, we'd finally have the money we needed to wage a court fight to break the original terms of Martha Paul's will. If we could convince the court that the priceless works of art were in physical danger in that old house, we could get a judgment permitting us to tear it down and build a new museum. Arnie's bequest was to have been the seed money for that grand construction project, too.

Disaster?

That's exactly what loomed if we didn't rescue those works of art from that collapsible stick house. One more hurricane, one good fire, and down she would tumble—and millions of dollars' worth of irreplaceable and beloved treasures with her.

The world would never forgive us.

It gave us nightmares thinking about the potential for loss; it had Simon Church reaching for the Maalox every hour on the hour.

We *had* to contest the will. We owed it to Rembrandt and van Gogh, to Caravaggio and Rodin and to all the other artists whose masterpieces were endangered by that cold, damp, rotting mansion.

"I don't want to talk about it anymore," I said irrationally. "Let's talk about something else. You, for instance. Why'd you get loaded tonight? I'm not mad, just curious."

"In two words, my father."

"Ah, the light dawns."

"But not the one at the end of the tunnel," he said. He slouched further into his coat and the bucket seat. "My father, according to reputable sources, is supposed to be retired. Now you tell me: If he's retired, how come he flies in from Tucson every couple of weeks to tell me how I'm going to be the first of five generations to run the company into bankruptcy? Retired, my foot."

"What does your mother say?"

"My mother is tired, Jenny. She's worn out from mediating between her son and her husband. So she doesn't want to hear about it anymore. Talk to your father, she says, and please don't upset him as you always do. Mother, I say, you know me fairly well—am I an unreasonable guy? A stupid jerk? A stubborn SOB? I don't wish to hear it, she says, and don't malign your father, he's worked hard all his life and now he wants some rest. No he doesn't, I tell her, but gently; he doesn't want to rest at all and that's the problem. He can't let go of the business, but I can't run it and cope with his interference, too. I'm not twenty years old, I say; I've been in this business all *my* life, too. He's got to trust me or *some*body, *some*time. Or else let go. Or else come back, take it over again and let me go my own way. And my mother says, I'm tired, Michael, let's have a drink, how's that nice Jenny Cain?"

"Poor Michael," I lifted a gloved hand off the gearshift knob and patted his knee.

"Damn right."

I applied the brakes, cautiously, to avoid a skidding van in front of us. When I could take my eyes off the road for a second, I glanced at him. In the pale light from the dash, his well-bred features were drawn; the gentle eyes were surrounded by shadows and fine lines, more deeply etched than I had ever noticed before. My heart, such as it was, went out to this kind man whose love I could not seem to return. "If you'd marry me, I wouldn't just be getting a beautiful woman," he had once teased. "I'd be getting an M.B.A. from the Wharton School of Finance. Why together we could wrest the Laurence Construction Company from the snapping jaws of my creditors."

The Jag straightened itself out of a skid. Trust, I decided then and there, is a man allowing a woman to drive his beloved and costly sports car on icy roads. Marriages have survived on less faith than that.

"I'm thinking of selling my house, Jen, and moving into a smaller place."

"Oh dear, surely it can't be that bad, not yet . . ."

"It is. According to dear old Dad, of course, it's all my fault. It seems to have escaped his notice that when I took over, housing starts were at an all-time low, mortgages were impossible to get, nobody was building or buying, and labor and material costs were sky-high, which they still are, I might add. *He* ran the company during the boom years. Hell, you had to be an idiot *not* to get rich then. But since then, a man's had to be a genius just to keep from going bust."

On that happy note we pulled up to the circle drive of the freshly built, gaily lighted Moshe Cohen Theater for the Dramatic Arts.

"Where is everybody?" Michael said.

I could hardly believe there were no crowds at the entrance. A few patrons seemed to be coming out, not going in. The lone car in the drive was Moshe's silver stretch limo, with no chauffeur in sight. I checked the clock on the dash.

"Oh, Michael, we *have* missed the curtain. Damn it! I guess that accounts for it; everybody's inside."

But still, something felt wrong. I had one of those absurd moments of paranoia that everyone gets at one time or another before a big party.

"This *is* the right night, isn't it?" I said.

"Of course it is, look at the marquee."

I looked.

"Port Frederick Premiere!" it bragged. *"Fiddler on the Roof,* Starring . . ." And it named the famous Broadway actor for whom Moshe had paid a king's ransom for this first proud week. Of course it would be *Fiddler*. Opening night had been sold out for weeks. Moshe's premiere was to be a grand social event, the only one Poor Fred had seen in some time. It was not, as they said in the beauty shops, to be missed.

"So where is everybody?" I demanded. A funny

feeling in my stomach told me something had gone awry, but oh, I hoped not. For Moshe's sake, I hoped not.

I drove slowly around the building and into the parking lot on the west side.

"There's your crowd," Michael said quietly. And soberly.

An eerie scene lay before us, as on an outdoor stage. Small clumps of people stood about in their overcoats like bit actors in a crowd scene; the principals moved with sure and purposeful strides across the icy pavement like stars who know their lines, having practiced this same scene many times before. Over it all was cast a luminous red glow—a reflection in the snow of the swirling lights of the police cars that had gathered at the side door.

With my heart in my mouth, I parked and we climbed out. Distraught voices carried to us over the crisp air. "It's not fair!" we heard a woman wail. "It's not fair!"

It was Francie Daniel and just as we recognized her, she spotted us.

"Jennifer!"

Her voice had a desperate edge that unnerved me. Quickly, I trotted to her side. I didn't know Francie all that well because she's of my mother's generation, but she's one of the few who'd stuck by Mom all those years. I was fond of her, and grateful. When I reached her side, she clung to my right arm with both of her hands.

"Moshe's dead," she said to my horror. "It's not fair! It's not fair!"

"We rode over with Moshe from the cocktail

party," Francie's husband said. Stanley Daniel's face, like his wife's, was pale with shock and his eyes were red-rimmed. Michael placed a comforting hand on his shoulder and I wrapped an arm around Francie.

"Moshe?" I said weakly. Neither Michael nor I seemed able to find our voices; they were lost in a fog of shock and dismay. But I remember thinking, Not Moshe, not dear funny Moshe . . .

Stanley was explaining to the police.

"He had too much to drink at the pre-party, Moshe did, and we noticed he was a little wobbly. And we wanted to make sure he'd be okay, so we rode over here with him."

"Jenny," Francie whispered, "he was almost passed out when we got here, but he *wouldn't* let us take him home. He just *insisted* on going in . . ."

"So we sat him down in one of the seats in the theater," Stanley continued, "and Francie went to call his doctor because we were really worried about him and I went for a glass of water for him . . ."

"And when we got back to him, he was—oh, Jennifer, he was . . ."

Dead.

It wasn't fair. Not fair for Moshe Cohen to have died on the biggest night of his life. Not fair for poor Francie to come upon the death of a friend twice in one week.

They thought he'd had a heart attack. So did the stagehands who came running to help. So did the director and the great actor from Broadway. And so, when they accompanied the ambulance just to be helpful on this night of bad traffic and slick streets, did the police. Until, that is, they went through the pockets of Moshe's tuxedo and found the odd little poem.

It had a nasty anonymous tone to it, just like the poem found earlier that day in a crack of the Testered Bed With an Alcove at the Martha Paul Frederick Museum of Fine Art.

Chapter 6

They were mean, smirking lines of doggerel. I didn't see them until later, of course, since they were evidence the police did not choose to share with us the night Moshe died.

In fact, I didn't know of their existence until the next morning when two policemen stopped by the office. Derek and I were there alone, sharing coffee and memories of Moshe. It being Saturday, I'd allowed myself the informality of wearing jeans and a red sweater that prompted Derek to recommend a bodyguard; he would, he said, be glad to volunteer for the job. There was a time, when I first hired him, that Derek made it plain he'd like to see me as more than a boss. I made it equally clear that I might sometimes mix business with pleasure, but not with my employees. He might have been a pleasure, too. Though younger and shorter than I, he's an appealing imp with his curly blond hair and elfin smile. He's also a smart, ambitious man and, as he loves to point out, one sexy little devil. Being nobody's fool, however, he proceeded to maintain a respectful if amused distance. The Foundation could only afford to pay him a fraction of his worth; I knew he would move on when he got a better offer. Meanwhile, I appreciated and trusted him.

I was more surprised than he when the two visitors in overcoats and business suits presented their badges to us.

"Geof Bushfield?" I hesitated before I held out my hand to the tall cop I thought I recognized. If he was who I thought he was, I wasn't sure I was glad to see him again.

"Hello, Jenny." He returned my handshake with a firm grip and a lopsided grin. "You look surprised to see me."

"Well, I am," I said, taken aback. Then I realized how rude that might sound, so I added quickly, "I mean, it's been years and years—since high school, I guess."

"Is that it?" Now his grin seemed to mock me a little and himself a lot. "Is that why you're so surprised to see me? And here I thought maybe it was because I'm the last person on this earth you ever thought would turn out to be a cop."

His younger partner looked startled. Derek looked intrigued.

"Well . . ." I shrugged. "You said it, not I."

"Thought I'd be on the other side of the bars, didn't you?" He removed his overcoat—I wondered how he could afford a Burberry—slung it over the back of a chair and sat down. He grinned. It was an incredibly infectious grin, impossible not to return. He waved his partner to a chair. "I know you'll feel safer now, Jenny, knowing that little Geoffrey Bushfield is the guardian of your public streets and morality."

"Have a seat," I said, "won't you?"

"Thank you," he said, straight-faced. "These days, I know that only means sit down. It doesn't mean I should take a chair home with me."

"Good," I said, equally poker-faced. "We can't afford to buy new chairs." Then I couldn't stand it anymore. "My God, Geof, you're a cop!"

"Yes, ma'am." He smiled. His voice had the slow, calm drawl of somebody who takes his own sweet time. It matched the sense of, not arrogance exactly, but confidence that he exuded and which seemed to emanate from some core of him. "And you, Jenny—it looks to me as if you're still the girl most likely to succeed. I'm glad to see you doing so well, although everybody always knew you would."

I felt oddly flustered. Irrelevantly, I thought of a poster I'd seen: "I know I'm efficient," it said, "tell me I'm beautiful."

"Thank you." I fiddled with the papers on my desk, then made my hands lie flat and still on the arms of my chair. I looked across my desk at him. The Geof Bushfield I remembered from high school was a wickedly good-looking kid who was, however, a shade too wild and rebellious to be popular, even for those loose days when we were growing up. I was a freshman when he was a senior, and, like most of the girls, I'd been a little scared and scornful of "that crazy Bushfield." He'd been a misfit who ran with a tight, defensive crowd of other kids who didn't quite fit in. Now I saw that in the thousand years since then, he'd grown up to be not only tall and a cop, but also a disturbingly attractive man with the lean look that spoke of good health and the outdoors and—though surely it couldn't be—character. It was extremely irritating to discover that little Geoffrey Bushfield still made me nervous.

"Why are you here?" I said.

The cool, intelligent eyes registered my every nervous twitch, but didn't seem to be laughing at me.

"You wouldn't have some more of that coffee, would you?" he said casually. While Derek played Stepin Fetchit, we belatedly made introductions all around. The other cop's name was Ailey Mason; I got the impression he was only tagging along to see how the big boys did things. He was young—maybe twenty-three—but he looked impressed with himself anyway. He moved stiffly, as if he couldn't unbend. He seemed to approve when Geoffrey the Cop finally got down to business with Jennifer the Executive Director.

"Jenny," Geof began, "I understand that Arnold Culverson was here the day he died . . ."

"Oh dear." I interrupted him. "Are you trying to find out why he killed himself? I'd like to know the answer to that myself."

I should have noticed that he ignored my question.

"How'd he seem to you?" Geof sounded only mildly curious. "Worried about anything? Frightened?"

I thought *frightened* was an odd word to use.

"I don't know about frightened," I said doubtfully. "Unless maybe of dying in general. Of course you know he suffered from high blood pressure and terrible migraine headaches. I think both his father and one of his grandfathers were killed by strokes, and Arnie was convinced that's the way he'd go, too." I turned to Derek. "But do you think he was worried about anything else in particular?"

"Well, he'd been acting funny all week," Derek said. "You know. We'd start to talk about the museum and he'd jump like a pogo stick."

"Because of the new will," I said. "We know that now."

"Yes," Geof said easily. I lifted inquisitive eyebrows at him. He explained that they'd just come from a thorough explanation at Edwin Ottilini's home.

"What were his plans for the rest of the day?" Mason demanded, managing to sound as pompous as he looked, which was no mean feat.

"Oh . . ." I glanced at my assistant again. "Well, I think he said he was going by Mr. Ottilini's office and, I don't know, I suppose to the museum?"

"Yeah," Derek agreed, "and he usually ate dinner at the club."

"Why?" Geof's question came quick and sharp enough to nudge a vague suspicion in my mind.

This time, Derek looked to me to supply the answer to the delicate question.

"Arnie didn't get along with his family," I said in as matter-of-fact a voice as possible. I saw no reason not to be straightforward. "He always said he'd rather eat alone than face Marvalene's . . . uh . . ."

"Marvalene's what?" Again, the fast, sharp follow through.

". . . poison," I finished weakly, feeling miserable for having to say it, but not quite sure *why* I felt so bad. I added quickly, "She's a lousy cook, I hear, but fancies herself a gourmet, so she won't hire anybody else to fix the meals." For some reason, I didn't want to divulge another of Arnie's favorite jests—the one about how it was a good thing he wasn't leaving Marvalene any money, because she'd probably poison him to get it. They had led separate lives, but had never divorced. "Bad habits are the hardest to break," was how Arnie explained it.

Then, oh so casually, Geof tossed the next unnerving query at me.

"I wonder," he said, "if Culverson got along with other people better than he did with his family. Would you know if he had any enemies?"

"Enemies?" Derek repeated the melodramatic word as if it were some astonishing and distasteful object he had picked up by accident. My formless suspicions began to roll themselves into a definite and malevolent shape.

"Why?" It was my turn for the hard fast ball.

Geof parried my thrust by the simple expedient of ignoring it. He said, "Were you surprised that he changed his mind about the will?"

"No," I snapped. I was tired of dropping live questions into dead space. "I was not surprised. I was dumbfounded, stunned, stupefied. The word *surprised* does not even begin to express my feelings."

"And resentful?" That from Mason.

"What?" I resented his unfriendly attitude, that's for sure.

"Did you resent his leaving his money to someone else?" Mason said.

"Well, in the first place, he wasn't leaving it to *me*," I said with exaggerated and, I hoped, insulting patience. "He was leaving it to The Foundation. But yes, of course, I felt some resentment. He promised the moon and we got eclipsed."

Geof's mouth twitched.

"We?" Mason again. He seemed to have a talent for picking up on all the irrelevant points. "You're taking this very personally, *Ms.* Cain."

If he thought he could irritate me with the exaggerated emphasis on Ms., he was wrong; it's what I prefer to be called. My marital status is nobody's business. What he did manage to do was amuse me.

I smiled openly at him and just shook my head.

"How about you, Mr. Jones?" Mason turned his impassive face toward Derek. "Were you pretty disappointed when you heard you weren't going to get the money?"

"*I* was never going to get the money," Derek said. His voice sounded amused, but his blue eyes glinted cold and angry. I wondered how long Geof would wait before he called off his idiot. "I think Jennifer has made it very clear that it was The Foundation that was promised the money. We were, naturally, ticked off to discover that all our work was wasted. But I think you can safely assume that neither Jennifer nor I nor any member of her staff had the slightest intention of going out and buying a new car with the money. Or fur coats. Or houses. Or tickets to Rio."

Mason forced a smile out of a face that wasn't used to the exercise. He said, infuriatingly, "Why are you so angry, Mr. Jones? I didn't imply . . ."

"Yes," I said, "you did."

Geof finally broke up the tension with his even, pleasant voice. He said, "Why do you suppose Culverson changed his mind? About the will, I mean?"

"Beats the hell out of me," I said. "And it also beats

the hell out of me why you're asking these questions but won't answer any of ours."

"I'm sorry, Jenny." He was as calm as ever. "Tell me your question again."

I went straight to the heart of my fear.

"Arnie was my friend," I said, enunciating every syllable to be sure he got the message. "And the two of you are scaring me very badly. What are you getting at? Did he commit suicide or did he not?"

"No," Geof said, "it doesn't look that way."

"Well, how does it look?"

"It looks like murder."

In the suddenly silent room, Geof reached into a pocket and pulled out two scraps of paper. He handed them to me. His eyes were full of searching and purpose.

"Look at these, Jenny," he said, "and tell me if you've ever seen them before."

They were about the size of postcards and they'd been neatly cut from a heavy weight of good bond typing paper. I read the first one twice. Each time the pounding of my heart got a little louder in my ears. It said:

> Now I lay me down to sleep,
> Devil take my soul to keep;
> Cross my heart and hope to die,
> If I tell another lie.

The second piece of doggerel took my breath away because of the unexpected evil it implied:

> If all the world's a stage,
> My script is at the final page;

This play is done because . . .
Shylock's dead. Applause.

"Moshe," I said, heartsick. Geof nodded. I passed
the rhymes to Derek. "I've never seen them before.
Do you mind telling us where you found them?"

"A maintenance man at the museum found the first
one yesterday. He was dusting the bed where Culverson's body was found. That poem was stuck down in
one of the cracks. The janitor took it to Simon Church
and Church called us."

Derek had read the ditties by that time.

"And the second one?" he asked quietly.

"In the pocket of Moshe Cohen's tuxedo," Geof
said. He added, "He died of a combination of wine
and hypertension medicine, like Culverson."

"But Moshe didn't have high blood pressure," I
said. "Did he?"

"No. And elderly people are known to react badly
even to standard doses of that medicine, if they're not
used to it. Alcohol increases the effects. It slows down
the heart, leads to stupor, coma . . ."

"Death," Derek said.

"But *rhymes?*" I could hardly believe the absurdity
of it; the classic, sinister, silly absurdity of it. "It
seems so ridiculous, so egotistical . . ."

"So obvious," Geof said, and those cool eyes
looked into my frightened ones. "Somebody definitely
wants us to know the two men were murdered."

The four of us sat silently for a long moment. We
sipped our coffee. We each looked speculatively at the
other three.

Chapter 7

After Geof and his partner left, Derek and I faced the fact that we weren't going to be able to concentrate on corporate bonds and market shares. So we locked up and waved each other off to our respective homes. It was a crisp, sunny day, which showed a definite lapse of good taste on God's part, I thought. A barometer reading of my mood would have indicated gray, wet and ugly.

At home, my answer phone greeted me with messages to call Ginger Culverson, Michael, Edwin Ottilini and my sister. There were also three hang-ups and a giggling teenager telling me that if I had Prince Albert in the can I'd better let him out. I decided to allow myself to procrastinate for once and return the most difficult call last.

First:

"Hi, Ginger, it's Jenny Cain."

"Jenny. Hi. Have you heard what the police are saying about my father's death?"

"Yes. I'm sorry."

"Strangely enough, so am I. But that's not really what I called to talk to you about. I wanted to tell you how much I appreciated your company the other night . . ."

"Me too yours."

"Interesting sentence structure. And I want to know if you can arrange for me to meet Simon Church . . ."

Oh golly, I thought.

". . . because I want to tell him personally how sorry I am about how the museum got screwed by my father . . ."

Oh yes, I thought.

". . . and, well, Jenny, I don't want to raise anybody's hopes, but I would like to at least *hear* about my father's plans. I mean, maybe *I* can help . . ."

Yes, please, I thought.

". . . if I get interested, that is. I mean, please don't say anything to Mr. Church that would even hint what I'm considering. I'd hate to bounce him back to earth again."

Oh you nice lady, I thought.

"How about Sunday brunch at the club?" I said.

"I'd love it."

"Great. I'll fix it up with Simon. And Ginger—I think your father would be very grateful."

"For whatever that's worth."

"See you tomorrow. I'll pick you up at your mother's house at eleven-thirty."

One call down, four to go.

I got a reluctant Simon to agree to brunch. He said he'd had enough of the Culversons to last him a lifetime; and why should the police grill *him* about the night Arnie died when it was *Ginger* who got the money?

Then I called Michael at the Laurence Construction Company general office.

"Michael. 'Tis I."

"Well, that's at least one good thing in this rotten, miserable day."

"Your father's at the office."

"You got it in one. Are you driving up to see your mother tomorrow?"

"Yes, in the afternoon." As usual. As always.

"May I drive with you? I need to get out of town for a few hours. And I'd like to see you."

"Oh Michael, I'm sorry, but I don't think so."

Silence.

"Michael? Please understand. You know these aren't pleasure drives for me. I wouldn't be good company."

"You don't want to have to deal with her problems and mine too."

I hated to hear him say it, but I couldn't deny it. Maybe love can be measured by how much of the other person's misery you're willing to share. Fair-weather friends need not apply. I was beginning to see that I was just that sort of friend to Michael. I cared about him, certainly; but I didn't love him enough to take him, misery and all.

"I'm sorry," I said again.

"Don't you ever get tired of saying that to me?"

I didn't like this new, self-pitying Michael very well.

As I hung up, I realized that I preferred the "saint" who persevered, smiling, through all my rejections of him. It wasn't fair of me, of course, but there it was.

"Good morning, Mr. Ottilini," I said next. "This is Jennifer Cain returning your call."

He said he understood the police had been to visit me; he assumed I knew that Arnie and Moshe had been murdered. I said yes to all of the above.

"Well, my dear," came the dry, whispery voice, "that gives us all the more reason to contest Arnie's will. It is very obvious that someone had much to gain from his death."

Ginger. Oh, I didn't like that implication at all. And I said so.

"We must be objective, Miss Cain," he said with his calm counsel. "As you so often remind our more emotional trustees when they bring their pet projects to you."

Touché, I thought.

"There is one other thing," he said. I always worry when lawyers say things like that. "I have heard rumors that the Cohen family plans to contest the will."

"Oh no." Moshe's will split his large estate between his family and The Foundation. Our half would help support his Jewish causes and the new theater, with a little left over for other charities. "Why?"

"They want all the money, my dear." Of course. Ask a stupid question, get an obvious answer. "And Miss Cain, I think we should be prepared for the possibility of other rumors . . ."

"Yes?"

"It's common knowledge that The Foundation has

61

been rather desperately hurt by Arnie's will. And now, you see, a second philanthropist has died—one who has left a generous bequest to The Foundation."

"So people will think *we* killed Moshe?" I would have laughed at the absurd notion if I hadn't heard the suspicion in Ailey Mason's voice that morning. "Who? Jack Fenton? You? Me? Faye Basil? That's the most ridiculous thing I ever heard."

"Let us hope that everyone agrees with you."

"Well, whether they do or not, this is all just marvelous publicity for The Foundation, isn't it," I said dryly. "Other donors will race to give us money now."

"Oh, they're just dying to give us money," he said grimly.

I was a little shocked.

After we hung up, I called my sister.

No one was home, so I didn't have to talk to her. Now *that* was good news.

Chapter 8

Moshe and Arnie. Murdered.

I focused my tired eyes on the screen of my home computer and realized with a shock that I had actually written the words. My fingers moved restlessly on the keyboard, seemingly of their own volition without conscious signals from my weary brain.

WHO? the fingers tapped and the angry capital letters glowed in the little screen.

WHAT? WHEN? WHERE? WHY?

And finally, HOW?

I thought I had sat down at my favorite toy just to play around and relax on Saturday night. I had even inserted a video game, but when the machine beat me four out of four at Star Warriors, I knew I didn't have my mind on the game.

I love that computer; it appeals to my sense of logic and order. Already I had it programmed to balance my checking accounts, track my bills and budgets, remind me of birthdays and chart my mother's medical history. Also stored in its gray discs were five chapters of the book I was writing in what I laughingly referred to as my spare time: a book about how to play the big league grants and foundations game. It is a game, as competitive and fierce as Space Battle with the big fast players remorselessly gobbling up the small slow players in the contest for big bucks from governmental and private sources. With Moshe and Arnie dead, and their bequests to The Foundation in question, I felt like the little orange space cadet who'd been blasted off the screen by the big purple monster from outer galactica. Pow, blooey, kabamm.

Who, what, when, where, why and how.

The classic five W's and H of journalism school and criminology. I had the questions all right, as evidenced on the little green screen, but neither the computer nor I had the answers.

I lifted my restless fingers from the keyboard and turned off the computer. Its screen glowed for a moment before it went dark, leaving the den unlighted except for the fire I had built in the old stone fireplace. The logs, still wet from snow, crackled and popped merrily.

I stared at the darkened screen, then turned around and stared at the fire. I got up and replenished my glass of dry red wine and stood by one of the four long, narrow windows. And stared.

Outside, Mother Nature was putting an exclamation point on the weather bureau's announcement that this was our worst winter in ten years. We hadn't seen thirty-three degrees in six weeks or the ground in five. It's about this time of year that I begin to feel claustrophobic, locked into the narrow paths of winter life by the rising drifts of snow and the forbidding cold.

I indulged in a moment of longing for Fort Lauderdale, Martinique, Acapulco, a warm bed, a warm body, Geof Bushfield. *What?* Where had that come from? More to the point, where did I want it to go?

I thought I had wanted to spend my Saturday night alone. I found I was glad when the doorbell rang.

"Michael! You look like a snowman!"

"Abominable or otherwise?" He grinned at me, those eyes the only warm part of him. Everything else, starting at the top of his ski cap and working down through his red ski jacket, snug blue jeans and waffle stompers, was white and icy.

"Otherwise." I helped him take off the top layers of clothing and reached up to warm his blue lips with a quick kiss. "Why are you covered with snow? Did you walk over here?"

"I am covered with snow because some people never shovel their sidewalks."

"Oh, Michael. You didn't fall down out there, did you? I'm so sorry!"

"There you go being sorry again. I swear, you are the sorriest person I know." His good humor was back, and with it his considerable charm. "I'd much rather you skipped the apologies and went straight to the drink."

"Whiskey?"

"Hot and Irish, please."

"You *are* a lot of trouble." I smiled at him over my shoulder as we walked toward the kitchen.

"But I'm worth it, or so the *other* ladies say."

"Yes, you are, and I'm delighted to hear you say so."

65

"No lectures, Swede. I'm here to charm and delight you, not alarm and affright you."

I groaned. "You're a poet, do you know it?"

"Of course, I'm a poet. All great lovers are poets."

In the kitchen, I pulled out a stainless steel bowl in which to whip the cream for his Irish coffee. I glanced at him as he perched on one of the stools at the counter . . . and experienced one of those jolting moments that had occurred occasionally in our friendship when I saw clearly what it was about him that left my secretary limp. Careful, I warned myself. You are merely horny; don't use the nice man.

"So you think you're a great lover." I tried to keep up the light, bantering tone. But I knew he'd caught that instant of awareness in my eyes.

He grinned at me. There was nothing even remotely platonic in his expression. "So they say, Jenny, or was it you who said that? Was it you, Jenny?"

Absurdly, I blushed. I felt a little incestuous about those few times we'd slipped out of friendship into something else.

"I may have mentioned something to that effect," I mumbled. I opened the refrigerator to get the cream and hid my pink face among the shelves.

"You have a terrific ass," he said.

"Michael!" I nearly bumped my head when I turned around to laugh at him. "I can't believe you said that; that didn't sound like you at all."

He sighed to the ceiling. "Oh that's right," he said, "saints don't have sex lives. Just cold showers."

He was laughing, too, by then.

"Fix my whiskey, woman!" he shouted and slammed a fist down on the counter top. He grinned wickedly, almost irresistibly. "I'll be in the den. Contemplating my saintly navel."

He walked out of the kitchen, leaving me collapsed in giggles and blasphemous thoughts about saints—definitely blasphemous, not to mention obscene.

Well, he had certainly taken my mind off the murders.

I felt compelled, however, to tell him about them when I joined him in the den. And that took his mind off me.

"But why would the killer *want* the police to suspect murder?" Michael said. "If they hadn't found that verse in the bed at the museum, they might never have suspected that Arnie was killed."

"Maybe the killer wants to be caught," I said doubtfully.

"Not *that* hoary old chestnut," Michael objected, but he couldn't come up with any better ideas, and shortly thereafter I kissed him goodnight in a sisterly fashion and ushered him back out into the snow and the dark.

I tidied up the den, turned down the thermostat and went to bed reflecting upon the fact that mature and responsible behavior is small comfort on a cold night.

Chapter 9

Hills and trees, your dog has fleas. Snow and ice, don't think twice. My thoughts flipped themselves into crazy rhymes the next afternoon as I drove the winding, two-lane blacktop to the Hampshire Psychiatric Hospital. Our crackerjack road crews had already cleared away last night's snowfall, so I drove as absentmindedly as I usually did on those Sunday trips, allowing my mind to wander over figurative hills and dales just as my car hummed over literal ones. I kept a corner of my consciousness alert for icy patches.

Red and yellow, catch a fellow. I was glad to be alone, even though Michael's mood had lifted so that he was an entertaining companion once again— maybe too entertaining. I didn't need any more confusion in my life than the week had already presented to me.

A jeep and a VW Rabbit whizzed by going the other way. I was not whizzing along. In the vintage Plymouth sedan in front of me, a very old and tiny driver pursued the minimum speed but couldn't seem to push the needle up quite that far. If he had a wife beside him she was too short to be seen over the car seat. Sunday drivers. Sometimes I think that ministers release their elderly flocks from church with the admonition: "Go ye forth this day and drive!"

Actually, I didn't mind.

Brown and gold, catch a cold. I should have enjoyed the scenery, beautiful as it is in all four seasons, but the recurring nightmare of my family's life waited at the end of the road. If a tree fell in the surrounding forest, I didn't hear it; if the pines were lovely with their heavy wet snow, I didn't see. My only identifiable emotion was tension, and that came from hoping that this day might bring a minimum of pain for my mother and me.

Mao Tse-tung, who'll get hung. The brunch with Simon and Ginger had been a great success. She loved his bawdy sense of humor; he liked her money. No, that wasn't fair, I chided myself. He'd probably have liked her even before she was rich. They had similar natures, Ginger and Simon—blunt, bright and damn-your-eyes. All I'd had to do was make the introductions, then sit back and enjoy their banter while I polished off scrambled eggs, hash browns, link sausages and whole wheat toast. My car was not the only thing that I fueled with plenty of energy before my Sunday drives.

At brunch, we had tiptoed around the subject of murder. Simon merely expressed his distress, Ginger accepted it, I seconded the motion and off we raced to other topics. What could we have said to each other: Did you do it? No, did *you?*

The great stone gates of the Hampshire Hospital frowned at me under heavy eyebrows of snow. I'd like to be able to use a more original figure of speech to describe them, but that is how they look. I frowned back and turned into the hospital grounds. As it always did, that quotation from Dante nudged its creepy way into my mind: "Abandon all hope ye who enter here." Yes, if one were writhing through the gates of hell; yes, for prisoners at the Tower of London. But not here, please God, not here.

My mother was waiting for me where she always waited for me—where the attendants deposited her in the big oak rocking chair in a private corner of the Recreation Hall. Some recreation: rocking, rocking, rocking.

"Mother." I smiled at her and bent down to kiss her cheek. The softness of her skin broke my heart, as usual. Unfortunately, as I raised up, she rocked forward, so the top of my head hit one of the hard back slats of the chair. She looked confused at the change in my expression from pleasure to pain.

It was going to be a long afternoon.

"Mom, you look so pretty."

I pulled a straight-backed armless chair close to her and sat down. I don't know, I suppose that unconsciously I thought that if I got as physically close to her as possible someday I might also penetrate the spaces of her mind.

She raised her lovely blue eyes to mine and tried to focus on my face and the question. I got my Scandinavian coloring from her side of the family. A dribble of spittle appeared at the corner of her mouth. I wiped it away with one of the tissues I always tried to remember to bring; the hospital tissues are so rough. She'd never notice the spit dribbling down her chin. It was I who couldn't stand it.

"Sherry, dear," she managed, finally.

"No, Mom, it's Jenny." Sometimes I let her think I *was* my sister, Sherry, so she'd think her other daughter had finally come to see her.

She nodded the long wise nod of the mentally ill.

I began to talk to her quietly, in one long continuous sentence that weaved in and out of the lives of people she might remember and places she had been. Sometimes she repeated a word I had said, and then I paused to say, Yes, Mom, yes, that's right. But mostly she just rocked, letting my voice flow over and around her like the familiar music from the symphonies she loved.

I murmured to her for an hour, until her eyes focused a bit more and she suddenly looked more aware.

"I have to go to the bathroom," my mother said.

I roused an attendant. While he and my mother shuffled off to perform one of the few of life's functions to which she still paid attention, I sat. If my chair could have rocked, I would have rocked in it.

I wanted to take a deep breath, but didn't dare for fear I'd swallow a great gulp of the smell of the place—that peculiar smell of the sick and the senile, that odor of the humiliation of human beings who don't know who they are.

"There now," my mother said when she was returned to me and resettled in her rocker. "There now."

A patient shuffled by—a boy about twenty. The shirttail of his regulation blue pajamas hung out. They all shuffle, all these strange lonely children of God, these mothers and fathers, sons and daughters, husbands and wives whose noisy aberrations are safely muffled now by drugs. They are safe now from the wild and fearsome rampages of their hallucinating minds, and all the rest of us are safe from them. But where there used to be too many voices in their heads, now there are none. In my mother's house and in her head, there was nobody home. She'd gone away, perhaps for good.

I sang my solo to her for a while longer, my monologue of gossip and memories, and then I stroked her hands and kissed her cheek and left. There was no use seeing the doctor; there was nothing to say. And what was said a few years ago had been said too late.

"Your mother is not an alcoholic," the doctors had told Sherry and me. "She suffers from a rather common chemical imbalance that just makes her act like one."

Too late. Too late to save Sherry from the humiliation of an adolescence spent with a stumbling, mumbling mother. Too late for the handsome husband whose strength was in his body, not his heart. Too late for the friends who watched her descent into aberrant behavior and sidled, shamefaced, out of the door.

"We might have been able to help your mother a great deal," the doctor had said, "if only medicine had discovered this chemical imbalance years ago when she was young."

If only. But they hadn't.

And so my mother joined the ironic fraternity of

children who caught polio before the Salk vaccine, of women who died in childbirth before surgeons learned to wash their hands, of all the victims of "if only we had known," the disease that is caused by being born too soon.

I pushed open the big glass doors of the hospital. It was snowing again; the roads would be hazardous. It would be a long drive home.

Chapter 10

The murders finally made the papers on Monday morning. Read all about it, as the boys used to yell on street corners. Read it and weep, as we used to say about our report cards in high school.

I sat in the breakfast nook, reading fast and gulping coffee. The impact of the story stole my appetite, which was just as well since I didn't have time for bacon and eggs. I knew I'd better hie myself to the office because this story would create a rumpus among my staff and clients.

I pulled open my mother's yellow curtains and let the thin, sharp winter sunshine puddle on the table-top. It's the sort of cozy breakfast nook that deserves a calico cat. I wished I had one to talk things over with. Cats are such good listeners, better than dogs because cats don't take personally everything you say. Dogs take your tone of voice to heart even when you're not talking about them; cats listen judiciously, without comment.

Good sense triumphed over my moment of anthropomorphic whimsey. I scatted my imaginary cat away and rinsed my cup in the sink. I would have loved to have a pet, but my schedule didn't have the cracks of time required for a cat or dog—or gerbil. I can't think of a pet as just a warm piece of furniture to leave casually behind me every day; if I ever own a Spot or a Tiger, I want time enough to love it.

I had learned a few things from the newspaper story. I considered them as I bundled up in brown leather boots, camel's hair coat, tan mohair scarf and the tan felt number that Derek calls my lady executive hat. A quick check with the hall mirror verified my qualifications for the Most Boringly Dressed List. Pat Nixon in her good Republican cloth coat had nothing on me. I looked professional, frugal and trustworthy; I could out-bland oatmeal. Little did the world know that my undies were red silk. Hah.

According to the paper, Arnie had gone to the museum that Monday night about eight-thirty after dinner at the club. He'd used the staff entrance at the South Wing; the guard remembered watching him sign in. He had that blue comforter and the pillow in a big sack under his arm; he said he'd brought them as "little gifts" for the women's staff lounge where there was a cot so the women could nap during lunch. Somebody had complained of the chill factor and voilà! sugar daddy to the rescue. How like him, I thought fondly, how wonderfully like him.

Simon Church reported having seen him, too, but only long enough to share a couple of drinks from a bottle of red wine that Simon kept in his desk drawer —for the chill factor. He wasn't drunk, Simon said; or at least he didn't act it. Arnie was still sipping the wine when he left the office, Simon said; the police had, in fact, found the wine glass where it had rolled under the testered bed.

Simon said that Arnie left his office about nine-thirty. The old man did not mention the change of wills, but Simon thought he had seemed fidgety and nervous. Several times Simon thought Arnie was about to tell him something, but each time Arnie opened his mouth he shut it again.

And that's the last time anybody admitted to having seen Arnie Culverson alive.

He had not signed out, but unfortunately the guard had not thought anything of it at the time. Frequent visitors to the museum often neglected to sign out, and he simply thought Arnie had left while the guard made his rounds of the building. With the guard gone from his post at the staff entrance, people inside the museum could still get out, but nobody outside could get in—unless, of course, Arnie or Simon had let them in.

If there was anybody else in the museum that night, neither the guard nor Simon knew of it, they said. And that didn't make things look too good for them. But Arnie could easily have let somebody in while the guard was out. And that somebody could have killed him and then waited to sneak out when the guard made his next rounds.

Ginger Culverson, the paper said, spent the night of her father's death watching TV in Idaho, but her only witness was a parakeet. Her mother and brother said they'd played canasta until midnight. No, they hadn't worried when their husband and father didn't come home, they said. Why should they care, they didn't say.

The police had no explanation to offer—at least publicly—for why they had not found the verse in the bed at the museum any sooner than they did. And of course, it wasn't really they who found it, but a janitor. I thought that delayed discovery was mighty curious. The testered bed is an exquisitely, elegantly simple piece of work; nasty poems on bright white paper ought to have stuck out like a Picasso head on a Vermeer lady.

As for Moshe, he'd been drinking too much wine the evening he died, in celebration of the theater premiere. He'd had those drinks with crowds of people at the cocktail party at the country club, the one to which Michael went and I didn't. Everybody, as they say, was there. Which meant that anybody could have doped his wine. The hypertension medicine that killed him—Soronal, the paper said—was what killed Arnie, too. It came in capsules, which could easily be opened and their powdered contents quickly dissolved in liquid. In sweet wine, the taste would not be apparent. The coroner was quoted as saying it probably took about nine capsules to kill Arnie because he was used to the drug and had developed some tolerance for it, but it took considerably less to kill Moshe. The murderer could have dissolved the medicine in a single glass of wine all at once, or spaced his poison out over several drinks. Easy and effective either way.

The newspaper article listed the beneficiaries of the

two men. The Foundation was mentioned twice. I can happily do without that sort of publicity, thank you very much.

I knocked snow off my boots as I got into my car. Then I slammed the door, started the engine and waited a bit for it to warm up.

I backed out of my parent's driveway. My radial tires crunched noisily into the crusty old snow that lay beneath the two inches of fresh. When I reached the edge of the street, I gave the car a little gas to get me over a hump of snow the plow had thrown.

I got over the hump all right.

And applied just enough brakes to throw me into a skid that twirled me deep into a snowbank in my own front yard.

So much for rushing to the office.

I left the car in the snowbank (well, it was my front yard and the car was in nobody's way) and got Derek on the phone just before he left his apartment.

"If you know what's good for you," I said as I stepped into his snappy red Toyota, "you will not mention that hunk of metal resting in the snow in front of the house." I closed the door and he accelerated carefully.

"You mean that interesting piece of modern sculpture?" He was trying not to laugh at his boss. "Wouldn't dream of saying a thing." But he couldn't resist. "Although . . . I might call Simon Church later and tell him how much I admire this new practice of placing large works of art around the community. What's this one called?"

"The sculpture, you mean?"

"Yeah."

"Car in the Yard."

He laughed and shook his head sympathetically. We followed the local (miniscule) variety of rush hour traffic in compatible silence for a while. The building which housed our office loomed ahead; at six stories, it's the town skyscraper.

"Interesting paper this morning," Derek said quietly.

"Um."

"To paraphrase a certain well-known book and movie, Somebody Is Killing the Great Philanthropists of Port Frederick."

I told him about the rumors that Mr. Ottilini had whispered to me over the phone. He wasn't surprised that the Cohens might contest the will.

"But I can't believe that people will suspect anyone connected to The Foundation!" he said. "That's crazy, is what that is. Why would any of us do it?"

"You and I know that none of us would," I said. "But consider it from the point of view of the general public. Or Ailey Mason, for that matter . . ."

"Speaking of limited points of view . . ."

"First, one of our major donors is killed . . ."

"But he did not leave us any money," Derek objected. "You'll notice the operative word is *not*. So where's our motive?"

I thought out loud, playing devil's advocate.

"Well," I mused, "maybe we killed him because we *thought* we'd get the money. Then when we found out the truth about the new will, we got desperate for funds to support the museum and so we killed Moshe for *his* money."

"But that won't help the museum, Jen, or at least

not directly. We're supposed to use his dough to support the theater. And B'nai Brith, etcetera, etcetera."

He signaled for a left turn into the parking lot.

"Yes," I said, "but I don't think the general public will understand those fine points. They'll just see that The Foundation gets the money, period."

He grunted, unconvinced, as he made the turn.

"With all due respect, boss lady, may I just say bull roar. You don't really believe people will believe something like that, do you?"

"Probably not anyone who understands how The Foundation operates, no. But Derek, if a rich person gets murdered . . . who comes under suspicion first?"

"The beneficiaries," he said grudgingly. He skidded over a patch of ice into an empty parking space. I held my breath as we missed the fender of a new Mercedes by a quarter inch. I yearned for spring, for dry streets, warm weather, green leaves. Derek said, "But we're not the only ones to inherit. How about Ginger Culverson? How about Moshe Cohen's family?"

It was my turn to look disbelieving.

"Oh come on, Derek. What do you think, that it's a conspiracy between those two families? I think I'd believe *you* did it before I'd buy that!"

He switched off the ignition. But instead of opening his door, he leaned his back against it, slung his left arm over the steering wheel and his right arm over the back of the seat and faced me.

"Jenny . . ." he said, with the tentative air of someone with a pregnant idea.

"Now don't get settled in for a long winter's chat, Derek. This car'll get cold fast."

"I know, but listen, okay? So far, all we've really considered is the crazy idea that someone connected with The Foundation has murdered two people in order to help us."

"That is crazy, you're right. So?"

"So . . ." He looked embarrassed. "Oh hell, this is going to sound nuttier than pecan pie." He turned back around in his seat and reached for his door handle. "Never mind, it's a dumb idea."

"Wait, Derek! What's your idea?"

"Oh hell, I'll just say it," he said. "What if somebody killed the philanthropists in order to *harm* The Foundation?"

The absurd notion hung in the frosty air between us.

I decided it was time to calm the troops.

"I don't think we ought to jump to any dramatic conclusions one way or the other," I said carefully, not wanting to put him down. "I know it sometimes seems as if the whole world revolves around The Foundation, but we're not *that* important. I'll grant you we've been seriously affected by the murders, but we're hardly the only ones. Whole families have been disrupted. The theater, the museum, other charities have suffered. Besides, if someone wanted to ruin The Foundation, surely he wouldn't have to kill two people to do it."

Derek's grin was shamefaced as if to say he knew he'd overreacted. "I knew it was a dumb idea," he said. "Let's go inside before we freeze."

As we walked over the snowy sidewalk, he said, "I notice they quoted your old high school buddy in the story about the murders in the paper this morning. I don't believe I'd want him chasing me." He threw me a sly, sidelong glance. "Unless I were female, of course."

I hardly heard him. I was thinking, instead, about the advice I had just given him. I believed what I had said, of course I did. It was absurd to imagine some anonymous fiend wished to destroy The Foundation and would commit murder to accomplish that end.

I reached the door first and held it open for Derek.

Absurd, I repeated to myself as he punched the button on the elevator. The murders don't have anything to do with The Foundation, I told myself, at least not in the way of a motive. It was sheer coincidence that by killing two major donors in one week, someone had just happened to demoralize my staff, wreck our projected growth, devastate our plans for the museum, force us into court fights we couldn't afford, frighten prospective donors, infuriate our trustees, disquiet our bankers, cast suspicion on all of us and generally disrupt business as usual. I felt like a winning quarterback who'd just been viciously sacked for a big loss, and it hurt.

I put a reassuring smile on my face as Derek and I walked into the office.

Still, I thought, absurd.

I continued to think that all morning, up until ten-thirty when Edwin Ottilini called to tell me that Mrs. Charles Withers Hatch had not appeared for a scheduled meeting with him that morning. He wondered if she might have called or stopped by The Foundation.

"No," I said, "we haven't seen her and she hasn't called. Did you try her home?"

"Of course. I'm afraid I frightened the maid. She

said that Mrs. Hatch went to a meeting last night and told her husband not to wait up, that she'd probably be late. Evidently Charles left for the office this morning without having seen her—I guess they keep separate bedrooms." He cleared his throat with embarrassment at that little bit of confidentiality. "By the time I called, Mrs. Hatch had not yet been down to breakfast. The maid went up to get her, and found that her bed had not been slept in. I told the maid to call Charles and see if he knows where his wife might be."

I thought of Derek's play on words . . .

Somebody Is Killing the . . .

Arnie had died at his favorite charity and Moshe at his. Mrs. Hatch might support the museum with small gifts now and then; she might donate funds to build a civic memorial or plant a garden. But her deepest concern lay with the Welcome Home for Girls. It was her pet project, the prototype of several other homes for juveniles that she hinted The Foundation might be able to finance with the generous bequest she might leave us. *If* she ever got around to making a will, which so far, to my knowledge, she had not.

I suggested that Mr. Ottilini might wish to meet me at the Welcome Home. I didn't offer a logical, rational reason and he didn't ask for one. He just said it would take him five minutes to rearrange his schedule.

Derek lent me his car keys when I asked for them. He also gave me a look of intense curiosity.

I walked calmly out of the office, gently closed the door and ran like hell for the elevator as if something possessed me.

It did—terrible, intuitive, gut-wrenching fear.

Chapter 11

I feel like a fool," I whispered to Mr. Ottilini. We sat on a dilapidated couch in the living room of the Welcome Home.

"I, too," he whispered back. "But if you don't tell anyone, I won't. Then they'll never know."

We traded sheepish grins. I'm not sure what hideous thing we expected to find there—Mrs. Hatch chopped up in little pieces and filed under "H," perhaps—but we hadn't. On the pretext of making a surprise inspection for The Foundation, we'd managed to examine every nook and broom closet, not to mention all six bedrooms, the kitchen, living room, dining room, staff offices, recreation room, sleeping porch and basement. The worst thing we found was an unmade bed.

"She undoubtedly forgot our appointment," Mr. Ottilini said, hardly any doubt in his voice by that time. "I will admit that is out of character for her, but

God help us if we can't be unpredictable now and then."

"Even you, Mr. Ottilini?" I dared.

"Even I," he said with more than a hint of a twinkle. He's the only trustee I called mister, but just because he was formal didn't mean he wasn't human.

"But how do you account for the fact that her bed wasn't slept in?" I persisted.

"As we age, we sleep less well, my dear." He patted the air above my hand. "I expect she dozed off on a sofa instead, and then got dressed and left this morning before the rest of the household was up and about."

"Well, I'm sure you're right," I sighed. I wished I could forsake this wild goose chase and return to my office. But we had to wait—to our mutual embarrassment—for the director of the home to bring the coffee she'd insisted we needed. After putting her to so much trouble, we could hardly refuse. Besides, I knew it was important to the director, Allison Parker, to make a favorable impression on the controllers of the charitable purse strings in town.

She rounded the corner from the kitchen, treading carefully on the worn carpet. With both hands, she carried a plastic tray—left over from Christmas, judging by the holly pattern around the rim—on which were balanced three cups full of coffee and napkins and spoons.

"What a tea service!" she laughed as she set it on a coffee table and then lowered herself into a lumpy armchair. "But you know how it is—everything we have is secondhand and cracked." She smiled brightly. "Not that we don't appreciate it, goodness knows what we'd do without secondhand and cracked! But I will admit, it's not quite the tea service my dear mother dreamed of for me!"

Allison spoke in exclamation points and dealt in guilt. She knew how to shovel it out in thick, rich piles so the more fortunate among us would ante up for her girls. She was just barely five feet tall with round blue eyes and curly red hair, and she looked more like one of the girls than the director of the program. Contrary to the appearance of sweetness and light that she tried to present, however, I knew her to be a tough twenty-five-year-old with sufficient steel in her backbone to discipline hard cases and a master's degree in social work to qualify her academically for the job. The mother she had spoken of had died when Allison was thirteen years old; I knew that much from the soap opera life story she'd told me soon after she was hired. The only thing she didn't say was what became of her father, though I gathered that he either had not been able to or had not wanted to take care of Allison and her two brothers. So they were placed by the state in juvenile detention centers—hard, tough places where they didn't deserve to be—of the very sort the Welcome Home was meant to replace. "I know what it's like to be one of these kids," Allison said in a rare moment of grim candor when she was hired, "I belong here." Still, she was young and probably immature for the load of responsibility she carried. But we had to hire young, cheap staff since the home budget did not allow for the luxury of more experienced and costly employees.

And yet somehow Allison managed. On a pittance of state aid and private donations, she managed to feed, clothe, educate, entertain and provide counseling for twelve girls. Most of what little private money there was came from Mrs. Hatch's pocketbook, which was irregularly and unpredictably opened now and then to the home. I knew that Allison was also going to have to learn how to wheedle donations out of the community at large, a community that didn't even like to admit it *had* poor or abused children, or, God forbid, both.

"I hope you don't take sugar," she said, just as Mr. Ottilini was, I guessed, opening his mouth to request that very thing. "Our government commodities are late this month, so we're making do with leftovers. And I'm sorry to say, there's no sugar left over." Her face brightened like a child's at Christmas. "Oh! But there's brown sugar, would that do?"

Mr. Ottilini bravely swallowed a gulp of the tepid, bitter instant coffee and said, No, he didn't need a thing, thank you.

"I'm fine, too, Allison," I said to the questioning expression on her round face. "Can you even spare this coffee?"

"Absolutely!" she fluted. "There's at least enough for the houseparents tonight. I can do without, quite easily."

As usual, I fell for her guilt games. I told her I'd drop off a pound of coffee and a box of sugar later that day.

"You're such a dear, Jenny!" she exclamation-pointed at me. "I don't know what this old house would do without friends like you and Mr. Ottilini!"

We generous ones shifted uncomfortably on the lumpy couch, thinking of our own plush furniture and the wasted coffee we'd poured down our sinks that morning. Allison did that to people—made them feel inadequate and guilt-ridden even while she gushed compliments upon them—and I found it a most unlikable trait. But I admired her dedication, so I just endured her like everyone else, and smiled fatuously back at her and gritted my teeth. And, of course, I handed down to her the secondhand and cracked of all my belongings.

"Well!" she said with the bright smile that the professional of any field uses to put laypeople in their places. You don't know beans, that smile says, but I'll condescend to pretend you do. "Well! How does our little house look to you good people this morning? I'm awfully sorry about that unmade bed. But of course, if we had known you were coming . . ."

She was all smiles and regret and helpfulness.

Mr. Ottilini apologized, on cue, for our having barged in.

I indulged in a delicious moment of fantasy in which Allison suddenly leaped to her feet, tired eyes blazing, and told us to go jump. In my fantasy, she yelled, "How dare you drop in here like you own the place, even if you practically do! Would you surprise your fancy friends early in the morning before they've had a chance to make their beds? Would you barge into an office without an appointment? Don't we deserve such simple courtesy, too? Out, both of you! My rug is not swept, my bathtub has rings and you can just get the hell out!"

"What's so funny, Jenny?" Allison turned her Little Orphan Annie eyes on me.

"Was I smiling? I didn't mean to smile," I said inanely. Then realizing how stupid that sounded, I really did laugh. She and Mr. Ottilini gazed at me with the tolerance usually reserved by the sane for the

looney. I tried to get my face under control. I said,
"I'm sorry. It's been a long week."

"But Miss Cain," said Mr. O, "it's only Monday."

"Oh God," I said, "only Monday."

"Oooonly Mon-day!" Allison chirped in an absurdly cheerful singsong that very nearly undid me. I had
to slurp coffee to keep from chirping back at her, "Tra
la! Tra la!"

One of the girls who lived at the house saved me by
appearing in the living room.

"Telephone, Allison!" she yelled.

"Who is it, do you know, dear?"

"Beats the fuck out of me," said the little girl. She
popped her gum and walked out again.

A frozen silence descended on the adults in the
living room. I prayed for deliverance from hysterics.
Allison located her most sincere smile once more,
pasted it on her face and turned toward Mr. Ottilini.
It must have taken some courage; I gave her full credit
for that. The old lawyer's face was scarlet, though I
detected that twinkle again.

"Well!" Allison said brightly. "If they were little
angels they wouldn't be here, would they?"

She excused herself, rather quickly I thought, and
went out of the room, either to answer the phone or to
pin one teenager up against the wall.

Mr. O pushed his glasses up on the bridge of his
bony nose.

"I think we may safely go now, Miss Cain."

"I'm sorry I suggested this." I stood and searched in
the pockets of my suit for Derek's car keys.

"No," he demurred, "I would have come anyway.
Better to err on the side of caution, as we lawyers

would have you believe. And speaking of caution, I suggest we depart by the back door. With any luck, we shall escape unscathed by further coffee or guilt."

He led the way along the narrow hallway with its peeling wallpaper to the back door with its broken storm window. Everywhere I looked, the Welcome Home for Girls cried out for massive infusions of money—the kind that a generous bequest from Mrs. Charles Withers Hatch would mean.

Mr. Ottilini, old-fashioned gentleman to the core, held open the door for me against the cold stiff wind that was huffing down from Canada. We walked down the neatly shoveled back steps, causing my guilt to rise again as I thought of my own hazardous steps that I still hadn't shoveled. And *that* reminded me of the modern sculpture in my front yard. I had not had time yet that morning to call the Standard station and ask them to haul it out for me.

I reached out a hand to the lawyer.

"Thank you for coming, Mr. Ottilini. I suppose it didn't hurt to tour the place."

"No, it's good for us, I think. Reminds us of how much there is to do for it. And how much The Foundation could help if only we had the money." He didn't shake my hand, but took it in a fatherly fashion between the two of his. "Let's don't tell Mrs. Hatch how foolishly we worried about her, all right?"

"Fine." As I returned his smile, I glanced over his shoulder. Snow was sliding in a small pointed avalanche off the roof of the garage. He turned to follow my glance.

"I forgot about the garage," he said casually, apologetically. "You don't suppose we ought to look inside, do you? Just to set our minds completely at ease?"

"Well, you know what lawyers would have us believe," I said and I started to wade through the foot of snow in the back yard to the detached garage that was used for storage instead of cars. "Better to err on the side of caution."

I heard his dry, whispery laugh behind me.

God, I felt stupid, plowing through the snow to open a frigid garage to see if Mrs. Charles Withers Hatch was among the items stored there. Of course, she was not.

We closed the garage door and exchanged those sheepish grins again. We were getting good at it. If Mrs. Hatch only knew, she'd die, I thought. And then I took one last look around the property—this time around a corner of the garage—and saw the second-hand badly cracked refrigerator. It was one that Mrs. Hatch had given to the home last year; obviously, it had not lasted long. It stood white and solitary in the snow under a low-hanging branch of a maple tree. Its aluminum shelves were propped against it; they sparkled in the cold sunlight.

"An abandoned icebox!" I was suddenly, fiercely furious. "They should *not* leave that out there! A child could lock himself in it!"

I didn't know why my heart was pounding so horribly. I only knew I was already in tears by the time I flung open the door of the empty refrigerator. Only, like the Testered Bed With an Alcove, it wasn't empty.

It was stuffed to the brim with Mrs. Charles Withers Hatch.

"She didn't suffer, Jenny." Geof Bushfield took time off from his unpleasant chores to walk over to where Mr. Ottilini and I waited in a forlorn and freezing huddle on the back steps. We had ignored Geof's advice to go inside. Inside held Allison and a houseful of frightened staff and nearly hysterical youngsters.

Geof's eyes were distracted, but kind. He said, "She was already dead or unconscious when she was, uh, put in there."

"How do you know?" I desperately wanted to believe he wasn't just saying that to make us feel better.

"Because I've seen what abandoned refrigerators look like when someone has been locked in them alive." His eyes held memories of unspeakable things. "There would be blood. There would be signs of a struggle to get out, to breathe . . ."

"How did she die?" Mr. Ottilini asked. Geof had to bend down to hear him. In the last hour, the old man had shrunk inside his expensive overcoat; the long lines of dignity and power in his face had drooped into furrows of grief. With the loss of this third old friend and client, something vital had seeped out of Mr. Ottilini. I was nearly as worried about him, standing frail and shivering beside me, as I was about the murders.

"I don't know, sir, and we probably won't know until we get the coroner's report." Geof scanned the lawyer's face, then glanced at me and then back at Mr. Ottilini. Geof chewed his lower lip. Our breaths turned the air to white fog. He said, "I'll tell you what, sir, we'll notify the family and . . ."

"No." But there was no spirit to Mr. Ottilini's objection. "I should do that. I will do that."

"Actually, sir," Geof interrupted smoothly, "it would be better for us to do it because we'll have to, uh, interview them anyway." He didn't pause long enough for the older man to get a word in. "You can call on them later today if you wish, how's that?"

Mr. Ottilini nodded his head as if at a dismal fate. "I'll be at my office," he whispered to the snow at our feet. He turned to leave, glancing back only once to attempt a smile at me and to stare with obvious pain at the white refrigerator in the snow.

I fought back the urge to weep. I looked up into Geof's concerned eyes. "There's a note, isn't there?" I asked him. "A verse, like the other two."

He hesitated only briefly before answering me.

"Yes, there was a verse. Stuffed in her pocketbook. Do you want to see it?"

I took a deep breath. It burned the inside of my nose and throat. "Yes, please," I said.

He pulled a clear plastic bag out of his inside coat pocket and held it so that I could read the typewritten words through the transparent plastic without touching the note.

It said:

> Depositor in many banks,
> Giving only where there's thanks,
> Now you're stuffed all dead and cold,
> Like a freshly frozen soul.

I swallowed my horror and disgust. With a deep feeling of regret, I said, "It's somebody who knew her."

"Why?" He slid the envelope back into the pocket.

I took in another breath of stinging air.

"Because Mrs. Hatch was a wonderful, generous woman, but . . ."

"But . . ."

". . . but she liked to feel appreciated. More than most volunteers or donors, I mean. If she gave you something, you'd better say thank you until your tongue got tired. She'd drop you like a hot coal if you weren't grateful enough to please her."

"Had she dropped anybody lately?"

I realized how important my answer could be, so I thought before I said, "I don't know, Geof, but I don't think so."

He nodded.

"Go home, Jenny," he said, and I was surprised by the gentleness in his voice. "We'll call you into the station or drop by your house to get a formal statement. You still live at your parents' house right?"

I supposed he knew that fact from his investigations of the murders.

"I can't go home," I said. "I've got to go back to the office. Call me there, okay? And yes, I'm at my parents'." I added giddily, "They're not. But I am."

"How's your mom?"

Amazing how much he'd learned from his investigation; of course, everybody in town knew about Mom.

"The same," I said. "No, maybe worse. I don't know."

"I think you ought to go home. Don't be brave."

"I'm not being brave, I'm being stubborn." I shoved my hands, whose fingertips were numb, into my coat pockets. "I'll be at The Foundation, Geof. Call me there, or come by, if you want to."

He shrugged and shook his head the way people do when they see I'm determined to have my way. His smile was tired and crooked.

"You never let the football team give up either," he said unexpectedly. "You were the cheerleader who kept yelling 'push 'em back' clear down to the last play."

"My gosh, is that true? How did you remember that?" I babbled. Cheerleader! How foolish it sounded in contrast to this serious, competent man standing in front of me. I felt suddenly embarrassed, inconsequential, naive, all those things I most hate to feel.

"I remember because you were so young to be a varsity cheerleader," he said, "and I thought you were the prettiest girl I'd ever seen."

That knocked me speechless, at least in part because the Geoffrey Bushfield I remembered had not been noted for his interest in varsity anything, though I remembered a snide joke about his having "lettered in hell-raising." I did manage to say, "Well, that was a long time ago."

His lips, which were slightly chapped, formed a smile that carried to his eyes with a message I couldn't decipher. Then he was gone, back to his men and the refrigerator.

I drove Derek's car back to the office.

I had a little breaking of bad news to do myself.

Chapter 12

After I told my staff about Mrs. Hatch, not much work got done. Marvin and Faye were too upset to concentrate on their normal routines—as if there were a normal routine to follow anymore. Derek, however, came into my office and closed the door behind him.

"You have to go to New York, Jenny," he said. I stared at him in disbelief.

"Tell me another joke," I said.

"I know." He sat down across from my desk. "It sounds crazy at a time like this, but you'll want to go when I tell you the why and the wherefore."

I waited for yet more bad news.

Only it wasn't bad. It was very nice. It seems a phone call had come for me while I was at the Welcome Home, a call from a lawyer in New York. Derek took the message. It amounted to the delightful fact that an old man from Manhattan, who had visited Poor Fred only once in his life had, on that trip, fallen in love with a certain distinguished painting by Degas which was displayed at the Martha Paul. And he just happened to have made a point of obtaining a second painting that the famous Impressionist had done of the same dancer. It further seemed that the old man had recently died—of natural causes, Derek said thankfully—and left us the second Degas!

"Why didn't he will it directly to the Martha Paul?" I wanted to know.

"That's what you're supposed to go to New York and find out." He tucked a forefinger in the neck of his navy blue turtleneck and tugged. "Seems there's a contingency clause to the will."

"Ah ha. The catch. The ever-popular, well-known catch."

"And the attorneys for the old guy have respectfully requested the presence of the executive director— that's you—in their offices tomorrow."

"Tomorrow."

"Yep. Nine o'clock and I do not mean at night."

"Do you realize how early I'll have to get up?"

"Early to bed, early to rise; that's the song of the boss who flies."

"Ugh. Have Faye get me on the best flight she can, okay? Preferably one that serves decent coffee. And ask her to get me a hotel reservation just in case I have to stay over. Anywhere as long as it's Central Park South. I'll pay the excess over the expense allowance. And have her arrange for a cab to pick me up at my house an hour before my flight, just in case my car's still in the ditch. Will you do all that for me, Derek?"

"Already done, done and done. Plus, I called the

Standard station and asked them to dig the modern sculpture out of the snow."

"You're a fine employee and I think I'll keep you. Now then, what was the old gentleman's name and what do you know about him?"

We talked business for the next hour. It was an effective defense mechanism that dammed the tide of my feelings. I couldn't afford to indulge my sadness or shock; I had to be a calm, reassuring source of support for the staff.

Somehow, the rest of the workday passed. When everyone else had gone—I told Derek I'd take a cab home—I remained at my desk. I took advantage of the chance to be alone to consider the frightening implications of certain questions that had occurred to me: Did Mrs. Hatch leave a will? If so, did she leave any of her money to The Foundation as she always hinted she would? If both answers were yes, did somebody kill her in order to cast more suspicion on us? If either answer was no, did somebody kill her to make sure her money stayed out of our grasp?

Either way, we lost.

I placed a fast, nervous call to Mr. Ottilini's office and caught him just before he left to visit the Hatch home.

Yes, he said, she left a will. She had, in fact, signed the thing last week, having been prompted to finally take action because of the death of her friend, Arnie Culverson.

"That's what it often requires, you know," he said dejectedly, "to motivate a person to write a will. When a friend dies, it occurs to us that the same thing *might* some day happen to us, too."

And yes, he also said, she left about $350,000 to

The Foundation for the purpose of founding residential treatment centers for adolescents. She also left $150,000 directly to the Welcome Home. The rest of the estate went to her family.

As to my other questions . . .

"I would not want to jump to any paranoid conclusions, Miss Cain," was how he carefully put it, "but I think that under the circumstances, we must consider the possibility that someone does not wish The Foundation well."

"Or," I said, and a shiver crawled down my spine, "someone wishes us all too well, in a rather misguided sort of way."

"Moshe's funeral was this afternoon," he noted. It had been a private service for immediate family members only.

"Yes." There was nothing else to say. So we said goodnight and hung up.

On my way out the door, I lifted a bag of drip coffee and a box of granulated sugar from the tray by the office coffee machine. I'd drop them by the Welcome Home and chalk it up as a donation from The Foundation.

Coward that I am, I jumped out of the cab when it pulled up in the driveway of the girls' home, stuck my head in the front door and tossed the coffee and sugar to the nearest resident. "Got to run," I lied, "give these to Allison, will you please?"

But I was foiled by the sudden appearance of the lady herself. When I looked into Allison's saucer eyes, I felt my own grief reflected back at me.

"Jenny!" she cried and reached out with her small hands to grasp my larger ones. "Oh, Jenny, how could anyone do this terrible thing to that wonderful woman! What will we do without her? She was the best friend this house ever had, Jenny, she was just the most wonderful, generous person!"

Gushers make me dry up like a prune that's been out in the sun too long. I felt my face go stiff and my voice go arid. "I know, Allison." I meant to sound sympathetic, but all I heard in my own voice was distaste. I tried harder. "I feel awful for you and the girls, just awful."

"Oh, the girls are so sad," she intoned mournfully. I doubted it; excited yes, maybe even scared, but not sad. For all her good works, Florence Hatch had not been a woman to whom a poor and troubled teenage girl would have been likely to get emotionally attached.

"I've got a cab waiting, Allison," I said rudely and tugged my hands out of her grasp.

"Oh, forgive me!" She was so contrite I could have kicked her. "I didn't mean to hold you up, Jenny, I'm so sorry!"

"Don't be sorry," I said, a little too loud and firm. A flicker of surprise showed in her eyes, but it disappeared as I stuttered my way out the door, saying, "I mean, it's okay, Allison, don't worry about it, call me if you need anything, good night."

But I remembered something important that would please her and I turned back to tell her.

"Do you know about the will?" I said, completely and unforgivably out of school. She looked blank, so I explained. "I understand that Mrs. Hatch left a generous bequest to this house."

"Oh!" she started to spout, but I fled back to the cab before the gushing cataract of her gratitude could drown me. It occurred to me as I waved goodbye to her that Mrs. Hatch's bequest not only ensured the future of the home, but also meant Allison might stop begging and fawning.

It seemed to me that was one definite if small blessing to arise from the greater tragedy.

The cab dropped me off at home a few minutes later.

Ginger Culverson was parked in her mother's Seville in the driveway, which made it fairly crowded since the local traffic also included a tow truck from the Standard station, my sister's BMW and Michael's Jaguar.

I'm too tired for this, I moaned to myself. I think I'll tell them all to go away and leave me alone.

"Hi, everyone," I called instead, of course. I threw Michael the keys to the house. "Let the ladies in, will you, while I talk to a man about a car."

Michael performed the chores of a host while I stood in the cold that was getting colder and listened to the man from the garage hypothesize about how I could possibly have got my car in such a fix.

"Your own front yard, too," he said wonderingly. The calculator in my mind deducted a dollar from his tip. "You really got 'er stuck as a buck in the muck, ain't you?"

That made me laugh, so I mentally added his dollar back. I said, "Can you get it out, please? I'll be in the house if you need me."

"Havin' a nice warm cup of tea, I suppose," he said bitterly. "While I'm out here freezin' my butt off, isn't that the way?"

"I guess it is." I wondered if he took guilt trip lessons from Allison Parker. I left him with his tip hanging precariously in the balance.

I walked gratefully into the cozy warmth the tow truck driver envied and closed the door decisively on him and his cold twilight. I peeled off coat, hat, gloves, muffler and suit coat and hung everything that was hangable on the brass coat tree in the hall, the one toward which my father used to toss his hat and usually miss so it landed on the floor for my mother to pick up later. So tired that even my face ached, I wished I could hang myself up by the scruff of my neck and dangle, limp and sleepy. I groaned just loud enough to let my guests in the living room know my feelings about the world at that moment. I unzippered and stepped out of my wet boots and—feeling put upon—padded barefoot in to greet them.

Michael had fulfilled the role of host to the extent of pouring drinks and hauling out the cheese and crackers. I wondered—but didn't much care—how my sister felt about being treated like a guest in what used to be her home. Michael had a Manhattan waiting for me in the hand that didn't hold his own Scotch and water.

"I can never get used to your drinking these things," he said and smiled as he handed it to me. I tasted it. Bless him, it was just the way I like it—up and "perfect," that is, a smooth-as-silk blend of bourbon and sweet and dry vermouth. He said, "It seems such an old-fashioned drink, like something out of the '20's."

"I'm an old-fashioned girl," I smirked. My sister snorted, thus making her opinion and her presence known.

"Hello, Sherry," I said lightly. "Did you have any trouble finding the place? Have to stop and get a map from a filling station?"

Ginger, who didn't know Michael or Sherry and barely knew me, looked startled. Maybe she was surprised to find that families other than her own also indulged in open animosity.

"No, Sis, I didn't have any problems finding it at all," Sherry snapped back at me. "I just followed all the signs that said 'dutiful daughter' and pointed this way."

Michael threw me a look that said "behave yourself," so I swallowed the supremely clever comeback that was on the tip of my bitter tongue. I turned to Ginger and put welcome in my smile.

"I would have called first," she said quickly. "In fact, I did call first. But your office lines have been busy all afternoon. So I just came on over. Hope you don't mind."

"Of course not." It was only a white lie; I may have been exhausted, but I was glad to see her open, friendly face. It offered such a pleasant contrast to my sister's closed, suspicious expression. I said to Ginger, "Have you met my sister Sherry, and Michael?"

"Yes, we've introduced ourselves." A hint of mischievous amusement lit her brown eyes. "I would have guessed the two of you are sisters, anyway, even without being told. You look remarkably alike."

I glanced at my sister's pale blond hair, her peaches-and-cream skin, her delicate features and tall slim body, and supposed I should have felt complimented by the comparison. "We are remarkably alike," I said wearily, "which is probably part of the problem."

Sherry's blue eyes—same light shade as our mother's and mine—looked startled, as if I'd caught her off guard. Then the perfectly made-up eyelids with their exquisitely drawn lines and shadows closed down again to shutter her thoughts. Everything about her was exquisite and expensive, from the cloud of shimmering hair to the Gucci belt and shoes and the Hermes handbag. It was as if she thought that by maintaining a facade of irreproachable respectability and class, she could rise above the town's memory of our mother as she had become in those last years before she was diagnosed and committed. Our lovely, sparkling mother had given up on everything including baths, deodorant, clean clothes, hairbrushes and toothpaste—and hope. Most of all, of course, she gave up on hope.

I've been told I'm no slouch myself when I really want to put myself together with clothes and makeup, but I was a slob compared to Sherry. She was as gorgeous as a trust fund, a well-to-do husband and the spur of shame could make her.

I came out of my reverie to hear Michael say that he, too, had been defeated by busy signals.

"I heard the news about Mrs. Hatch and wanted to make sure you knew," he said tentatively, gently, as people do when they're not sure if you know your dog is dead. "You do know, don't you?"

"I was the one who found her."

That got their attention, even Sherry's. I avoided Michael's sympathetic eyes and my sister's cool ones and told my horrifying story to Ginger.

"Oh God," she said at the end of it, "it's tied to my father's death, isn't it? And the murder of Mr. Cohen?"

"Oh Swede, how awful for you," Michael said and

wrapped a warm and comforting arm around my shoulders.

"Quite the center of attention, weren't you?" my sister said, arched eyebrow and all. "Aren't you. Always."

I leaned into Michael's side and absorbed his affection into my wounded spirit while he and Ginger stood by looking awkward and uncomfortable. I wished I were six years old again and could stick out my tongue at my bratty little sister. I knew, however, that what I *should* do was ignore her because that was the best of all possible ways to aggravate her. It was attention she craved as an alcoholic craves drink; but like the fed-up-to-here family of an alcoholic, I knew I shouldn't indulge her insatiable need. "Stop being her patsy," a psychologist had advised me. "Don't allow her to make you pay for the failings of your parents. Does she think it was easy on *you?* Stop being so sweet and patient with her—give her back some of her own and see how she likes it. She has to learn to accept the natural consequences of her actions; and it is *not* natural for you to swallow your hurt and fury when she abuses you. She knows you don't mean it, anyway, and that only makes her despise you more. Jenny, the past is not your fault. Your sister has to get on with her life as it exists today, without demanding payment from you for yesterday."

He didn't tell me I would *enjoy* giving it back to her; it was a shocking and humbling experience to learn that. We had both, my sister and I, a long way to go toward forgiving.

"Stuff it," I said angrily, without a hint of wit or self-control or good nature. I even raised my voice. "I didn't ask you to visit me, Sherry, but if you can't control your snide tongue in front of my friends, I *will* ask you to leave. Make up your mind."

I could feel Michael's intake of breath; Ginger looked at me as if she *really* didn't know me at all. As for my sister, she couldn't have looked more shocked if I had hit her. She looked so surprised it was funny. So, true to the psychologist's advice to let my natural feelings show, I laughed.

"I'm sorry, Ginger and Michael," I said briskly and moved across the room to take a seat in my father's armchair. "It's no fun to witness family squabbles, I know. Are you leaving or staying, Sherry?"

Her blue-eyed glare was vivid with hate.

"Leaving. But not before I tell you why I came. Not before I have the pleasure of telling you the hospital called me today—because of the busy signal on your popular phone, I presume."

I stiffened and prayed she wouldn't indulge her considerable capacity for cruelty. My prayers went begging.

"Mother's gone catatonic again," she said as if she took it as a personal affront, which of course she did. Then she twisted the corkscrew further into my heart. "It happened last night after your visit with her. You don't suppose there's a connection, do you?"

I looked away from her, unable to cope with her venom and my pain at the same time. When she saw she wasn't going to get a response—or maybe had already got the response she sought—she raised her perfect little chin in the air and marched elegantly out of the house. My only satisfaction lay in knowing how much she would later regret having shown her worst side to strangers. My God, we were hideous to each other; my God, how we needed each other and how sadly that need cried in vain.

"Jennifer, I'm so sorry." Michael's voice was as gentle as his eyes.

"I'll come back later if that would be better." Ginger spread her plump hands in a gesture of helpless embarrassment.

"No." I stood and tried on a smile for size. It seemed to fit, if a little raggedly, so I kept it there. "Just let me make a quick phone call and then I hope you'll both stay for supper. I'd be grateful for your company. Will you?"

They would.

I shut myself in the den and called the doctors. I got about as much response out of them as they were getting from my mother. "Wait," they said. "Be patient. She's come out of it before. She'll come out of it again."

But I didn't believe them, not this time. My mother didn't have a reason to come out of it this time, except possibly for the sake of life itself, and that held no rhyme or reason for her anymore. No reason at all.

Chapter 13

I paid the man from the garage when he came huffing and puffing to the front door.

"You ought to shovel your walk," he said.

"You ought to shove off," I said, but with a smile and a tip. One mustn't alienate one's service person. Or one will be, someday, stuck as a buck in the muck with nobody to bail out one's ass.

He stuck the extra money in his wallet and nodded complacently as if it were only just. He didn't say thank you.

"Better shovel this before you get sued," he said in farewell.

I made a classic Italian gesture of disrespect behind his back.

I shut the door on the cold night and turned back into the house to organize the troops for dinner.

While Ginger poured the wine and Michael washed

the lettuce, I alternated between the oven and the phone. Simon Church called to say that he, too, had received a summons to appear in New York the next day. He sounded aggrieved that the bequest of the Degas was being routed through The Foundation; I told him truthfully that I didn't have the vaguest notion why.

"I hear you found Mrs. Hatch," he said in his blunt way, but not unkindly. His big voice boomed out into the kitchen for everyone to hear. "Uh, Jenny my love, would you happen to know if she left anything for the Martha Paul? You know she always hinted she might give us a little something."

"Simon, Simon . . ." I looked over at Ginger to find her shaking her head and smiling. She'd heard him, too.

"I know," he said cheerfully. "I know I'm a crass bastard, but I learned a long time ago that if you don't ask the question, you won't get the answer. So did she?"

"She left some money to The Foundation for the purpose of providing care for adolescents," I said, sounding rather like a will myself. "And she left some directly to the Welcome Home. So if you benefit at all, it will only be indirectly, Simon." (Sometimes a large bequest enables us to increase our overall purchasing power, so that we can invest in something that pays better interest or dividends. When that happens, there's a trickle-down effect that benefits all the charities we support—because whenever we earn more, we have more money to give away. As the old saying goes, it takes money to make money.)

The sound of his large, disappointed sigh filled the

kitchen. "Jenny, Jenny," he complained, "Arnie promises the world and gives us zippitydoodah . . . Moshe Cohen didn't give a rat's ass about us compared to his precious theater, or the goddamn Golan Heights, for Pete's sake! . . . and Florence Hatch drops hints like an outfielder drops flies, but she doesn't leave us a pot to piss in! I'll tell you, Jen, people are so irresponsible."

It was almost comical. For Simon, the axis upon which the world revolved was the Martha Paul; nothing happened that he couldn't connect in some way, for good or ill, to the museum.

"Just think about that Degas, Simon," I said soothingly. "Just think about that lovely painting and how it's going to be all yours."

"All *yours*, you mean," he said bitterly.

"Simon," I said, suddenly beset by the trepidation born of experience, "you will be good tomorrow, won't you?" He was a superb museum director in many ways, but a lousy diplomat. I always held my breath during his dealings with donors; they have to be handled with kid gloves and he didn't have a pair to his name. I said nervously, "You won't get mad and do something I'll regret?"

He laughed, a shade wildly, I thought.

"Oh ye of little faith," he said, "you can count on Simple Simon. I'll be good as gold, Jenny love, I'll be . . ."

"You'd better be," I threatened, "or maybe The Foundation will find some other museum in which to hang that Degas."

That blackmail sobered him up.

"I'll see you at the airport, Jennifer," he said,

reproof in his voice. Simon could dish it out, but he didn't easily tolerate jokes about his sacred cow.

"Thanks for calling," I said, all business, and hung up just in time for the phone to ring again.

"Jenny," a male voice said. "It's Geof . . . Bushfield."

"I know which Geof you are, Geof." I wondered if he could hear my smile. But then I stopped smiling. "Oh dear, I forgot you wanted to interview me today. I'm so beat. Can we do it tomorrow instead?"

"Well, we need your statement," he said. "I'd suggest taking it first thing in the morning, but as it happens, I'm going to New York tomorrow."

"Me too."

"No kidding? That early bird commuter flight?"

"Yes, God help me, the one that cracks the dawn."

"So am I," he said. "Okay then, how's this for a compromise? I'll take your statement on the flight down."

"There won't be enough time, will there?"

He laughed. "Why? Do you have a lot to say? Okay, here's a better idea. I'll get what I can on the flight, then I'll meet you later in the city and we'll finish the job."

"Sold."

"Thanks, Jenny." There was a pause. "Are you all right?"

"Pretty well," I said. "Thank you. Uh, Geof, can you tell me what you've found out about Mrs. Hatch?"

"Sure," he said calmly, "I don't see why not. We found her car for one thing. It was still in the parking lot at the hotel where she went to that meeting. The guy on the switchboard at the hotel remembers getting a call for her, but he can't remember if it was from a man or woman. At any rate, he had her paged out of her meeting and that's the last anybody knows about her. Evidently she took the call on one of the house phones and then got her coat from the rack outside the meeting room. She may have left the hotel with somebody in another car, but nobody saw her, unfortunately."

"Well, that hotel lobby's a busy place," I said. "I suppose there's no reason anybody would notice one old lady leaving. But didn't she go back to her meeting and tell them she was going?"

"No," Geof said. "There were close to a hundred people there and she was only in the audience, so she could have just picked up her coat and left without anyone knowing."

"So now you have to try to trace her movements from the time she took the telephone page to the time I . . . I . . ."

"Right," he said quickly. "We've interviewed the girls and the staff at the Welcome Home, and their neighbors."

"And?"

"And nada," he said with an air of frankness. "On Sunday night, the staff at the home always take the girls out to a movie, so the grounds were conveniently empty for at least two hours. And the neighbors say there's always so much activity at the house—people coming and going—that they've got so they don't pay attention anymore."

"Somebody must have known those facts," I suggested. "The same person who knew Mrs. Hatch well enough to write that rhyme about her."

"That's what we think, too," he agreed. "If you get any ideas on the subject, will you let me know?"

"Of course," I said. "See you in the morning."

After I hung up, I switched on the telephone answering machine. Whatever else anybody had to tell me could just darn well wait until tomorrow.

"Who was that?" Michael looked up from his work at the salad bowl. He'd created a crisp jumble of lettuce, radishes, sliced Jerusalem artichokes, cucumbers, red onions and Italian dressing. I pulled the rib eye steaks out of the broiler.

"A cop," I said. I slit open the baked potatoes and slathered them with butter, sour cream and freshly snipped chives. "The one who's in charge of investigating the murders."

"Sounds as if you know him pretty well," he said casually. I watched him carry the salad bowl to the table and I wondered what it was he had heard in my voice during the brief conversation. Ginger tactfully kept her head bent over the wine bottle as she poured the rest of it into an open-necked decanter to set on the table.

I said, "Oh well, you know. Murder breeds familiarity."

"And familiarity," he said, looking straight at me, "breeds contempt."

Not tonight, Michael, I thought as I removed the pumpkin bread from the microwave. Please don't start on me again, not tonight.

We were ready to eat at the round oak table in my mother's dining room.

"L'chaim." Ginger smiled and raised her crystal goblet of California burgundy. "To life."

Too late, she realized that might not have been the

113

best toast for that particular day. There was an awkward moment in which we all glanced at each other with dread in our eyes. Then the instant broke apart into rueful, understanding smiles.

"I'll have to remove my foot from my mouth before I can eat," she said. The corners of her mouth turned down in apology.

"Don't worry about it," Michael said and rewarded her with his kindest smile, the one that left my secretary limp and speechless. "The way things are going in this town, there's hardly a subject that isn't uncomfortable to somebody." He munched on a bite of salad before adding, "I mean, we can't talk about business, because I'll get depressed. We can't talk about parents, or we'll all cry. We can't discuss money or wills. We can't mention sisters or brothers or dying or sickness or health. So what's left?"

"The weather?" I suggested between mouthfuls of potato.

"No!" Ginger said. "We're sick of it!"

"Religion, politics?" I said.

"Nope," Michael said. "Didn't your mother always tell you—oh boy, see what I mean? I'm sorry, Swede."

I was, too, because the reminder of my mother took my appetite away. I put my fork down and smiled—bravely, I thought—at him.

"S'okay." I hoped the tears I felt were not visible.

Ginger saved me by asking me to pass the salt and pepper—and then the butter and the sour cream—and then the bowl of chive bits. Michael and I stared, fascinated, as she glopped her potato two inches high with fattening condiments.

"I haven't had a decent meal in a week!" she said defensively. "My mother has stopped cooking entirely, which I must say is a blessing. And she and Franklin eat at the club every night. I don't want to join them, God forbid, so I batch at home on peanut butter and eggs."

"Together?" Michael, whose tastes run to the gourmet, was horrified.

"No," she laughed, "peanut butter one night, eggs the next. So this is Nirvana! I shall now proceed to make a pig of myself."

We settled down to serious eating.

After dinner, we formed an assembly line by which the dishes got removed from the table, scraped and placed in the dishwasher. Then, still in a mood of comfortable, satisfied companionship, we carried big mugs of decaffeinated coffee into the den.

I made a fire while Michael and Ginger settled back into opposite ends of mother's big comfy chintz couch. I sat on the rag rug on the floor in front of them and leaned against the green leather library chair. It was an odd mix of furniture, but it worked somehow.

"This is nice," Ginger said softly.

They watched the flames. I stared at the random patterns in the rug and thought of the now-useless hands of my mother that had woven it almost thirty years ago.

"Well." Ginger lifted her shoulders in a sigh that said she was ready to talk. "I'll tell you why I came by this afternoon, but I hope it doesn't ruin this lovely mood. I heard The Foundation is going to contest my father's will."

I gave her a direct look and a direct answer.

"Yes," I said.

And then she surprised me.

"Well, I just want you to know that's all right," she said. "I told you I never wanted the money. Well, now that I'm within dreaming distance of it, I'm not so sure I was honest with myself about that. You know how it is, you get to thinking maybe you could do some good in the world. Pay for the money, so to speak. But I want you to know I understand your decision and I don't hold it against you. I'd do the same thing if I were in your position. I know it's nothing personal against me; it's for The Foundation and the museum. You're only doing your job."

I winced at the phrase. Only doing my job: Damn the torpedoes and the consequences no matter who got hurt in the process? How badly would Ginger suffer if we won?

"That's very good of you," I said.

"However." She grinned wickedly. "I *am* going to fight you for it! Who knows? Maybe I could do as much good with the money as you and The Foundation could. And maybe I'd enjoy a little luxury that money could buy me. I've never had luxury since I so proudly left home. My jobs have been menial and my budget's been tight."

I read amusement in her eyes, and challenge. She had her father's competitive spirit, all right; it just took a cause to galvanize it.

"So be warned, my friend," she said and winked at Michael. "I'll give you a fight for your money—a fight for *my* money, that is!"

"So be it." I raised my coffee mug to her. "And may the most cunning attorneys win."

They stayed another half hour, chatting idly, avoiding unhappy topics, before bundling up to face the frozen tundra outside. Ginger tactfully left first.

"Thank you, Jenny," she said softly, just to me. "This is the second time now that you've provided an oasis during a rough time. It's meant a lot to me, just to get away from my near and dear for an evening and to talk about something besides death and taxes."

"It's been nice for me, too," I said inadequately. "You were kind to stick around tonight."

"Kind had nothing to do with it." She grinned and patted her stomach. "I figured I *had* to get a better meal here than I would at home."

She closed the front door behind her, leaving Michael and me alone in the hallway. He pulled me in toward his puffy ski jacket.

"Will you be all right, Jenny?"

"Yes, fine." I had the feeling he was going to kiss me in something other than a brotherly fashion. I shoved my better judgment to one side, and let him.

A few moments later, he said, "My father's coming back permanently to take over the business, Jen."

"No!"

"It's okay; in fact, it's a relief. It's what he needs to keep him happy and alive. And maybe now he'll finally see that our problems have not been entirely of my doing."

"What about you?"

He chewed on the outer edge of his lower lip and gazed at me in an evaluative sort of way. I could imagine him looking just like that when he was estimating construction costs—and coming up with a price the client would not be willing to pay.

"There's nothing in Poor Fred for me," he said, "at least not in business. I've decided to look for opportunities elsewhere. I've got a friend who has a construction business in Colorado and it's booming. He wants me to come in as partners with him and help him run it. It might be my chance to prove myself to myself . . ."

And to your father, I thought, but didn't say it.

"Come with me, Jenny," he said. My secretary would have dissolved, but then she reads Harlequin romances. I, on the other hand, reader of the *Kiplinger Report* and the *Wall Street Journal,* froze. Still, he managed not to look foolish as he said, "Come with me, and we'll make a new start together."

I pulled away from him.

"I don't need a new start, Michael. I have the job I want and the future I want right here."

"You won't have me right here."

"Can we talk about it later, Michael? Let's talk about it after I get back from New York."

"That's what people say when the answer is no, isn't it?" he said bitterly. "They say we'll talk about it later. But later the answer is still no."

"I don't know . . ."

"Sure you do."

He lifted his ski cap from the coat tree.

"Good night, Swede."

"Thank you for coming over." I tried to soften my tone. "It was sweet of you to be concerned about me. Believe me, I do appreciate the fact that you're so often there when I need someone."

"You might consider returning the favor," he said and slammed the door behind him.

I let the fire in the den die down and the room get cold before I stumbled to bed. I set the alarm early enough to allow me time to pack the bag I might need if I stayed the night in New York.

The bed—the four-poster I'd slept in all the years of my growing up—was soft and warm as my mother's hug. I went to sleep quickly, but woke in the middle of the night crying from a dream of loss and desolation.

Chapter 14

I read the morning paper in the cab on the way to the airport the next morning, having decided not to risk my car and neck on streets which had been freshly iced in the night.

The cabbie heard me unfold the paper. He glanced back in the rearview mirror.

"I don't buy that sensational crap," he declared. "A mass murderer in Poor Fred? Come on, what do they think we are, idiots?"

I peered over the top of the *News* at the back of his big head of neatly trimmed gray hair. His cab was immaculate; he looked spiffy in black wool slacks, a red plaid Pendleton with a green turtleneck underneath, and a tan suede jacket with a matching billed cap. "It's My Cab," a sign on the visor announced, "and I'm Damn Proud of It. Wipe Your Feet. Don't Smoke."

"I don't know that I'd call three a mass," I said. "But what do you think happened, if it wasn't murder?"

"They were old and they died, period, end of quote."

"In an abandoned icebox!"

"People get senile, they do weird things. I'm telling you, it's just the press making a murder out of a molehill, so to speak."

It was rather comforting to know there was at least one person in Port Frederick who hadn't panicked. From the tenor of the stories in the paper, it seemed everyone else had.

"But what about finding the same medicine in all three victims?" I demanded of him. "Especially in the two who didn't have hypertension?"

"So how do we know they didn't have high blood pressure?" he rebutted. "You get old, you get hypertension. Maybe nobody knew they had it."

I sorted out the pronouns.

"Not even their doctors?"

"Maybe they only *thought* they had hypertension, the victims, I mean. You know, hypochondriacs. Listen, all it is, is it's a conspiracy to sell more newspapers and get more money out of the Town Council so's they can beef up the police force. You mark my words, now anytime some old coot kicks off, they'll say he was murdered! Well, my aunty's booties, that's all I can say. Which airline you want? The commuter flight, right? I'll drop ya at the gate."

"Uh, yes, fine," I said and returned to reading the paper. Opening a cab door is like walking into an adventure; you never know what awaits you.

I tipped him well when he, unnecessarily, carried my overnight bag to the ticket counter. He smiled a benediction on my generosity.

"See?" he said to the public at large. "Women tip just fine. Just treat them nice like they was human like everybody else, and they'll do you right. Thank you, ma'am, don't be scared of getting killed or anything, they're just selling newspapers."

With a tidy tip of his suede cap he was gone, leaving a variety of bemused, amused and offended expressions on the faces of the people around me. I picked up my ticket—open seating—and checked through security to the gate. Simon and Geof were there already, separated from each other by a blue plastic seat and their respective raised newspapers. I supposed they knew each other, since Geof would have had to interview Simon about Arnie's murder at the museum.

Simon saw me first. Slowly, like a striptease artist, he lowered his paper down past his nose, his mouth, his neck, the collar of his conservative white shirt that nicely complemented his conservative and proper dark blue suit with its thin red pinstripe, and . . .

"My God, Simon." I must have sounded strangled. "A cravat?"

He grinned and stroked the red and silky thing. He crossed one leg over the other so that his matching red socks showed vividly at his ankles.

"We are going among the Philistines, my dear," he said. "And they think all artists are strange; they *expect* artists to dress in a nonconformist manner. I shall not disappoint them! I shall epitomize the popular misconception of artist as fool."

Geof lowered his paper and looked bewildered. Simon does that to people.

I set my briefcase and overnight bag on the seat between them and took the empty seat next to Geof. I leaned over him and glared suspiciously at Simon.

"Simon," I said, "are you doing this to drive me crazy? Because if that's why you're doing it, I want you to know it won't work. I know you for the simpleminded practical joker you are, and I know perfectly well that you will remove those offensive objects and put on proper socks and a tie before we get to their offices."

He looked as if I'd run over his tricycle.

"You're no fun anymore, Jenny," he said lugubriously, "you haven't been any fun since I refused to sleep with you."

"Simon!"

Geof shifted uncomfortably in his already uncomfortable seat; other passengers looked away from Simon's purposely loud voice, hiding smiles.

"We were lovers, you see," Simon lied straightfaced to Geof. "I don't suppose many people know that, but it's true. But she's so demanding, Detective Bushfield, such an insatiable woman, well I had to get my rest . . ."

"Simon Church, you lying, rotten, lousy . . ."

"You're sputtering, Jenny, it's getting all over your blouse. Disgusting habit, sputtering. Try to control yourself, my love, I don't want you embarrassing me in New York."

He finished the process of folding his paper, which he had begun while we talked, and stood and placed it on the seat. Then, with an innocent smile, he strolled off toward the coffee machine across the hall.

"Infuriating man," I said to Geof, but loudly enough to amuse Simon as he walked away. "One of these days, I'll lose my sense of humor and my patience and I'll turn him over my knee and spank him."

Simon heard that and quickly turned around.

"Oh, promise!" he simpered, so that I had to laugh.

Geof smiled and said quietly to me, "It seems to me that geniuses are often childish. I've never yet met one I'd care to live with. It's only after they're dead that they become lovable."

"Well," I said, "I will grudgingly admit to his genius. I don't know if you know it or not, but Simon has an international reputation as an art historian and scholar. And he's really quite a talented artist in his own right, which I don't suppose many people know. Oils, pastels, photography, watercolor. Simon is one of those rare birds who can *do* as well as teach."

I gazed at the artist in question, watching him pound the coffee machine when it failed to release the correct change.

"But you're right about childish." I sighed the sigh of experience. "I've seen him throw temper tantrums that would shame a two-year-old—yelling, throwing things, the whole scene. And then sometimes a silly mood comes over him, like today, and that's when I really watch out. He's totally unpredictable when he's in this mood."

"Not much fun playing parent to a grown man," Geof said sympathetically. And on that bit of wisdom we stood, gathered our belongings and joined the line of passengers to board the plane for New York City.

We found seats together in nonsmoking. Simon took his foul French cigarettes to the rear.

"Behave yourselves, children," he said as he squeezed past in the aisle. "Tell her to keep her hands to herself, Detective Bushfield."

Absurdly, I blushed. Geof frowned in the exasperated way that people do around Simon. It reminded me of the way that our high school principal used to frown whenever he saw little Geoffrey Bushfield in the halls.

By mutual unspoken accord, we waited until after lift-off and the passing out of coffee to talk about the murders.

"Hold my coffee cup for me, will you, Jenny? Thanks." He lifted his black briefcase from under the seat in front of him and used a key to open the lock. As he removed a small tape recorder, I glimpsed several small packages in the same sort of plastic envelope in which he had placed the poem about Mrs. Hatch. He saw my glance.

"That's why I'm going to New York," he said. "Their crime labs can do tricks we can't afford to do."

"That's why they call us Poor Fred," I said lightly. I was nervous. I'd never been interviewed about a crime before. And I was having a hard time adjusting to the fact that the juvenile delinquent I used to know was the experienced cop sitting next to me.

As if he read my insecurities, he gave me a reassuring smile. If the boy is the father of the man, I had certainly missed something back in the days when I had looked down my nose at Geof the teenager. I squirmed inwardly at the memory of my snobbishness and hoped he didn't remember me as well as I remembered him.

He plugged a small microphone into the machine, slipped in a fresh cassette and turned the recorder to

On. Then he took back his coffee from me, leaned back in his seat and made me a thoughtful present of that same nice smile.

"Interview with Miss Jennifer Cain," he said into the mike just loud enough for it and me to hear him. The noise of the twin props kept our conversation private. "Miss Cain is the executive director of the Port Frederick, Massachusetts, Civic Foundation, address . . ."

He told the mike that he was asking me to explain my finding of the body of Mrs. Charles Withers Hatch.

I did, closing my eyes now and then as I tried to recall accurately the horrifying details he wanted. He did not interrupt, but let me answer each question until I ran out of words. By the time I was through, the stewardess had announced preparations to land. Geof took the microphone back from my hands and put the recorder back into the briefcase and stuffed the thing back under the seat.

"That was fine, Jenny," he said. The stewardess came by and reached across for our empty cups. She left behind a provocative, subtle wave of perfume. Geof sniffed appreciatively before he said, "Now, when and where can I meet you today to finish this business?"

"What's to finish?" I pulled my seatback "to a full upright position" like a good little passenger.

He smiled. "Well, if I'm doing my job right, one or two questions may occur to me. I'll want to get the answers while they're still fresh in your mind."

"Okay, how about the Plaza for lunch?"

He looked as if I'd just displayed a surprising lapse of good taste. "Uh, Jenny, my police department expense account won't cover the Plaza. Schrafft's, maybe, but not the Plaza."

"Neither will my expense account from The Foundation." I smiled winningly at him. "It's on me, please. I like to pamper myself when I'm in New York. You may as well take advantage of my self-indulgence."

"Lunch at the Plaza." His eyes had a hungry, yearning look. "This couldn't be construed as bribing an officer of the law, could it?"

"Absolutely not!" I said firmly. "It can't be a bribe, because there's nothing I want from you."

"I'm sorry to hear that," he said lightly. We tightened our seat belts and the plane landed.

Chapter 15

I love New York," I said to Simon in the back seat of our shared cab. Geof had departed in a different direction in the patrol car that picked him up at La Guardia.

"Unoriginal, my love," Simon said. "It's already been done."

I grinned at a Hare Krishna bicycling past; flimsy saffron fabric flowed from beneath his Salvation Army coat and draped the boots that rode the pedals. He threw a kiss at me. I said, "If I live to be a hundred . . ."

". . . which is getting harder to do in Poor Fred . . ."

". . . I will still love New York. It sizzles, Simon. And how many things still sizzle in this jaded world, I ask you."

"Steak, bacon, eggs on a sidewalk on a hot day . . ."

"Look at that!" I pointed as a girl whirred by on

roller skates; she was dressed in wool and warm raccoon—*live* warm raccoon. The creature—a young, small one—was snuggled into the front of her coat with only its bright-eyed, pointed head visible beneath her chin. They both looked as if they were enjoying the ride. We whisked past a street corner where two vendors argued territory. I heard one of them bellow: "I'll show you where to roast your chestnuts, buddy!"

I leaned back, deeply satisfied.

"Oh, Simon, New York makes me feel alive and electric! Port Frederick is so conservative it's barely breathing. Look at this! It's exciting, they live on the edge, they take risks, they . . ."

"They pay exorbitant rent," he said. "They rob and mug and murder each other. On second thought, I guess they're not so different from us, are they, my love?"

"Splat," I said. I turned away from the fascinating view to frown at him. "A little reality therapy, eh Simon? Thanks a lot. There goes my good mood."

"Good." He didn't bother to look my way. "I hate to pout alone."

He'd calmed down considerably since our departure from home, even loosening the cravat in what I fervently hoped was a first step toward removing it. But instead of settling into a congenial mood, he'd plunged straight down to sarcastic and depressed. I was worried about the impending meeting.

I looked back out the window and tried to recapture the happy, anticipatory feeling. We passed the canopied doorway of an exclusive condominium where a uniformed doorman struggled to untangle the leashes of one Doberman, two Pekingese, a dachshund and a

Brittany spaniel. The trees of Central Park emerged, bare and beautiful as a Japanese print, between the buildings ahead of us. I opened the window a crack to admit the crisp, invigorating air—an aromatic blend of espresso, fresh bread, Italian sausage and the smell of snow filled the cab.

"I don't care," I said softly. "It makes me sizzle."

"Well, don't splatter on me," Simon said, having the last grumpy word.

Our meeting with the lawyers was quick and hard and to the point. Simon and I sat in orange leather chairs facing three gray attorneys across an intimidating expanse of walnut table in a conference room that smelled of lemon oil and money. Simon had, at the last possible minute, exchanged the crimson cravat and socks for the proper socks and tie he had stuffed in his briefcase.

"Mr. Church," the youngest lawyer pronounced, "are we correct in our understanding that under the terms of the will of Mrs. Martha Paul Frederick, all the art that has been purchased with funds from her estate must be displayed in her ancestral home?"

Simon managed to follow the sentence and said, "Correct."

"Mr. Church," the youngest lawyer then said, "are we further correct in our understanding that since the bulk of the collection consists of works of art that have been purchased by using the funds from her estate, there has never been a large enough collection of art that has been purchased through the beneficence of other sources to allow for the construction or locating of a second or other museum?"

That one was tougher to track. Simon hesitated and

then said, "Right again. It's almost all stuff we bought with Martha's money, so we have to keep it in her house."

The attorneys blinked at the use of the word *stuff* to describe masterworks of the quality of the Degas they were empowered to protect. The eldest actually flinched when Simon called the redoubtable Mrs. Frederick by her first name.

"Mr. Church," continued Junior, "is it also true that the house—the museum—is an eighteenth-century structure that is rapidly deteriorating? And that the works of art are, themselves, in danger of deterioration because of inadequate temperature and humidity controls; fire hazards; danger from severe storms; inadequate maintenance, storage and protective displays and shortage of trained staff?" He said all that without once referring to his notes. *I* was impressed.

Simon clenched his big red hands in his lap and looked defensive. "Correct," he said through a visibly stiff jaw.

"Mr. Church." Really, the man was most irritating. I felt sorry for Simon and wondered when my turn for the inquisition would come. The lawyer said, "It has also come to our attention that you cannot hope to move the works of art to another, safer facility without an attempt through the courts to break the original terms of Mrs. Frederick's will." All three lawyers frowned at the mere thought of such temerity. The whippersnapper continued, "The museum, we understand, has no funds to finance such an attempt. We may, therefore, safely assume that the works of art will remain where they are—in clear and present danger—for some time to come."

Simon and I looked at each other, and the thought of Arnie Culverson's money and what it could accomplish passed between us. I felt Simon struggle with the question of whether to broach that delicate subject; I was relieved when he decided to leave it well enough alone.

"That is correct," he finally said.

My turn.

"Miss Cain." The middle-aged lawyer took over. "Let us state a hypothetical situation. Let us suppose that an extremely valuable painting came into the possession of The Foundation. Let us further suppose that The Foundation chose to lend said painting to the Martha Paul Frederick Museum of Fine Art. Now, my question to you is this: If it became apparent that the painting was in danger of suffering damage because of adverse conditions at the museum, what would you do? Would The Foundation choose to leave the painting at the Martha Paul? Or would you have it removed to storage or to another museum where it could be kept in a safer fashion?"

I froze, chilled by the sudden realization of why the painting had been left to The Foundation instead of bequeathed directly to the Martha Paul. This had never happened before; it was an ominous precedent for the museum. I couldn't bear to look at Simon, though I knew he was staring at me.

"We would remove the painting from the Martha Paul," said I, the traitor. "We would place it in another museum where it could be maintained in greater safety."

The three lawyers were the only ones in the room who relaxed. They would need the assurance in writing from my trustees, they told me. And then the young one smiled and became a person as well as an attorney.

"You can see," he said, "why our client left the Degas to The Foundation." He smiled at Simon, innocent of the pain his words caused. "Our client had seen for himself how your museum is crumbling. He didn't want to risk keeping his beloved painting there past the time when it is safe to do so. You'll have the Degas for a while, Mr. Church, at least until The Foundation finds a better spot for it. Our client did wish it to be displayed with its sister painting, at least for a while. Perhaps you can lend *your* Degas to the museum that gets *our* Degas!" His bright, friendly smile faltered in the face of Simon's expression. He said, "Really, it is too bad about that will of Mrs. Frederick's. People can be so shortsighted in their last testaments. I'm sure you'll get other bequests routed through The Foundation, too, as the museum continues to deteriorate. Really, it is a shame, Mr. Church, and most unusual, but it can't be helped, can it?"

They thanked us for our time.

I took the papers they wanted my trustees to sign.

They closed the heavy oak doors behind us and we took the elevator forty-eight floors down to the street.

"Simon . . ." I looked up at his stricken face.

"You'd really take that painting away from me?" he said wonderingly. "You'd do that to me, Jenny?"

"Rather than see the painting harmed? Of course, Simon, how could I do otherwise?"

"That goddamn house!" His large, handsome face twisted in anguish. "That goddamn house!"

He stalked away from me, pushing against the flow of the early lunch crowd.

"Simon!"

I wanted to remind him that we might successfully contest Arnie's will and be able to start the process that might lead to a new museum. But he didn't turn around.

I stood in the cold for a moment, full of sympathy for Simon. But I didn't regret my answer. The lawyers' client—that smart old man who loved Degas—had known what he was doing. So did I.

Chapter 16

The Plaza Hotel was within walking distance, so I did. Geof was waiting for me—looking remarkably at ease, I thought—on a chair in the lobby, his briefcase with its depressing reminders tucked unobtrusively behind his legs. His thick brown hair looked as if he'd recently combed it; his tweed sport coat, yellow shirt and brown wool slacks compared favorably with the designer and preppy attire strolling by. It occurred to me as I walked up to him that I didn't know much about his family or background. Plumbers, I seemed to remember, probably good ones.

"Have any trouble finding the joint?" I asked him, and smiled.

He looked amused. "No problem," he said. "I knew I was getting closer as the mink coats and limousines got longer."

I laughed and gazed around us at the opulent lobby

with its matching guests. "The wealth *is* astounding," I said. "It's hard to reconcile with the beggars and bag ladies outside."

Geof bent to retrieve his briefcase and then put a surprising hand under my elbow. I felt a disconcerting flush go through my body at the nearness and maleness of him. He was saying, "Well, that's one good thing about your job, isn't it, Jenny? Through The Foundation you *can* reconcile some of the disparities of the world. You find ways for the rich to give to the poor, don't you?"

"We try, God and the IRS willing." I looked up at him. "You seem to be leading me straight into the Palm Court. There are other restaurants in this hotel, you know. Would you rather try one of them?"

That amused look crossed his face again. "No," he said, "there's a table waiting for us here. I hope you don't mind, but I went ahead and arranged it so we wouldn't have to compete with the lunch crowd."

"I don't mind at all; I think that's a fine idea." I did, too, though I was surprised at the aplomb with which he was handling this bastion of privilege. I mentally kicked myself and told myself not to be such a snob; even policemen and plumbers' sons have social graces.

The maître d' escorted us to a table for two, set beautifully with linen and crystal. Ah, the Plaza. I unfolded a yellow linen napkin and covered my lap with it.

"How do *you* reconcile the disparities, Geof?"

"Cops only reconcile domestic disturbances," he said wryly, "and we're not even very good at that. As for the poor and hungry and troubled of this world, I stopped trying to reconcile them with the idea of justice a long time ago. Goes with the territory, cop territory, where there is law but little justice."

I fiddled with the heavy silver knife at my right hand.

"So here we sit," I mused. "We will order caviar and wine . . ."

"We will?" He looked delighted. "I'm glad to hear it."

". . . and we will pay for it what a beggar collects in a week . . ."

"Some beggars make $30,000 a year, I think you should know," he said.

". . . and why doesn't that knowledge ruin my appetite?"

"What, that some beggars make good money?"

"Come on, Geof, you know what I mean."

He met my serious gaze with one of his own. How did we get in so deep so soon, I wondered.

"Do you always get guilt spasms when you go to the Plaza?" he said. "I told you, Jenny, cops don't worry about inequities. We can't, I can't. I'll eat my caviar and drink my wine while the beggar whines, because I don't know what else to do and because there's always one more beggar. And after that, one more and one more. What? Shall I righteously refuse to dine here? Shall I insist on Schrafft's and dedicate my chili dog to the bag ladies of the world? Hell, they'd be glad to eat at Schrafft's, much less the Plaza! And my hot dog might be more than they'd get all day. So where do you draw the line, Jenny? At steaks or hot dogs or dog food? Maybe we should all starve to death; then we'd be equal for sure.

"Look." Still his voice was low and calm. "I do what I can, as you certainly do. Sometimes we're selfish and sometimes we're generous; sometimes we screw up and sometimes we get it right. But mostly we're human. That's all I know. Do you mind if we order now? I'm starving."

I stared at him.

"It has been said, you know," I said, "that the real sinner is not the man who kicks the beggar, but the man who ignores him."

"All right," he said.

"All right, what?"

"All right, I agree, I'm a cynical bastard."

I couldn't help but smile, I was so startled. And he couldn't seem to help but smile back at me. "You put on a good act," I said, and he laughed as though I'd told a marvelous joke. A couple of elegant heads turned. I was suddenly, ridiculously pleased to be seen with this contradictory, opinionated, intimidating, appealing, good-natured man.

"Oh, Jenny," he started to say when a waiter materialized at our table. He stood at a tactful midway point between us. It used to be so easy for waiters to take the order from the male of the party and present the bill to him, too. Now, poor things, they don't know where to look first or whom to thank. I've had some who thanked my male dining companion after *I* signed the charge slip!

Waiters at the Plaza, however, always know precisely what to do at all times in all situations. That's why they're waiters at the Plaza. I was irreverently tempted to ask this one to solve our philosophical conundrum. Instead, I ordered lunch for both of us. Thinking Geof might enjoy a sampling of the Plaza's most famous dishes, I ordered a veritable smorgasbord of delicacies.

His smile was gratifyingly beatific.

"I have died and gone to heaven," he said. I complimented myself for giving him a treat that so obviously delighted him. I hoped it would be a unique and special experience for an underpaid policeman. His eyes were dreamy as he said, "That's what my mother used to order for us kids when she'd bring us to town for Christmas shopping."

"Your mother brought you here?" I'm afraid my voice rose on the last word.

"Yep." His eyes were still dreamy with fond memories. "We had a favorite suite, too, with a separate bedroom for us kids. We'd stay and play with our nanny while Mother shopped."

I swallowed some water and chagrin.

"Geof," I tried to say casually, "your family's in the plumbing business—am I remembering right?"

"Right, and hardware. Bushware, Inc., you know."

Bushware, Inc., was the third or fourth largest hardware and plumbing supply company in the Northeast. I felt as dense and small as the drain in a stopped-up sink as I said weakly, "But you're not headquartered in Port Frederick, are you?"

"I am," he said firmly, "at *police* headquarters. The rest of the family, you're right, has been stationed in Boston for years. That's why nobody in Poor Fred connects me with the firm, thank God."

"Stationed?" Our wine arrived and the waiter, bless his correct little heart, presented the cork to me to sniff and the glass to me to sip and approve. I did, vigorously.

"That's how I think of it." The corners of his mouth pulled down in disgust. "A family business is like the army, you know, at least ours is. You start in basic training at the bottom and rise through the ranks to the top. And you're in for life unless you're willing to go AWOL and face the consequences."

"Which are?"

He grinned. "You are looking at the Bushfield black sheep. If you get too close, you'll find little tufts of black wool stuck to your clothes." He grinned even more hugely.

"Baa," he said. "Baa, baa."

He looked so silly and smug that I giggled.

"Well, you make light of it now," I said, and thought of Michael, "but I'll bet it took some courage at the time."

"Some," he said mildly. "But it's much easier to go your own way when you have enough money to grease the alternate path. I have the best of both worlds, Jenny—a profession I like as well as generous trust funds to compensate for the lousy pay." He paused and looked a little embarrassed. "Uh, back home I don't talk about my family much. I mean, you can see how the other cops might resent my privileges. I don't blame them. Why should I be so lucky? But then, we've already decided life's not fair."

"*You* decided," I said. "I still suspect it all works out somewhere along the line."

"Well," he shrugged, "I guess you have to be an optimist in your line of work. You know, my father says I'm still in the plumbing business—only I can't fix the kind of sewers I walk in."

On that appetizing note, lunch arrived.

Just before the first bite, I finally asked the single question I'd been dying to ask.

"Geof?"

He gave me that little mocking grin again.

"Yes, Jenny?"

"Why did you become a cop?"

He laughed. "What you mean to say is, *How* in God's name did I ever become a cop, all things considered."

"Okay," I laughed, "okay, that's what I mean."

He raised his glass of red wine to me. "I'll tell you about it sometime if you're really interested." There was an unexpected seriousness about his gaze. "Are you?"

"Yes," I said, and lifted my glass to his.

By another of those unspoken accords into which we seemed to fall naturally and easily, we proceeded to avoid unpleasant subjects—like death and sewers —while we voraciously, unabashedly devoured every delectable morsel.

Ah, the Plaza.

The waiter cleared away the plates that we had all but licked clean. He wiped the tabletop of crumbs and spills. He supplied two cups of excellent coffee. I took a sip of mine and waited for the detective to take the conversational lead.

"Jenny, you think the killer knew Mrs. Hatch personally, that he'd have to have known her to have written what he did."

"Yes, or knew about her from other people."

"Was that trait of hers—that need for gratitude— was it widely known?"

"I wouldn't think so. It's the sort of thing you'd only recognize after you'd known somebody quite a while, don't you think? Her family probably recognized it, although you can never tell about families, and a few of us who'd worked with her on charitable causes knew about it."

"Who?"

I didn't like specific, incriminating questions like that. I tried to be fair in my incrimination by spreading it around town: "Oh, the director of the Welcome Home for Girls . . ."

"Allison Parker. She had quite a bit to gain, didn't she? Now she has money to secure her job and the future of the home."

". . . and my staff." I didn't even argue with his comments on Allison; they were obviously such weak motives for murder. "Edwin Ottilini. My other trustees. And just about anybody else in the world to whom any of us had gossiped, I guess."

"So we're back to widely known."

I leaned my forehead on my hand and smiled apologetically. "Yes," I said, "sorry."

"What about the other two verses?" He took copies of them out of his coat pocket and laid them on the table in front of me. "Do these make you think the killer also knew Culverson and Cohen?"

Like graffiti on a chapel wall, they profaned the genteel atmosphere. They were simpering, leering slashes of malevolence. They infuriated and frightened me. I wrapped my hands around the warm coffee cup to hide my craven trembling as I read again:

> Now I lay me down to sleep,
> Devil take my soul to keep;
> Cross my heart and hope to die,
> If I tell another lie.

"I don't know what lie Arnie might have told," I said, "or what lie he might have been *perceived* to have told . . ."

"That's an interesting, subtle point." He smiled at me approvingly. "You'd make a good detective, Jenny."

I felt a pleasure in his approval that was all out of proportion to the event. I very nearly shuffled my feet and said aw shucks. He continued, oblivious of my inner wackiness: "But Culverson *did* lie to The Foundation and the museum, right? What about that?"

"Well, he didn't so much lie as change his mind about who he would give his money to. And we didn't even know about that until *after* he was dead. I suppose the only person who knew was his lawyer."

"Ottilini."

"Yes."

"Okay, so everyone else *claims* not to have known," he said, giving me pause and making me realize there was only one real detective in the crowd. "We'll leave it at that for now. What about the rhyme that was left on Moshe Cohen's body?"

I reread it:

> If all the world's a stage,
> My script is at the final page;
> This play is done because . . .
> Shylock's dead. Applause.

I shook my head in frustration.

"It doesn't tell me anything," I said, "except maybe whoever wrote it was anti-Semitic."

He put the notes away.

"Geof, there is one thing, though," I said hesitantly. He paid me the compliment of looking interested. "All three of them were killed at their favorite charities. Arnie's passion was the museum—that bed in particular—and that's where you found him; Moshe Cohen's passion was the theater; and Mrs. Hatch loved the Welcome Home."

"Who else knows that?"

"Oh lord, anybody who knew them and a lot of people who didn't. They were all prominent, public sorts of people."

"Jenny, do you see any other connection between them that I might not see? Anything besides the facts that they were rich and given to doing good works?"

"Well, there are some connections, but you've probably already considered them." I felt shy about asserting my thoughts in police territory.

"Tell me anyway," he said encouragingly, "and we'll see if I missed one."

Given as I am to making lists, it was easy to oblige.

"They lived in the same neighborhood," I said. "Same lawyers, same accountants, same country club. They were likable, all of them, but demanding and accustomed to privilege. They went to the same parties, but then how can you help it in a town our size? They probably shopped at the same grocery stores and department stores. They knew the same people, at least socially. And they were all committed to or at least interested in The Foundation . . ."

I stopped. I stared at the empty spot on the table where the offensive notes had been.

"Culverson, Cohen and Hatch," I muttered to myself. I was trying to snag a loose end that floated tantalizingly at the edge of my consciousness. "Hatch, Cohen and Culverson. Cohen, Culverson and . . ."

"What?" Geof pounced on my hesitation.

"No." I shook my head, dismayed. "No, it isn't, I don't believe it."

"What? Cohen, Culverson and . . . *what,* Jenny?"

I raised my hands to my lips as if they could keep the hideous idea safely buried in my head. But it spilled out of my mouth anyway.

"It's the order, the alphabetical order," I said. My voice seemed to have disappeared; Geof leaned forward to hear me. "Cohen, Culverson and Hatch."

I stopped again. My God, I didn't want to go on.

"We, uh, keep lists at The Foundation, Geof, lists of potential donors. It's a common practice among fund raisers, no big deal. Well, we have long lists of the names of people and corporations from whom we plan to solicit grants and bequests. For instance, there's a list of Port Frederick people, and another of potential donors in the county, and there's a national list and even an international one, mostly of people who've expressed interest in the Martha Paul. And . . ."

His eyes said keep going.

"And there is one very short list of potential major donors. They're not necessarily the richest people in town, but they're the people who are most likely to contribute the largest amounts of money to The Foundation. They've either indicated a firm commitment or shown a strong interest. It's a very private list, you understand, and they might not like to know they were on it, though we don't mean any harm by it . . ."

"How many people are on this list, Jenny?"

"F-five. We call it the Big Five. Or at least we used to—several months ago, I told my staff to quit using that term because I was afraid one of the people on it might hear about it and be offended. I haven't used it myself in a long time—I suppose that's why I didn't think of it until now." It was not only getting harder for me to talk, it was getting harder to breathe.

Geof helped me out.

"And Cohen, Culverson and Hatch were on the list?"

"Yes, in alphabetical order, like that. It's almost a joke, a chant . . ."

"What is?"

"The names of the Big Five, the names in alphabetical order. We used to say them so often and so hopefully they became like a ritualistic chant . . ."

"How does the complete chant go, Jenny?"

I swallowed and saw that he was shocked at the look in my eyes when I finally raised them to meet his own.

"Cohen, Culverson, Hatch and Mimbs," I singsonged. "Cohen, Culverson, Hatch and Mimbs."

"But that's only four names, Jenny. What's the fifth?"

I licked my very dry lips. I said, "The whole chant goes like this: Cain, Cohen, Culverson, Hatch and Mimbs. Cain . . ."

Geof had become very still. The only part of him that moved was his mouth.

"Which Cain?" he said stiffly.

I pointed miserably at my own chest.

"This one."

"Oh Jesus," the detective said.

Chapter 17

Mrs. Mimbs, please."

"Speaking." Minnie held her free hand to the light and critically examined the pale grape polish on her nails. Yes, it was just the right shade for the lilac jersey dress. She patted her newly-lavendered hair. "Who's this?"

"James Turner, ma'am, sorry to disturb you at home."

"James?" The church custodian didn't sound at all like himself and she said so. "For heaven's sake, James, you must have the most awful cold. I hope you're not washing floors or doing anything cold and damp."

"No ma'am." He coughed and excused himself.

"What can I do for you, James?" she said briskly, helpfully. He never bothered her with anything less than important concerns; the Grand Old Man of Spic and Span he called himself, and she agreed.

"It's the roof, Mrs. Mimbs." His reedy voice had coarsened with the bad cold. "The snow load is too heavy; I think it's going to crack the roof."

"Oh my word!" She'd warned them about that roof; she'd even offered to pay for a new one. But oh no, we need the money for a new vestibule, they'd said, and then it was an addition to the Sunday School and then repaving the parking lot, thank you very much. There's nothing wrong with the roof, they'd said, as if prayers alone could mend the leaks and support the icy weight of Port Frederick winters.

"I don't suppose you can get anybody else to listen to you," she said knowingly. Really, that young priest was a nice boy, but he didn't know a thing about capital improvements. She'd *told* the bishop they ought to teach architecture and economics at the seminary, but he'd only smiled that pious, patronizing smile and patted her hand.

"That's right, ma'am." His voice was so weak and hoarse it sounded very near to laryngitis.

"Well, you stay there, James," she said. "I'll be right over."

"Uh, I'm sorry, ma'am, but my daughter wants to take me to the doctor this afternoon. Could you come over this evening, do you think?"

"You don't think the roof will cave in between now and then, do you?" She wasn't joking.

"No, ma'am." Neither was he.

"Well then. I'll meet you at the chapel at seven o'clock. Now you take care of yourself, James, you do what the doctor says."

"Yes, ma'am, thank you," he said. "You won't tell anyone, about my calling, will you Mrs. Mimbs? Not just yet, I mean. I don't want to get into trouble, going over the reverend's head and all."

She assured him she would be discreet.

Funny what being sick will do to people, she thought as she hung up the phone. Makes them weak and subservient, even old James. Imagine him calling her Mrs. Mimbs and ma'am, when they'd been on a first-name basis for all the twenty-five years she'd been chairwoman of the House and Grounds Committee. The poor man must feel frightfully ill.

Well, she'd inspect that roof and be quick about it so she could send him home to that nice daughter who took such good care of him.

She looked at her watch, a fortieth anniversary present from her husband. Good. With five hours to go until seven, she had plenty of time to climb the stairs to her bedroom and lock the door and have a good cry.

She needed it. She felt awful and bewildered about Arnie and sweet Moshe. And she missed Florence Hatch very much—they'd been friends for so many years, they'd had so very much in common.

We walked north on Fifth Avenue—Goef and I—until the cold nagged us into hailing a horse and buggy. Then for an expensive half hour—his treat that time—we huddled under the gypsy red blanket in the carriage and murmured about murder.

He recalled enough of my family history to save me from having to explain in boring detail how I happened to be the fifth of the Big Five. Most everybody in town knows how my great-grandfather got rich canning clams, how his son expanded the business and our wealth, and how my dad—in the grand, sad tradition of third-generation failures—mismanaged the business so it finally had to be closed. That happened when I was seventeen years old, too young to try to take it over myself and run it. At any rate, thanks to the foresight of my grandfather—or maybe to his disappointed understanding of his son's deficiencies—my sister and I had long ago been provided with hefty trust funds. So even after the closure, she and I could still afford to move among the country club set into which we'd been born. (Perhaps I should say here that I'd like to be able to claim that I won my job on the basis of my sterling qualifications alone, but the truth is that my upper crust connections didn't hurt me none, as they say in Texas.) Even my father had trust funds on which to support my mother and to enable him to live out the rest of his lazy days in California.

Of course, the people he put out of work were not so lucky. It was they who suffered the most from the collapse of Cain Clams. I don't know if my father ever allowed himself to admit that fact—it isn't like him to take any blame for anything—but it shamed my sister and almost killed my already sick mother then and there. As for me, it was probably that incident as much as anything that propelled me toward this strange combination of high finance and social work. I guess I thought that through good deeds I might make partial payment toward the debt my family owes this town.

Having said all that to Geof, I then said that I thought the idea of someone killing the Big Five was ridiculous.

He said he'd heard stranger things.

I told him it was only coincidence.

He asked me how I'd like to be the fourth coincidence.

I said it made a nice theory, but there wasn't a motive behind it. Rhyme, yes, but no reason.

He asked me if I only believed in things I could see.

"Okay," I gave in temporarily, "suppose, just for the sake of not arguing, that it's true—what now?"

He pulled up another dirty, gaudy blanket from the floor of the carriage and tucked it around us. We were, by that time, heavy with blanket.

"*I* will continue to look for the connection that gives us the motive," he said. His earlobes were red with cold; mine were numb. "*You* will take pains to be extraordinarily careful with your life."

The horse's hooves clip-clopped in a steady, soothing rhythm; I heard the driver hail another driver in a passing carriage. I huddled and was still.

"Jenny?" His voice was sharp and brisk as the wind. "What's *your* passion?"

I looked at him, startled.

"My what?"

"If Culverson's passion was the museum and Cohen's was the theater, and Mrs. Hatch's was the home, what's yours?"

I knew what he was getting at and I didn't want to go there.

"The Foundation," I said reluctantly, "though I don't know that I'd call it a passion. Certainly, it's my overwhelming interest in life these days. But don't tell me to stay away from it, because I'm needed and I can't."

"Stay away from it."

"No."

"Just for a few days."

"And what if you don't catch the killer in just a few days? There are other ways of giving up your life, without dying. I'm not going to give mine up to fear."

His legs shifted impatiently under the blankets. His calm seemed to have vanished; he looked cold, worried and aggravated. He said to my stubborn profile, "Then don't be alone in the office. Not even with just one person. I want two people with you all the time while you're there. And I am not speaking as a friend you can shrug off; I am speaking as a cop who knows better than you do how to protect you."

"Hmmph," I said, or something to that effect.

"Listen, Jennifer, if I ever want to bequeath money to The Foundation, I'll come to you and ask your advice. You're the expert; I'll do as you say. Well, when it comes to murder and mayhem, I'm the resident expert. Please return the compliment and do as I say."

A grin slipped out from beneath my fear and fury.

"Think you might give us some money, humm?" I said. "Well, I just happen to have with me a little brochure that explains all the benefits and tax advantages that will accrue to you and your family if you . . ."

He laughed and literally broke the ice by flicking an icicle off the edge of the carriage window. The driver turned his ruddy face around and smiled benevolently at the nice young couple who were crazy enough to pay him to ride around and freeze.

"I have to go back tonight," Geof said. "For one thing, I want to talk to Mrs. Mimbs as soon as possible . . ."

Minnie. I thought of that dear, funny lady and the

Episcopal church to which she was emotionally and financially devoted. I hoped God was as caring of her as she was of Him.

Geof was still talking . . .

". . . and I suppose I'd be wasting my breath if I asked you to stay over in New York for a few days."

"Actually, we're probably going home on the same plane," I said helpfully. He didn't look helped. Then for some mischievous reason that must have reached way back into my subconscious, I turned to face him and smiled.

"What's *your* passion, Geof?"

He looked at me for a very long moment.

"I wish," he said, "that the weather would turn bad. I wish it would turn so bad they'd have to close the airports. And then we'd have no choice but to spend the night."

I let him get nervous for a moment, *if* indeed he ever got nervous about anything. Then I said, "Well, who knows—maybe the cab that takes us to my house will not be able to get back through the snow to yours."

He did what any red-blooded boy is supposed to do when he's riding in a buggy in Central Park.

He kissed the girl.

"Where are you off to, Minnie Mae?" Her husband had never liked the nickname HaHa; he said it degraded her dignity; she said she didn't have any dignity and didn't want any, thank you, how boring; he said she had more than she knew, so he called her by her real name which she said wasn't any too dignified itself.

He smiled up at her from his invalid's bed. Or

rather, half his face smiled; the other half hung, useless and expressionless, from the strong bones of his face, paralyzed by stroke.

"I'm off to church, my darling," she said and smiled fondly back at him. Really, people shouldn't tell her secrets they didn't want her sweetie to know. "James Turner called and he said the chapel roof is about to fall."

"You told them, didn't you dear?" he said proudly. "They should have listened to my Minnie Mae."

She sighed in put-upon agreement.

"Well, just you be careful, dear," he said. "I don't want that old roof caving in on my girl."

She blew him a kiss and promised to be home within the hour. His voice stopped her once more at the door of his bedroom.

"You look mighty pretty, Minnie." He flopped his good arm at her. "I surely do like you in purple."

Simon was cheerful again by the time we met him at La Guardia. He would have been talkative, too, if either of us had responded to him, but Geof buried himself in a police journal and I pretended to read a tourist guide to This Week in New York City.

"Well, did she behave herself?" Simon boomed, so that every passenger within fifty yards looked up. "Did she manage to control her libidinal urges?"

Geof withered him with a watch-it-buddy cop look and Simon slouched into a plastic seat across from us. He didn't see the twitch of a smile that Geof hid behind his magazine.

"Well, hell," Simon complained to no one in particular and everyone in general. He lifted an abandoned newspaper from the floor and propped it ostentatiously between him and us.

I read, or tried to. Every now and then a word identified itself to me as something I recognized. Bobby Short was playing at the Carlyle, I read, and saw myself there with a certain detective. Leonardo Print Exhibition at the Metropolitan Museum, the magazine announced, and I imagined us strolling the vast halls. I read that the Museum of Holography was open from ten to five weekdays, and that the Frick was open on Sundays and I thought of Sunday mornings in bed. I was as sensitive to the feel of Geof's tweed arm against my wool one as though I wore a short sleeved summer dress and my arm was bare.

Read the magazine, I commanded myself, but the voice sounded like Michael's and was aggrieved. An advertisement advised me to dine at the World Trade Center; I saw myself gazing over the rim of a glass of champagne at a man who was not Michael. Other ads invited me to stay at the St. Moritz, the Algonquin, the Hyatt . . . comfortable suites, soft beds, soft lights, smooth skin, soft lips . . .

By the time they called our flight my fancy was taking heated flights of its own. Funny what the twilight hour will do to the human imagination.

"So did you learn anything?" I asked Geof, and nodded my head at his magazine. "From the article?"

"What article?" he said and smiled. He ran a hand along his chin and the side of his face. "I need a shave."

"Yes," I said sweetly, "I'd appreciate that."

He had to turn away quickly so Simon couldn't read the amused and intimate message in his eyes.

Chapter 18

The snow was decoratively banked up to the bottom of the stained glass windows of the chapel, so the little church on the hill above the ocean looked like a New England picture postcard. Its steeple pointed out the right direction to heaven-bound Episcopalians. Its back yard was a rocky cliff which descended steeply and picturesquely to the de rigueur pounding waves below.

Minnie viewed with favor the Chamber-of-Commerce, tourist-approved quaint scene. But it was the immaculately cleared sidewalks and steps that were, to her elderly perspective, far more beautiful. She preferred her traction under foot rather than in a hospital bed. As she walked safely up to the double doors, she offered a silent prayer of gratitude—not so much to God as to James Turner for his conscientious labor on the snow plow.

The doors pushed open easily to her gloved hands.

My heavens, it was cold inside, much too chilly to remove her mink coat or lavender knit hat. Then she remembered it was, of course, Tuesday, the one day of the week when no activities were scheduled in the church and the thermostat was turned down to save a few pennies on fuel.

She and James would have the place to themselves. Good. Fewer interruptions meant greater efficiency.

It was so still inside the chapel that she could hear the snow shift on the roof. She peered up into the darkness at the suspect ceiling, listening for creaks and looking for cracks. Well, she didn't hear or see any signs of impending disaster, but James would show her. And then *she'd* show that well-meaning young whippersnapper of a priest.

She'd get some action, she would, or her name wasn't . . .

"Mrs. Mimbs."

Her old heart jumped violently as the figure walked out of the shadows at the front of the chapel. She laughed a little in surprise and relief when she saw who it was.

"Glory! You startled me," she said and sank into the hard seat of a walnut pew. "I didn't expect anyone but James Turner."

"I'm waiting for him, too."

"Oh, for heaven's sake. I can't imagine why James would bother you about our roof. I must say, it's nice of you to come over in this weather, at this time of night."

"No bother. But it's freezing in here, don't you think? I've brought a thermos of coffee—here, I'll pour some for you."

"I never drink coffee after six P.M.," she said

regretfully. "Oh, be careful, you've spilled some! You didn't burn yourself?"

"No. Just got a little on the floor, I'm afraid. Actually, it's decaffeinated, if that's what you're worried about."

"Oh, well in that case, I don't mind if I do." She reached out grateful hands for the steaming plastic cup. "If it's decaffeinated, I don't think I'll have any trouble sleeping tonight, do you?"

"No, you'll sleep just fine."

Minnie sipped. Goodness, the coffee tasted awfully sweet, but the warmth was wonderful. Where *was* that James Turner?

"You make wonderful coffee."

I looked over at Geof who was seated on a stool at the counter of my mother's kitchen. He smiled at me over the rim of his steaming mug.

"And you look like a commercial for Maxwell House," I laughed. "I feel as if I ought to know if you take cream or sugar, but I don't. Do you?"

"No." He set the mug down and reached for the telephone. "I should have called Mrs. Mimbs from New York, or at least from the airport. For some reason, I can't seem to keep my mind on my job."

"Do you know, I've been assuming you aren't married," I said in what was not entirely a nonsequitur. "You don't act married; you never mention a wife or girl friend. So?"

"Divorced," he said. "Twice."

"Oh." That gave me pause and he could see it. Well, I wasn't going to marry him after all, so what was I worried about?

"Better you should know," he said, some of the

light edge gone from his voice. "And better now than later."

"Yes." So he was counting on a later, was he? I said, "Thanks for being honest," and meant it. I told him I had never married.

"I know," he said gently. "It would be hard to bring someone into your family, wouldn't it?"

His quick perception unnerved me. Here was a man who was capable of surprising and maybe even understanding me. Watch out, I warned myself, watch out.

"Your phone call," I reminded him.

While he dialed Minnie's house, I ambled into the den and switched on the answering machine to find out who'd called while I was gone.

Michael. Four times.

"Hi, Swede," he said the first time. "This is the bad loser calling. I want to apologize for last night. I'm sorry. Love, Michael."

"Me again," he said the second time. "Will you be home tonight? I'd like to see you, okay? Maybe I'll just drop by when I leave the office. More love, Michael."

"Surprise," said the third message. There was laughter in his voice. "I just called to tell you I'm crazy about you and I'm tired of being your friend. What this world needs is fewer friends and more lovers, that's what I say. And what do you say to that, my pretty?"

By the last call, he'd switched from teasing back to glum. "Dear Ann Landers," he said, "my father is taking over my business and running it and me into the ground. I have an opportunity to chuck everything and run away to fame and fortune in Colorado. Only my best girl won't go. What should I do? Signed, Morose."

Dear Morose, I thought, your best girl doesn't love you in the way you want her to. Pack up and leave the ungrateful wench before she breaks your noble heart.

I curled up in the green leather chair and wondered why two people so rarely fall in love with each other with the same intensity, in the same way, at the same time.

"Jennifer." Geof appeared at the doorway, filling the frame of it. He looked pale and urgent. "Jennifer, get your car keys and come with me. Now."

As we threw on our coats and hats and scarves and ran to my car, he told me why we were rushing. He slid into the passenger's side, I slid into the driver's side. And then three things happened at once.

I turned the key in the ignition to find my car would not start.

He found the poem propped up on my dashboard.

Michael pulled up behind us in the driveway.

Chapter 19

It was like Friday night at the theater, only this time there were three of us in the Jaguar and the flock of police cars was congregated at the church. As soon as Geof had learned that Minnie had been summoned to the chapel, he had phoned police headquarters to request assistance, pronto.

I introduced Geof and Michael on the way over; it was obvious from the expressions on their faces that the introduction raised more questions than it answered for them. Hunched in the vestigial back seat of the Jag, I felt tense and frightened; I wondered what had happened to the firm control I'd had over my life only a week ago. The rhyme still lay on the dashboard; there hadn't been time to read it. The thought of it there did not settle my nerves.

"I don't know what we're doing," Michael said when we commandeered him and his car, "but when a cop gives me permission to speed, I'm not going to miss my chance."

He took full advantage of that opportunity, skidding around icy corners and sliding past slower cars as if someone's life depended on it. As, of course, it might.

"Stay here, both of you." Geof unfolded himself from the sports car. Then he was gone, racing up the front walk to the church before we could protest.

"I'm getting out," I said, and did.

"So am I," Michael said. "What the hell's going on?"

We hustled up the walk and I told him as much as I thought I should. Geof saw us approach and threw us an irritated look. We heard a uniformed policeman say, "We found a back door open, but there's nobody inside. No body, either."

"Positive?" Geof looked as if he didn't believe it.

"Yeah. This church is so small, it only took us a minute to search it."

I should have felt relieved. Instead, tension continued to build inside me until I thought I'd burst with the gassy uncomfortableness of it. Geof's next question didn't help.

"Jennifer," he said sharply, all business. "What is it in particular that Mrs. Mimbs loves about this church? Any special room or activity?"

"I don't know . . ." I tried fiercely to recall things she had said in the past about her affection for the place.

"Think, Jenny!" Michael's eyebrows shot up at the peremptory, familiar tone in Geof's voice.

I stared at the house of God as if He might suddenly

step out the front door and provide the answer. Failing that, perhaps the solution might appear on the bulletin board, that announced next Sunday's sermon. Port Frederick ministers cannot resist seafaring metaphors of the Bible and evidently the young Episcopal priest was no exception. According to the bulletin board, next Sunday he would command his flock to be "Fishers of Men."

My eyes lingered on the announcement.

"That's it," I said. "The sea. She loves this church because of its setting by the sea. She says she loves the sound of the waves on the rocks at the bottom of the cliff."

I don't think Geof heard any more than my first four words. They were no sooner out of my mouth than he and the other policemen were gone, racing again, this time for the edge of the cliff.

"But we already looked down there!" I heard a woman cop shout.

"Look again!" was Geof's reply.

It took them ten minutes—in the dark, stumbling down to the rocks—to reach the bottom. And that's where she was, terribly battered and bruised from her tumble down the rocks, and lying in the only soft patch of weeds and sand.

She was alive.

"But just barely," a panting Geof told us after he'd climbed back up the cliff face. "Her breath is shallow and her pulse is about as weak as it can be without quitting altogether."

They put her in a body sling and used ropes and strong backs to push and pull her to the top. Paramedics took over from there. The last I saw of Minnie that night was a glimpse of her face—pale and slack—on a stretcher. She might not have been dead, but she looked it.

"So what now?" Michael said. I was too stunned to speak.

"You go home," Geof said, "and I stay here for a long night." His eyes told me he was sorry he wasn't going to be spending it in another place, in another way. He turned to Michael and held out a hand.

"Thanks for the ride. You couldn't have come along at a better time."

"Glad to help." Michael shook the hand. "Nice to meet you, Detective. When this thing's over, maybe Jenny and I can take you and your wife to dinner some night."

"I'm not married."

"Well, your lady friend, then." Michael's expression was all innocence. He smiled a little too charmingly, placed a possessive hand under my elbow and began to steer me back toward his car.

I, angry at his presumption, shook off his hand and turned around to look at Geof.

"Call me," I said, "if you want me."

The message could not have been more clear if I had posted it on the church bulletin board.

"A cop, Jenny?" Michael slammed the door on the driver's side and twisted his mouth in scorn. "Come on!"

"You're a snob, Michael."

"Oh? I thought I was a saint. Long-suffering, ever-loving Michael, the celibate saint."

"Your halo has slipped down around your ego."

"How long have you known him? Five days?"

"About fifteen years." I let him stew over that one and I didn't explain. I felt mean and defensive.

"I've never heard of him," Michael said accusingly. "You've never mentioned him."

"Well, now you've heard of him."

"Is he why you won't go to Colorado with me?"

"Oh Christ, Michael! No! He is irrelevant to that issue. The fact that I won't go with you has nothing to do with him or any man. It has to do with *me*. Just me!"

"And the goddamn Foundation."

"And my life and my choices about it."

"And the fact that you don't love me."

"Yes," I said, but softly. I slumped back in the hard leather seat. "That, too."

We rode in silence until we reached my parents' house.

"Michael . . ." I turned toward him.

"Jenny, sweet Jenny." He reached over awkwardly to hug me and we clung together in the front seat that was never constructed for such activities. "Don't cry, Jenny, don't cry."

"I'm not crying, I'm sobbing."

When we finally looked at each other, there were tears on both faces. I said, "I'm sorry, Michael, I'm sorry for everything."

"I know. You can't help it that you don't love me."

"No."

"You need to wipe your nose."

"I was mean. I'm sorry."

"You *were* mean. It hurt."

"I'm sorry, I'm sorry. Oh God, I'm starting to cry again. It's not just you, Michael, or us. It's everything —Moshe, Minnie . . ."

"I know. Everything stinks."

"It's horrible, and we've been so petty—having a stupid fight when the world is falling apart."

"I don't care about the rest of the world. I love you."

"I know. Good night, Michael."

I didn't kiss him goodbye.

It was only after he drove off and I turned to face my parents' dark house that I realized how very much I didn't want to be alone. I wished Michael had thought to wait to see me safely inside the house.

But first, before I could unlock the front door and turn on the comfort and security of lots of lights, I had to get that poem out of my car.

Chapter **20**

I slogged through the snow to the car and opened the door with cold, fumbling fingers. I felt like a child who's afraid of a bogeyman under the bed. I checked the back seat—no one was hiding there—and jerked my head around every few seconds to reassure myself that I was truly alone.

I had a feeling there was no need to worry about fingerprints on the note, but if there *were* any, my gloves would protect them. I carried the note, unread, up to the front door.

Inside, the phone was ringing.

The keys that always slid so smoothly into the locks, didn't for several frustrating moments. The door which never creaked, did. The hall light switch which was always at my fingertips, wasn't. Every familiar, comforting thing seemed to have moved—perversely, infuriatingly, frighteningly—an agonizing quarter inch out of my reach.

I didn't close and lock the door—my route of escape—until I had raced around the first floor and turned on every light in sight. I even locked the basement door in the kitchen. Then I answered the phone which was still determinedly ringing.

"Hello?" What if it was an anonymous caller to match the anonymous note? My voice sounded breathless and high pitched.

"What's wrong, Jenny? Are you all right?"

"Geof." I sank onto the stool beside the phone. "I'm fine, yes, I'm fine, I'm fine."

He laughed, but only a little and that little had a tense sound to it.

"Who are you trying to convince?" he said. "Did you just get in?"

"Yes. I did. Yes."

I laughed, too, a shade hysterically.

"Oh Geof, this is crazy. Do you know, I'm just scared to death? When Michael dropped me off, I got spooked. I feel like a kid who's afraid of ghosts."

"He should have gone in the house with you." I heard anger.

"Don't be mad at him," I said. "He was distracted."

Silence at the other end of the phone.

"We had an argument," I said quickly.

"I guess that's none of my business," he said carefully.

"I think it is. I'll tell you about it sometime."

"Thank you," he said simply. The stiff, hard edge of his voice softened and relaxed. He said, "You don't have much to thank *me* for though. Hell of a cop I am, letting you go home alone. I'm sending somebody over to take you someplace else for the night."

"Okay." I was just scared enough to be meek.

"*Okay?*" His laugh was deeper, and unbelieving. "Did you say okay? Just like that? No argument?"

"Where should I go?"

"You have a sister, right?"

"Not there."

"A good friend?"

"They'd ask too many questions," I said. "How about your house?"

"Now *that* would sure as hell raise questions," he laughed. I waited for him to consider it. "But if you don't mind what it does to your reputation, I certainly don't mind what it does to mine."

"Tell them I slept on the couch," I suggested.

"I'm not a good liar," he said softly. "Uh, Jenny? Give the rhyme to the officer, please, when he comes to pick you up."

"It's out of sync, isn't it?" I said. "I mean it doesn't fit the previous pattern of leaving a note with the body. What do you think it means?"

"Uh," he said and hesitated. "Jenny, maybe it's not the rhyme that's out of sync."

"What do you . . ." I said, and then when his meaning came through to me, "Oh God, you mean maybe there was supposed to be a body to go with the verse, don't you? Maybe I'm supposed to be dead."

"Well, you're not," he pointed out. "But do not eat or drink anything until you get to my place, got that?"

"No," I said weakly. "I mean yes. I mean no I won't."

I perched on a stool in the well-lighted kitchen at my mother's house and stared at the blasted rhyme and willed my hand to stop shaking. It wouldn't obey me, so I set the note on the counter top.

Snow fell off the roof and hit the ground with a sudden thud. I jumped the proverbial foot, discovering that a person's heart, when said person is frightened out of her wits, really does stop beating. When it starts again, it's with a, no kidding, sickening lurch. Whoever coined that cliché knew whereof he spake.

I longed for the cop to come fast, soon, now.
And I read:

> Jennifer Cain, beauty and brain,
> Her father is Greed, her mother's Insane;
> Jennifer Cain, giver of pain,
> Gave her life, but not in vain.

I put my head on the counter with the note and wept.

Chapter 21

The policeman who rang the doorbell five minutes later insisted on identifying himself fully with his badge. "It wouldn't do for you to go with just anyone, miss," he said kindly, if unnervingly. As I locked the door behind me, I heard the phone ring inside the house. I had forgotten to switch on the answering machine; well, it would just have to ring until whoever it was gave up.

I climbed into the front seat of the squad car beside the officer. He was about fifty, gray and ruddy with that bulbous red nose that comes to heavy drinkers as they age. Pretty, he was not; but he was quiet and considerate. If he thought my destination interesting, he didn't show it by word or expression. I may be a child of the '70's, but I am also my mother's child enough to have been obscurely grateful for his lack of leering.

Geof's home turned out to be one of a number of

enormous contemporary houses in a new and expensive part of town. From the outside, his was all graceless angles that pointed off in every direction as if the architect hadn't been able to make up his mind which way was up.

"Must be nice," the officer said as he walked me to the door. "You'd never know he was rich, though, the way he acts I mean. Never puts on no airs."

He preceded me into the house and turned on so many lights that I had a feeling he knew I'd been frightened at my own empty home.

"Snazzy, huh?" It was obvious he was waiting for my dramatic reaction to the interior of the house.

"Good grief," I said. I didn't mean at all what he thought I meant, but he was pleased with the look of astonishment on my face.

"Well, Detective Bushfield said to tell you to make yourself to home and that we'll drive by every now and then just to see you're all right. We won't bother you or nothin'—I'm sure you need your sleep—but maybe you'll feel better, just knowin' we're there."

"Yes. I will." I jerked my wondering eyes away from the scenery and smiled as largely as my exhausted muscles would permit. "I can't thank you enough, Officer. Really, I'm so grateful."

"No problem," he said, prophetically I hoped. "Take care now, Miss Cain."

I locked the door behind him and turned around.

To my right was Geof's living room. Beneath the vaulted roof there was only one piece of furniture: an enormous redwood hot tub, with no water in it.

To my left was his dining room. There was *no* furniture there—only Nautilus equipment for body building. Well, that accounted for the broad shoulders and muscular legs. But from the looks of his house, there was *no* accounting for taste. His kitchen, in which he evidently neither cooked nor dined, was straight ahead down the hallway: hardback and paper-back books lay neatly stacked on every available inch of counter space and floor. There was only a single thin path through which he evidently strolled from barbell to book to tub.

Bell, book and sandal.

The mind boggled at what the bedrooms might reveal.

I walked cautiously forward until I could see the family room just the other side of the literate kitchen. And there, thank goodness, lay the answer to that eclectic decor: packing boxes. Geof, it appeared, had only just moved in.

I breathed more easily. Before I jumped to unflat-tering conclusions, I'd wait and ask him if maybe his last wife got all the furniture in the last divorce.

A phone rang somewhere.

I found it in the kitchen between stacks of Le Carré novels and a yellow pile of *National Geographics* which looked as if they had actually been read.

"How do you like the house?" Geof asked as soon as I'd said a cautious hello. I thought I detected a grin in his voice, but I wasn't sure, so I settled for tact.

"Well, it's certainly . . . new . . . isn't it?"

He guffawed.

"Ain't it awful?" he laughed. "I suppose I should have warned you, but I was afraid you wouldn't go if I told you I was in the middle of moving out."

"Out?"

"Um. That house was the supremely bad idea of wife numero dos, name of Melissa. Her taste was all in her mouth."

"Now, now. It's not nice to speak ill of the departed."

"Oh, that was one of the nicer things I could say about her. That was a compliment compared to what you will undoubtedly hear some time at great and boring length."

"You seem a nice enough guy to me. How come two wives couldn't get along with you?"

"My fault," he said, the laughter gone. "I'm told it's not much fun to live with a dedicated cop."

"Is that a warning?"

"I suppose." He sounded as tired as I felt. "I'm sorry things are such a mess, Jenny. I hope you'll find your way around well enough to be comfortable."

"I will. Don't worry about me."

"I'll make my own choices about that."

Sadly, it only took a moment for him to tell me how little more was known about the attack on Minnie. "She's still alive," he said, "but unconscious. They pumped her stomach at the hospital, on the assumption that she'd been doped like the others."

"Why didn't it kill her, too?"

"Well, she'd eaten fairly recently and that slowed the action of the drug, plus we got there soon enough and we knew what we were dealing with."

"But she's still in danger, I take it?"

"Yes, and possibly in more ways than merely medical. I've got a twenty-four hour guard on her. I am *not* going to let anybody get near her to harm her a second time."

"Did you find a rhyme?"

"On Minnie? No." He sounded puzzled. "But I guess it'll turn up."

He told me to sleep well and we hung up.

It was two A.M. by the luminous clock on his bedside table when I woke and became aware of him sitting on the bed beside me.

"You're staring," I said sleepily and smiled. "Have you been staring long?"

"Years." He looked older in the dim light from the moon that shone around the edges of the window shade; the long night had temporarily aged him. He reached out a gentle fingertip and stroked my eyelids. "You're the one who just woke up," he said, his voice husky, "but I think I'm the one who's dreaming."

He stood up slowly and began to remove the tie he had loosened hours before at my house. I raised my hands to shake the tangles from my hair. The sheet and blankets fell away from my shoulders.

Geof's hands paused on a shirt button and his eyes moved down from my face.

I looked down at myself.

"I don't wear a nightgown," I said.

"Yes," he said, "I see that."

His fingers moved at the buttons again.

"What," I said suspiciously, "are you grinning about?"

"I was just thinking about the guys I used to know in high school." He slipped off his loafers and socks, then removed his shirt and draped it over the back of a bedside chair. When his handsome head emerged from the white T-shirt he pulled off over it, he was still smiling. "We used to watch the cheerleaders bounce up and down and we'd make bets on which

175

girls were for real and which weren't. You were always so proper in high school—friendly, of course—but proper, so we never had the benefit of anybody's firsthand account to tell us the truth."

"Well?" I was trying not to laugh.

He stepped out of the rest of his clothes.

"Just wait until my reunion," he grinned. "Finally, I can tell them you're for real."

I threw a pillow at him.

Things happened fast after that, the first time; then things happened beautifully slowly.

"Darling Jenny," he said softly before he slept.

Chapter 22

You're staring again."

I woke in the morning, too few hours later, to find him propped up on one elbow and turned toward me in the bed.

He said without preamble, "I opened my eyes and the first thing I saw was the wall and the first thing I felt was exhaustion and depression over this damn case. But then my foot moved so it touched you"—he smiled—"and then I remembered . . ."

He kissed me a sweet good morning.

". . . and isn't it amazing how rested and optimistic I suddenly feel. Love's even better than a good night's sleep."

I pulled him down so we snuggled together under the covers. I said, "A little early for talk of love, isn't it?"

"Early in the morning or the relationship? It's

neither for me, Jen. I've been in love with you since I was seventeen years old."

I was—I have to admit it—charmed, although of course I didn't believe a word of such blarney.

"Oh Geof, that was only a schoolboy crush."

"Maybe, but I've fantasized about you ever since," he insisted, to my surprise. He brushed a clump of hair from my forehead, then ran his finger down my nose and cheeks and across my lower lip.

"In your fantasies, have I always been a fourteen-year-old girl?" I teased.

"Give me some credit," he laughed. "I've seen your picture in the papers now and then through the years; I've kept up with how you've grown up."

"And have I changed a great deal? From the girl you remember?" Suddenly it was important for me to know what he thought of me now as compared to the bubble-headed child of then.

"You're more beautiful," he said simply, and then when I thought my heart couldn't race any faster, he floored me by adding gently, "Sometimes sorrow does that to a person, and trouble." When I didn't say anything, he continued in a much lighter tone. "You were always outgoing, but now you're, well, confident. I like that. Very much. And you're still the ambitious girl who wanted to be the best at everything." He paused and grinned. "Now you tell me how I've changed. I'll bet you can't even remember me well enough to do it."

"You must be kidding."

He raised an eyebrow.

"You were a memorable kid, Geof, don't you know that? Anybody who knew you would remember you. Vividly."

He lay back and groaned.

"For all the wrong reasons," he moaned.

"Well, you did all the wrong things!" I reminded him, laughing. It was my turn to roll over, prop up on one elbow and peer down at him. "Why did you? Was it rebellion? Your own personal war against the plumbing and hardware business?"

He glared at me.

"Damn it, Jenny, you weren't supposed to get it right on the first try! I was all worked up to spend at least a week in justifying for you my years of juvenile delinquency, and you hit the nail on the head in the first five seconds."

"Don't say nail," I deadpanned, "you hate the hardware business, remember?"

He chuckled. It had that deep, delicious sound that laughter has when a person's lying on his back. I found the rumble irresistible and leaned over to kiss the source of it, in the middle of his rib cage.

"Mmm," he said. I slid up with my kisses, spacing them about an inch apart until one landed on his mouth. He would have pursued the subject further, but I was for the moment more interested in the previous topic.

I propped myself upright again.

He sighed resignedly and crossed his arms behind his head on his pillow. "So," he continued with mock seriousness, "what we have so far is your basic poignant story of misunderstood youth. He knows he doesn't want to do what his parents want him to do, but he's too dumb to know what he wants to do instead."

"So he kicks."

"And generally raises hell, yes. Until one day, the

179

good fairy drops by and waves her magic wand and says, 'Hey Bozo, wise up.'"

"This is not the same good fairy that paid a visit to Cinderella."

"I don't think so. But this old gal knew her fairy business, because when she waved her wand it suddenly occurred to Bozo that although he thought he was hurting his family, he was—ta da—" We finished the sentence together. "Only hurting himself!"

"Geof, you idiot, was there really a good fairy in your life?"

"Yeah." He smiled reminiscently and it was obvious he liked the person in his memory. "She was a cop."

"Ah."

"She caught me shoplifting one Saturday, but she didn't arrest me. Instead, she blackmailed me into riding around with her every spare minute I had for two solid weeks."

"Ah ha," I said. "And her magic wand was probably a nightstick. And after that illuminating experience, you knew in your black little juvenile delinquent heart that what you really wanted to be was a cop, just like your fairy godmother."

"You're very perceptive," he said, and smiled at me. "Not to mention silly. I think that all my life I've been looking for a woman I could be silly with."

"Do I look as ridiculously smug as you do right now?" I asked him.

"Yes."

I ran a hand lightly over the impressive muscles of his chest and upper arms and laughed at the look in his eyes.

"Okay," I said, "you're just waiting for me to say it, aren't you? You want to hear me say how wrong we were about you; how you've grown up into a gorgeous, respectable, capable man. And if the other cheerleaders could only see you now, they'd eat their hearts out."

He loved it. He laughed from deep down in his flat belly, until I rolled toward him and gave him something more current than memories to consider.

The sweet dream ended and reality returned when he drove me to The Foundation on his way to the station that morning.

"You're positive there will be at least two people in the office with you all day?" he said, a cop once more.

"Yes, Geof, I'm sure."

"Come on, Jenny, don't be impatient with me," he said easily. "Surely you're convinced by now that you might be in considerable danger."

"Yes. Okay. I'm sorry." I frowned at the gray sky; I was heartily sick of gray skies. "I'm not mad at you, I'm mad at whoever has put me in the position of having to circumscribe my life. It infuriates me."

He didn't have an answer to that. We were compatibly quiet until he pulled up to my building.

"There are a lot of things we haven't discussed," I said tentatively, my hand on the car door handle, my mind on the anonymous notes.

"Yes," he said, "I know. Expect a visit from Ailey Mason today. I may not be able to come too, but I'll try."

"Kiss me, please."

"Yes, ma'am." He obeyed me very nicely, just as

Simon Church drove by, smirking, with Derek Jones in the passenger's seat beside him.

Simon and Derek and I walked into the elevator together. I said a terse good morning, then busied myself with the elevator buttons, my coat, my briefcase, anything.

"Good *morning,* Jennifer," Derek said.

"Yes, isn't it?" Simon was equally arch. "You know, Derek, I always feel better about the day when I know our police force is out there protecting us, don't you?"

"Absolutely, Simon. A citizenry can feel so safe in the embrace of our guardians of the law."

"Well put, my man. Safe in the strong arms of the law, as it were, kissed by the sweet breath of justice."

I felt the red at the back of my neck rising faster than the elevator.

"You know, I tried to call Jennifer this morning, Simon."

"Did you, now?"

"Um. Nobody home. Early, too."

"Maybe her phone machine was turned on and she was trying to sleep?"

"No, that's not it. The machine wasn't on and the phone just rang and rang."

"My, my, where *do* you think she was?"

"Don't know. Worried me a little. Do you think I should have called the police?"

"I wouldn't think so," Simon said as the elevator door finally, mercifully opened. "I'd guess they already had the situation well in hand. So to speak."

"All *right."* I turned on them, having had enough of their smarmy vaudeville act. "Enough. Please. Thank you."

Derek, the employee on my payroll, was instantly contrite. "Sorry, Jenny," he said to the person who buttered his bread. "We were out of line."

But Simon was merely egged on to further depths of lunacy and tastelessness. "Speak for yourself!" he said. "*I* only stepped out of line for a minute, and look what happens—some dumb gumshoe steps in front of me!"

I could literally have struck him. I settled for a figurative hit below the belt.

"Simon." I turned reproachful eyes on him. "I'm not in a good mood this morning . . . I feel so bad about Minnie. You've heard, haven't you? Yes, well, I hope you understand my feelings. We could all use a little kindness today, don't you agree?"

It worked, but then I'd meant at least some of it sincerely.

"Oh shit, Jenny." His voice and face filled with remorse. "The Tactless Bastard Strikes Again. I'm just sorry as hell."

"That's okay," I said magnanimously. "I understand."

"Big of you," Derek murmured in a wry sotto voce that Simon didn't hear. I, taking firm control of the scene, held open the office door for them. This was my domain. They could like it or leave.

"Why are you here, Simon?"

I indicated a chair beside my desk, after I'd stalled the outer office by telling Faye and Marvin I'd talk to them about Minnie later.

"A little more graciously if you please, my love." He crossed his athletic legs and lit a cigarette—*not* one of the French ones whose smell he knows I abhor.

At least he knew better than to push me *that* far that morning. He said, "Derek called me and asked for a ride to work. His car won't start. So I thought I'd drop by and say hello to dear *sweet* Jenny."

He smiled ingratiatingly.

"Must we be flip?" I was fast running out of patience and time. "I have a startling idea: Let's address whatever it is that's on your puerile mind and get it over with. And let's do it now."

He wasn't offended; as long as you didn't insult or threaten his museum, it was impossible to hurt Simon's feelings. "I want to know where the Martha Paul stands with The Foundation," he said bluntly, getting down to the brassiest of tacks. "I want to know how these murders affect me."

"Minnie's not dead," I said angrily.

"Yet."

"Oh, Simon." I put my elbows on my desk and hung my chin in my palms and felt forlorn. "You think she's going to die, too?"

His shrug was a gesture of helplessness.

"It sounds like it, Jen, although I can't fathom who'd want to kill a terrific old gal like Minnie. Do they know who did it?"

"Nope, except it must have been the same monster who killed Arnie and Moshe and Mrs. Hatch. They've got Minnie under armed guard at the hospital to make sure he doesn't get a second chance at her."

"Armed guard?" Both his complexion and his sangfroid faded all at once. "This can't be real life! This can't really be happening to people we know!" He shrugged again, but it had an air of depression about it now. "Hey listen, I'm sorry I was such a jerk this morning. But I'm upset, too, you know. I don't know

how to handle it. I mean how do you *handle* murder, for Christ's sake? So I concentrate on the one thing I do know—talk to me about my museum, Jenny love."

"You want to know where you stand, Simon? You stand in a big, fat, deep hole that I'm going to try to get you out of. Here, my friend, is how it is . . ." I straightened the papers on my desk as I quickly gathered my thoughts.

"If Arnie's new will stands up in court, The Foundation will not get any of the $8 million. If we go to court and challenge the will and win, we might get it all . . . but more likely, we'll only get some of it. If we get *any* of the money, we'll abide by the terms of the old will and invest the money and distribute the earnings to you. Are you with me so far?"

He nodded, deadly serious now that we were talking about *his* life's blood.

I continued: "If we go to court and *lose,* you might as well pretend that $8 million never existed. You won't see a penny of it unless Ginger Culverson falls in love with you or the museum."

"Oh well, then there's still hope." He managed a grin.

"Humility, thy name is Simon Church," I said. "Okay, that explains the Culverson bequest. Now for Moshe Cohen: The money he left to The Foundation will be funneled to the theater and some Jewish organizations. You gain only because The Foundation as a whole gains. Do you understand why that is?"

"Don't be condescending, love," he smiled. And then, robot-like, he recited, "When-you-add-funds-to-the-general-assets-of-The-Foundation-you-increase-your - investment - capabilities - and - that - benefits - every - charity - on - your - list - because - the - more -

money - you - make - the - more - you - have - to - give
- away - to - beggars - like - me."

I had to laugh.

"Right," I said.

"Okay." He leaned forward in thought. "That's
clear even to my right-brained artistic mind. As The
Foundation goes, so goes the Martha Paul."

"Well, sort of," I semi-agreed. "That's true as long
as we continue to be your principal source of funding,
which I suppose we will unless these murders kill us,
too."

"Is that a possibility?" He looked a little wild. "You
don't mean it."

"I mean it, this publicity is doing us no good at all.
But let's talk about Florence Hatch and her will. Mr.
Ottilini says she finally did get around to writing
one—just the week before her death, as a matter of
fact. She left some money outright to the Welcome
Home for Girls and some to The Foundation so we
could found other treatment centers in addition to
continuing to support the Home. Again, you only
benefit indirectly if at all."

"Shit, I lose again."

"I wish you'd at least use French obscenities,
Simon." I smiled. "You'd fool some of the people
some of the time into thinking you're cultured."

"Fou of the dog," he said and laughed.

"As to Minnie," I concluded, "she is not going to
die, please God. But when the day comes—years from
now—that she does, half of her estate will come to
The Foundation and the other half will go to her
church."

"How will you use the money, darling Jenny?"

"It's unrestricted funds, dear Simon, which means

she trusts us to use our discretion and spend it as we see fit."

"Would you see fit to spend it on me?"

I smiled. "I can't speak for my trustees, but I think you can be fairly sure you'd get your share, Simon. We've talked about Minnie's will before this, haven't we? I thought you already knew where you stood with the Big Five."

"I *thought* I knew where I stood with Arnold P. Culverson," he said bitterly. "Since then, I don't take anything for granted." He checked his watch and abruptly stood up. "Thanks, Jenny love. As long as I'm already on the *Titanic,* I like to know how soon it's going down."

"Are you on budget this quarter, Simon?"

"Surely you jest. As you know perfectly well, my budget is an exercise in wishful thinking. We're going under, my dear. I needed that money from Arnie, bad."

"But he might have lived for several more years, Simon. You still wouldn't have got his money as soon as you really need it."

"He wouldn't have let us drown."

"He as good as did, Simon."

Despair crossed the museum director's strong, mobile features. He made one of his silent, sudden exits, leaving me alone with my own unhappy thoughts.

Chapter 23

Before I could follow him out the door to talk to my staff, the phone in my office buzzed and presented me with a complication I had stupidly failed to foresee.

"I've been worried sick about you." It was Michael. His voice had that quality that mothers get in their voices when they're glad their child is home safe, but they could kill him for having worried them so.

"You didn't answer your phone," he said accusingly. "I called and called last night. I even drove by and rang the doorbell, but the house was dark. You weren't there this morning either."

I dodged the obvious if unspoken question.

"Oh, Michael," I said, "I'm sorry you've been concerned. It just didn't occur to me that you might call after you left last night. But I'm fine, really, I'm perfectly all right."

"People are getting murdered left and right in this town and you disappear!" He wasn't through being aggrieved. "What was I supposed to think? Of *course* I was worried!"

"Of course you were," I said soothingly. "I would have felt just the same way. And I'd have been furious at you for putting me through such a bad night."

That mollified him a bit.

"Damn right," he said, but more mildly. "I was so worried I almost called the police."

I gathered my courage and asked the most leading question of all.

"Why," I said, "didn't you?"

A long pause.

"Because," he said, "I would have felt pretty embarrassed to find out the police already knew where you were. I suppose you get my drift?"

"Got it."

"Well?"

"I'm trying to figure out if I think you have a right to ask that question and if I have an obligation to answer it."

"You have an irritatingly legalistic mind, Jennifer. Right now, I'd rather you had a merciful heart."

"Then the answer is yes," I said quickly, and got it over with. "Yes, I spent the night with Geof."

"Thank you," he said, without irony, and my heart ached. "One of the things I'll always love about you is your honesty, brutal though it sometimes is. You've spoiled me for other women, Swede."

It sounded like a farewell. For him, emotionally, it probably was. And I—perverse creature—felt suddenly lonely and afraid to lose him.

I didn't say so. Sometimes the hardest cruelty is to show a temporary mercy that seems to offer hope for a future that cannot be.

We said a few trivial things, promised to get together soon, said careful and gentle goodbyes and hung up. I sat with my hand on the phone and consoled myself with the thought that it had to happen sometime, if not with Geof then with another man. Unfortunately, that same thought was probably no consolation at all to Michael.

I buzzed Faye and asked her to call the staff into my office. *She* would say I was the bigger fool; I wasn't so sure she'd be wrong.

Faye was crying and Marvin, the controller, looked as if he'd like to. Seeing them, and Derek, seated in a half circle around my desk brought home to me as nothing else had the larger context of the tragedies.

I saw it clearly in Faye's tears.

"Poor, poor Mrs. Mimbs," she said. And, "What is the world coming to?" And, "I'm so frightened. Everybody I know is just so frightened."

They weren't aware of any threat to me, and I didn't fuel their fears by telling them. Things were bad enough without their knowing their boss was next on the list.

"What do the police say, Jennifer?" That was Derek, without a hint in his voice or face that he knew I had unique reasons to be privy to police knowledge. He said, "Can we believe what we read in the papers?"

"I think so," I said. Then I added cautiously, "Although I'd imagine they're not telling us everything they know."

"What *do* they know?" That was Marv, sitting as straight and precise as the long columns of figures he loved. He spoke rapidly and enunciated every consonant, so his sentences had the efficient, staccato sound of an adding machine.

"Well . . ." I started to review the depressing situation, but stopped myself when I saw the outer door open. "Here comes the man who can tell you better than I." I raised my voice so the newcomer could hear me. "Come in, Mr. Mason. We're having a staff meeting. Pull up a chair, if you like."

His inexpressive face made it impossible to tell if he ever liked anything, but he did place a chair just behind and to my left, neatly usurping the position of authority in the room. It occurred to me that I might have underestimated him. I wheeled my chair around to face him. He might be young, but he must not be a total fool, or Geof wouldn't have sent him out alone.

"We're worried, Mr. Mason," I said, "and scared. We'd like to know what's going on. Can you tell us?"

He didn't like that, though I hadn't been peremptory. Evidently he only *asked* direct questions; he didn't answer them. I'd be more devious next time.

"What's the Big Five?" he said abruptly, and it was then I decided he was a fool after all. When I heard three separate exclamations of understanding and horror behind me, I very nearly told him so.

"No!" Faye actually stood up and leaned her tense white fingers on my desk. "Oh no, Jenny!"

Marv clacked his tongue several times, a sure sign of his distress and consternation.

"You should be in the theater, Mr. Mason," I said acidly. "You have quite a little knack for the dramatic moment."

"I hear you have some little talents yourself, Ms. Cain," he, unbelievably, said.

Derek, bless his irreverent heart, laughed at that

and winked at me to remind me the man was an idiot. I smiled sweetly and said, "Why thank you, that's very flattering and nice of you to say so. Now what is it you'd like us to tell you about the Big Five? If you already know enough to call it that, I'm surprised you don't know the rest as well."

"I like to hear things firsthand," he said, somehow managing to insinuate double meanings even into that simple sentence. "Who are the Big Five?"

"Moshe Cohen, Arnie Culverson, Minnie Mimbs and Florence Hatch," I said.

He waited.

"And I."

"Why'd you call them the Big Five?"

"Of all the potential donors to The Foundation, they're—they were, are—the ones from whom we're most likely to get generous bequests." Verb tenses were getting to be distressingly confusing.

"They'd promised to give money to The Foundation?"

"Yes," I said, "or else they'd dropped strong hints to that effect."

"How much money?"

"We were supposed to get $8 million from Arnie Culverson," I said. "That was the whole of his estate."

"Nothing for his family."

"No. You already know this, don't you?"

"But the wife is independently wealthy, so she didn't need his money anyhow," Mason asserted. I've always disliked people who refer to the female spouse as "the wife," like "the table" or "the chair."

"Need is a relative term, Mr. Mason," I said. "What you or I need and what Marvalene Culverson thinks she needs might be two very different things."

"Are you accusing Mrs. Culverson of something?"

"No." I could be every bit as terse as he. Out of the corner of my eye, I saw the resentful expressions on Faye's and Marvin's faces; they didn't like this grilling of their director. Derek wore that deceptively amused look that conceals contempt. He liked it when I said, "It would be stupid to accuse Marvalene of killing Arnie, when she didn't stand to gain a penny from his death."

"But she didn't want you to get the money either," the detective pointed out in his nasty, personal way.

"*I*, as I have said before, was never going to get the money. But you're right in thinking that she didn't want The Foundation to inherit. At least that's the impression I always got from Arnie. I never heard it directly from her, so I don't actually know for a fact that she gave a damn."

"What about Cohen?" Mason said.

"What about *Mr.* Cohen?" That was Faye. I smiled at her and answered the cop's implied question.

"Moshe left The Foundation a half million in his will," I said.

"Why'd he leave you the dough?"

"He wanted to provide financial support for the new theater," I explained. "But he didn't want to establish a separate trust to do it. Establishing a trust is an expensive and complicated procedure, and he didn't see any need to go through that process when he could use the mechanism of The Foundation."

Marv cleared his throat.

"Yes, Marv?" I said, knowing he wanted to add something to my explanation.

"There's the matter of ROI," Marv said.

"ROI," Mason repeated stiffly. He didn't like being presented with terms he'd never heard of.

"Return on investment," Marv explained patiently. "Mr. Cohen was a successful businessman. He knew he'd get a better ROI from The Foundation than from a separate trust set up just for the theater."

"Why?" Grudgingly.

"Because whenever someone leaves money to The Foundation, they are, in effect, adding their pile to a larger pot. We, in turn, invest the whole pot in stocks, bonds, securities or whatever, in the hope of earning a good return on the investment. Obviously, the larger the pot we invest, the greater our potential for a larger return. The smaller the pot, the smaller the return."

"Obviously," Mason said nastily.

"Common sense," Marv agreed pleasantly. "So Mr. Cohen knew his money would make more money if he placed it with The Foundation. And that would mean there'd be more money to spend on his theater."

"Mrs. Mimbs and Mrs. Hatch?" Mason was eager to get out of the unfamiliar realms of high finance and back to motive and murder.

I told him about Mrs. Hatch's will and about Minnie's.

"They didn't like their husbands?" Given his choice among several possible conclusions, I felt sure Mason would always leap to the most unpleasant one.

"They loved their husbands," I said politely. "But those men have plenty of money of their own, so the women could give theirs away."

"You do-gooders." Mason's face finally showed an emotion—disgust. "You sit up here in your ivory tower dispensing largesse and you think everyone's innocent and the world's just clean and wonderful."

"Dispensing largesse," Derek murmured. "Such big words for such a . . ."

"Derek." I cut him short, though of course Mason got the insulting point.

"It is precisely because the world is *not* clean and innocent that The Foundation exists," I said calmly.

"So what will you clean up with *your* money, Ms. Cain?" His tone was as full of envy as anybody's I'd ever heard. Finally we'd got to the core of his resentment.

"My bequest is designated as unrestricted funds," I said. "That means The Foundation can apply the money however or wherever it wants."

"How much?"

"Right now, I suppose my estate is worth about one million."

"Where'd you get the loot?"

"Rich grandparents."

"What's it in?"

"You mean, what are my holdings? Blue chips, mostly. But I don't have control over them yet. They're held in a revocable trust that pays me quarterly dividends. When I turn thirty, I'll be able to take over the administration of the trust and manage my own investment portfolio."

"When will you be thirty?"

"Sunday."

"This Sunday?"

"Yes."

"Uh, Jennifer." Derek suddenly had an odd, hesitant look about him. "Sorry to ask this, but, uh, what if you died between now and Sunday? Would The Foundation still get the money?"

"No," I said. "Under the terms of the trusts that my

grandparents set up for my sister and me, if either of us dies before we turn thirty, the other one gets the money. All of it. After we turn thirty, we can do whatever we want with it."

"So," Derek mused, "if somebody wanted to harm The Foundation . . ."

"They'd better kill me before Sunday," I said.

"Interesting," said Ailey Mason.

"That's one way of looking at it," I said dryly. I avoided the horrified expressions on the faces of Faye and Marv.

"Well, well." Mason tugged his black topcoat—which he had never taken off—more tightly around him and slipped his leather gloves back on. "We'll be in touch, Ms. Cain."

"How nice," I said politely.

When he reached my office door he turned back to face me.

"Happy birthday," he said.

"I certainly hope so," I replied.

Right after Mason left and the others filed out of my office, I got a call from a highly excited member of The Foundation board of trustees.

It was Jack Fenton, phoning from his office at the bank, where he still went to work every day despite his seventy-seven years.

"Jennifer," he said, "I don't want to frighten you unnecessarily, but I've been doing a lot of thinking about the attacks on our friends. I've come to a startling conclusion."

"The Big Five," I said tiredly, stealing his thunder.

"Yes! You've thought of it, too!"

"I've mentioned it to the police, Jack."

"Good, good. Very wise, Jennifer, very wise. I think we have the answer, don't you?"

"It could be coincidence."

"Bosh," he said succinctly. "Who knew about the list? Who knew about the Big Five?"

I told him what I had told Geof the day before in New York City. "I knew," I said. "Naturally. And all of you trustees, and my staff. And I suppose anyone we might have told, like wives or husbands."

"Who else?"

"Well, it wasn't a term we should have used outside the privacy of The Foundation, but I have a feeling we bandied it about rather loosely."

"Bankers never bandy," he said amusingly. "Although I seem to have a vague memory of having discussed the Big Five with our priest one Sunday."

"You go to Minnie's church, Jack?"

"Um." He clucked, distressed. "Poor Minnie HaHa."

"You told your priest?" I said patiently.

"Yes, Dr. Priestly, if you can believe it. Ian Priestly. Nice enough young fellow, but doesn't know beans about money management. I've tried to give him the benefit of my experience, sticking the old nose in, don't you know."

"It's a nice nose, Jack," I said. He was one of my favorite trustees. "I'm sure he appreciates your advice."

"Don't you believe it," he said astringently. "I'm just a nosy old codger to him. At any rate, be that as it may, I told him about the Big Five. We were talking about the church's money problems, and that led to talk of potential donors which led to The Foundation, and you see how we got to the Big Five."

"Sure. I take it we don't know if he mentioned it to anyone else."

"No. I'll ask him."

"Maybe," I suggested tactfully, "we'd better leave the asking to the police."

"Bosh," Jack said. "Cops can't hold a candle to bankers when it comes to weaseling information out of people. Bet I'd have made a helluva detective."

"I don't doubt it," I laughed.

"Who else knew about the Big Five?" asked the banker-cum-detective.

"The directors of our charities. I'm sure we discussed it with them. Not particularly discreet of us, I suppose . . ."

"But natural," said Jack, who understood the byways of charity and the symbiotic relationship between givers and getters. "So that means the museum knew . . ."

"Simon, yes. And Allison Parker . . ."

". . . the Welcome Home . . ."

"Right, and the directors of the boys' home and the historical society and the home for battered women and the local AA and the hotline for runaways and . . ."

"If I ran down the list of the agencies we fund, I'd know who knew about the Big Five," he said.

"I'm afraid so."

"Well," Jack summed up, "we know who's being attacked, don't we. And we have a list of potential suspects . . ."

"A *long* list, Jack. And we still don't know why."

"Why somebody's trying to kill off the Big Five? I think that's perfectly clear, Jennifer: Somebody wants to ruin The Foundation. When the newspapers make the connection between the victims and the Big Five—and they will, believe me—they'll publish it. And then nobody will want to give us a blooming cent. We'll get written out of so many wills so fast you won't see the ink dry."

"But *why?*" I persisted. "It doesn't make sense."

"That's only because we don't have all the facts yet," he said. "When we get the rest of the facts, then we'll know."

I wasn't persuaded, but I didn't argue with him.

"Uh, Jennifer," he said in a very different tone of voice from the businesslike one he'd been using. I could feel his concern and the warning before he voiced it. "I think you ought to have police protection."

"I do," I said and smiled to myself. "In a manner of speaking."

"See that you do," he said sternly. "It would be hell to try to replace you, young lady."

I was touched.

My phone was busy all morning.

The other three trustees called, of course. Mr. Ottilini said he'd put two and two together and come up with the Big Five; he'd even told the police last night, but hadn't wanted to frighten me at the time with what he hoped was an erroneous conclusion.

"I'd rather have been wrong," he said over the phone. He sounded the way he had looked when he walked away from the Welcome Home for Girls the day we found Mrs. Hatch's body—that is, old, sad and tired.

"We don't *know* that you're right," I reminded him.

"Be careful anyway, Miss Cain."

"If I err, I swear it will be on the side of caution."

A dry chuckle whispered its way over the phone.

"How is Minnie?" I asked, knowing he'd know.

"She's still unconscious," he said. "She was discovered before the drug had time to stop her heart."

"Is she unconscious because of the drug?"

"No. Because of the knock on the head, which she might have sustained when she rolled down the cliff."

"Or which might have been inflicted on purpose?"

"Possibly."

"Bastard."

"Indeed," the old lawyer whispered. "Indeed."

After Roy Leland and Pete Falwell called, it occurred to me that Michael was the only trustee who had not yet connected the Big Five, the murders and me.

How ironic, I thought.

His mind was so preoccupied with the fear of losing me and with murder in general that he hadn't realized he might lose me in a rather more permanent way to a rather more specific danger.

Having accomplished exactly nothing in the way of regular Foundation business, I went to lunch.

Chapter 24

Nobody tried to kill me at any time during the rest of that day. Nobody tried to kill me on Thursday. Nobody tried to kill me on Friday or Saturday. Early Sunday morning, I rolled over in bed and nudged Geof to wake him.

"Wish me happy birthday," I said.

He stretched and yawned and turned on his side to return my attention.

"Happy birthday, Jenny."

"Do you notice anything special about me today?"

"You're alive."

"Quite. Why *is* that, do you suppose?"

"Because we protected you so well?"

"From what?" I tweaked his long, handsome nose. "Nobody tried to kill me. It's anticlimactic, isn't it?"

He laughed and said, "I'm not disappointed. I hope you're not."

"I've ruined your case, you know. Now you're

going to have to look for another motive." I lay back on the pillow and sighed. "If somebody wanted to wreck The Foundation, they should have killed me by now. Ailey Mason will be furious."

"He's not so bad."

"He's an ass."

"He's young, he's got a lot to learn." He scooted closer to me under the covers and kissed my bare left shoulder. "I'm glad you're alive, Jenny."

I returned the compliment with a kiss on his bare and slightly hairy right shoulder. "How's about a little hanky-panky?" I leered.

"Brazen hussy," he laughed. He threw the covers off, revealing two people who would put the night-gown and pajama industries out of business in no time.

"Can you wait until I've brushed my teeth?" he said. "And fixed some coffee?"

I threw my feet over the side of the bed, sat up and sighed theatrically. "Dear Abby," I said, "what does it mean when he wants coffee before hanky-panky? Have I been seeing too much of him? Do you think the thrill is gone?"

His answer was to push me gently back down on the bed and kiss me, as they say, lingeringly. No, the thrill definitely was not gone.

"You're right about the toothpaste," I said, however. "And I'll take my coffee black this morning, please."

"Here." He held out his hands. I grabbed them and he pulled me off the bed to a standing position. We strolled, arms around each other, into the bathroom where we companionably brushed our respective teeth at the double sinks and washed our respective sleepy faces. I felt fey, and electrically, gratefully alive.

While Geof shaved, I brushed my hair back into a ponytail at the nape of my neck. I dabbed on enough makeup to cover the blue beneath my eyes. Funny how troubles show up in shades of blue around the eyes—got the blues, they sing, and blue Monday and feelin' blue. Appropriate, but remarkably unattractive on the human female face. I dabbed on the makeup with a heavier hand.

"You're quiet this morning, Detective Bushfield."

"I'm counting my blessings." He wiped off the remnants of shaving gel from under his chin. I like to watch men shave. His hand with the double-edge razor moved in quick, sure, efficient strokes. He rinsed the razor and set it on the edge of the sink. I thought he was going to walk past me and on into the bedroom.

Instead, he stopped behind me, lifted my ponytail and kissed the back of my neck.

"That's one blessing," he said.

I smiled back at him in the mirror.

He turned me around and placed a second kiss on my lips.

"That's two blessings," he said.

He moved his kisses downward.

"Three blessings," he said. "Four . . ."

I pulled his head up until his mouth was even with mine again and kissed him back. "Mustn't lead a girl on," I said, "with words of coffee, if you don't intend to produce."

We hugged, gaily, happily, gratefully.

Ten minutes later we were in bed again, but this time we were perched against pillows we had propped against the headboard. Geof had wrapped a thick navy blue robe around himself and pulled the covers up over our legs. I wore a white chenille robe left over from a previous wife.

The coffeepot sat on a table on his side of the bed; he'd carried it up from the kitchen, along with buttered English muffins, a jar of honey that smelled like fresh clover and a wrapped and beribboned birthday present.

"For me?" I said idiotically. I was delighted; I love birthdays.

"Yes," he smiled, "unless you know of somebody else in the room whose birthday happens to be today and who I happen to be nuts about."

And that's what it was: a little box of mixed nuts with a card that said, "Little Geoffrey Bushfield is nuts about pretty Jenny Cain." There was a P.S.: "This card and one cashew redeemable for one fabulous weekend in the New York City of your choice."

"I'm a fool for birthdays, you know," I said. I couldn't seem to stop beaming.

"Somehow I guessed as much," he said dryly. "Beneath that beautiful and efficient exterior beats a sentimental slob of a heart."

I ate a Brazil nut while I got the heart in question under control. "I can see why they married you," I said. "It's not every man who makes coffee as well as he makes love."

"I butter a pretty mean muffin, too," he said between satisfied munches.

"Um." I licked butter off my lower lip.

"But married life," he said with mock seriousness, "if I may say so . . ."

"You may say so, particularly in light of your employment history as outlined here on your résumé . . ."

". . . is not all love and muffins."

"What then, oh wise one, *is* married life?"

"Well, my first wife said it's not the time you spend together, it's how you spend the time."

"Together."

"Precisely." He sipped and smiled. "Quite the philosopher, my first wife. She also said, she who hesitates is lost, and so she didn't hesitate to divorce me."

"She's not lost then."

"No. Found herself in California."

"Regular national lost and found department, that state," I said. I chewed the muffin, but eschewed further comment. If this was how he wanted to introduce the topic of his divorces, that was fine by me. I didn't have to see tears to appreciate the pain beneath the banter. He'd get to all of it, given time and trust.

"Wife numero dos, on the other hand," he said, "was of a practical rather than a philosophical nature. With her it was not the quality of the time we spent together, but the quantity of it."

"Not enough, huh?"

"Not by your basic long shot. I worked too many weekends and too many nights."

"She got lonely."

"Only for a time, but she solved that problem."

"Found a friend, did she?"

"Yep. Married him, too."

"Oh, Geof."

"Don't feel sorry for me, Jenny. You get what you ask for in this life, and I got mine."

I licked my fingers before I said, "Did you ask for me?"

He put down his cup of coffee. He took hold of the fingers I had just licked and he kissed the inner tip of each one of them.

"Yes," he said finally. "The first time I asked for you I was about seventeen years old. And I guess I've been asking for you ever since in all the women I've known. None of them was you, of course, and maybe that's been the problem. It never occurred to me that I'd ever get the real thing."

"Didn't your fairy godmother ever tell you?" I said in a voice so husky I hardly recognized it as my own.

He looked at me.

"About what?" he said.

"About happy endings."

We set down the rest of our plates and got down to the business I had tried to initiate earlier that morning. It was nice—after toothpaste, coffee, muffins and conversation—very intimate, very comfortable.

It was very wonderful to be alive to enjoy it.

Only a couple of hours later, I took the wheel of Geof's car for my weekly drive to the hospital. My own testament to American ingenuity still sat idle—but not idling—in the driveway of my parents' home. I'd had a few rather more pressing things to worry about that week, and a willing chauffeur in Geof.

He sat beside me in his BMW. I'd never taken anyone with me to visit my mother before, but I didn't think I'd tell him that, at least not yet. We talked of other mutual concerns as I negotiated the unfamiliar car onto the all-too-familiar route.

"So," I said, "if he wasn't going to kill me, why'd I get one of those poems?"

"Well, I wasn't really kidding about the protection we've given you." Geof pressed the lever that lowered the passenger's seat so that it and he leaned back comfortably. "It's just possible that he couldn't get *to* you to get *at* you."

"So to speak." I pointed at one of my favorite views along the road—a "typical" New England barn attached to a farmhouse. Geof made satisfactory, appreciative sounds.

"You're a good tourist," I said. "I like people who react to things."

"Wow!" he said. "What a *terrific* farmhouse."

"That's the way," I laughed. "So then you still think the murders are connected to the Big Five, even though nobody murdered me?"

"I suppose," he said agreeably.

"You're awfully relaxed about this, Mr. Crime Fighter. You don't suppose you could act a little more alert, do you?"

"Um." He closed his eyes. "If the price of liberty is eternal vigilance, the price of eternal vigilance is exhaustion. Besides, I've just had the most wonderful morning . . ."

"Anyone I know?"

"And I'm limp as a deflated blimp. Drive on, sergeant, you're doing a fine job."

A Don Williams country/western tape was sticking halfway out of the cassette player, so I pushed it in and turned the music down low. Geof was asleep by the time mellow Don was singing ". . . and I believe in you."

I let him nap all the way.

We sat on opposite sides of my mother's hospital bed and talked over her prone body. She might as well not have been there, which to all intents and purposes she wasn't.

"How long has she been like this?" Geof asked. His chin rested on his arms, which he had crossed on top of the metal side railing that had been raised to keep my mother from falling out of bed.

"A week."

"This isn't the first time she's gone catatonic?"

"No."

"She'll come out of it then."

"That's what the doctors say."

"The tone of your voice says the doctors are fools."

"No, but they don't know everything."

"What do you know that they don't?"

"She won't come back. There's nothing for her to come back to."

"You? Your sister?"

"That was good enough when we were young and needed her in order to survive. We haven't needed her in that way for years, though, and somewhere inside her I'm sure she knows it. Nobody needs her with a strong enough need to keep her alive for their sake."

"What about for her own sake?"

"That was never enough, not for her."

"Yes," he said, "it isn't, for some people."

We sat silently then. I stared into my mother's open, vacant blue eyes; Geof stared over the bars at me. She'd lost weight in a week, even with the tube that

208

fed nourishment directly into her stomach. And she looked flaccid as a coma patient; maybe it *was* coma rather than catatonia. It hardly mattered; either way, she was far away from me.

"Where are you, Mother?" I whispered to the cold metal bars. "Is it warm where you are? Are you comfortable and safe? It's okay, you know; don't feel guilty about anything. It isn't your fault, none of it has been your fault. I know you can't fight anymore, I don't blame you. You hung in there for so many years for Sherry and me, and once upon a time for Daddy. I know you're tired and you want to rest. Mother, I just want you to know that if you want to go—it's all right with me. I love you, no matter where you are or where you go. So you do what you need to do, and don't worry about me. I know you love us, somewhere in there you do."

I stood and leaned over the bars to kiss her forehead. My tears splattered onto her nose and ran down her cheeks so that it looked as if she were crying too.

Geof stood too and reached for me over my mother's bed. He held me until I stopped shaking, and then he drove me home.

Chapter 25

We drove first to my parents' house to water the plants and get me several changes of clothing. As Geof remarked on the way over, it might be safe for me to stay alone now that my birthday had come if not yet gone, but we couldn't be absolutely sure of that.

"Besides," he added lightly, "I hate to make a bed by myself."

"I didn't know it mattress to you," I said and he groaned.

"That was a hit pillow the belt," he said.

"No sheet."

"Obscene language in public is a pun-ishable offense."

"All right!" I laughed. "Truce!"

"Say uncle," he demanded. So much emotion in so short a time had rendered us both a little goofy.

"Aunt," I giggled.

"That'll do."

"Pun-k!" I yelled as I slammed the door and slogged, laughing, through the snow to the front steps. I walked in the postman's several tracks, slurring them as I kicked my way home. Thin layers of snow had fallen in my absence, so the house had a freshly powdered if rather forlorn look about it. I fantasized that it was glad to see me. The evergreen bushes my mother had planted years before bowed low to me under their white load; icicles sucked determinedly at the eaves. Except for the tracks of the postman and those of a roaming dog or two, the yard spoke eloquently of no-one-home.

I climbed the postman's footprints up the front steps and onto the porch, fumbled in my purse for my big brass key ring, the one I bought so I wouldn't have to fumble in my purse for my keys. Geof whistled his leisurely way up the walk behind me.

The feel of the house key in my hand was like the feel of welcome-home, which is where I was rather glad to be, Geof's company notwithstanding. I smiled happily to myself and looked up at the big front door of my parents' home.

It was open.

Not wide open, but definitely ajar. The small pane of glass nearest the lock was broken. Funny, I'd never noticed how vulnerable my nice sturdy conscientious bolt was, and how easy it would be for a hand to reach in through the glass and switch the lock I had so carefully turned. I noticed now.

"Geof."

He came running at the alarm in my voice, lifting his long legs high through the snow I had never shoveled. When he saw the door he said quietly, "Get back in the car, Jennifer." It was impossible to see inside the hallway because of the curtains I had neatly closed before I left with the policeman several nights before. I watched Geof pull a gun I didn't know he had from a holster I hadn't known he was wearing. I didn't have the slightest idea what kind of gun it was, but it looked as efficient as the man who owned it. He said, "Get in the driver's seat. I left the keys in the ignition. Do not start the car. Wait five minutes. If I don't come out this door, or if you see or hear anything that frightens you, drive immediately to the police station and tell them to get here fast."

"I could run to the neighbors'."

"They're not home," he said, proving how little I knew about how alert he was. "Go now, please."

I went.

But only as far as my own car, where I quietly opened the trunk and reached in for the tire jack that was stored beside the spare. I set my purse in the trunk, which I left open, and walked back through the silent snow to the front porch. I waited there, off to one side, with the jack raised high in both hands like the racket of a tennis player at the net. It did occur to me that I must have looked pretty ridiculous and that I wasn't all that sure what I thought I was doing. But I didn't see any need to spend my five minutes unprotected.

Sooner than I expected, Geof stepped back out on the porch. He saw me just as he put his gun back in its holster.

"Expecting someone?" he said. "Maybe the villian running out the front door with me in hot pursuit?"

I dropped the jack in the snow and breathed again.

"You might have needed me," I said defensively.

"I do need you." He gestured for me to join him on the steps. I wondered why he wasn't angry at me for ignoring his undoubtedly wise instructions. He seemed, instead, gentle.

I understood why when I stepped into the house.

"Bastards," I whispered when I saw, and then my whisper turned into a banshee scream. "Bastards, bastards!"

"Yes," Geof said coldly, rather like Edwin Ottilini before him, "yes, indeed."

I've heard that bomb and burglary victims experience similar feelings of violation and fury, of fear and grief and helplessness. That may be so, but frankly, I think I'd rather be bombed, provided no one was home at the time. I wonder if it isn't a little less excruciatingly personal when yours is only one of several devastated houses on the block and the hit was merely a vicious stroke of fate, not purpose. If you're bombed, at least you can't imagine the pilot and the bombardier had it in, personally, for you. They didn't smile meaningfully at each other, six thousand feet up, and say, "Coming up on Jenny Cain's house. Let's annihilate it, old boy. Bombs away!"

There wasn't any doubt that somebody had it in, as personally as possible, for me. The proof lay scattered about my parents' house in tiny shreds of family photographs and scissored pages of favorite books; it snuggled in the cozy down that spilled out of the slashed cushions of the chairs and sofa in the den; it nestled evilly among the pieces of broken crystal in the dining room. My mother's twenty Wedgwood dinner plates were neatly lined up in four rows in front of the hutch. Something hard—the heel of a shoe? the leg of a chair?—had carefully stepped down in the center of each one, smashing it to pulverized dust.

"This took a lot of time," Geof said as he walked me through the house. He'd already called the station. I asked him if he'd thought to tell them to bring brooms.

We climbed to the second floor.

Out of the corner of my eye, I glimpsed the damage to my room—clothes pulled out of drawers and closets, probably ruined. But I walked on down the hall to the only room my mother had known in her adult life besides various ones in various hospitals.

"Wait, Jennifer!"

But I didn't.

I stood in the doorway of my parents' bedroom and stared.

"This took a lot of time," I said finally, unconsciously parroting Geof. "Somebody certainly took a lot of time to do this."

It looked as if a tornado of frenzied malice had ripped through the room. Clothes lay everywhere, having been yanked from their hangers and drawers and tumbled to the floor. But that wasn't what had taken the intruder so much dangerous time, it wasn't that task over which he or she had labored so painstakingly. There were in that room other marks of wickedness so painful to me that my eyes could only briefly register them and then skitter away . . . the last hooked rug on which my mother had been working was carefully and completely unraveled so that the colorful ribbons of material lay limp among the devastation . . . my parents' wedding pictures which my mother had never removed from the room were still intact, but for their two heads neatly scissored from every single one of them . . . my Grandmother Cain's eyelet pillowcases had been cut into ragged squares of dead lace . . . the funny little ceramic sculpture of a clam that my mother had made for Dad when he took over his doomed company was smashed into unrecognizable shards . . . my bronzed baby shoes, and my sister's, were lined up side by side on the floor where somebody had defecated on them . . .

I turned blindly away from that awful room and ran back down the hallway, looking neither right nor left, nor at Geof who waited anxiously for me at the head of the stairs. I ran down the steps and out the front door. I plowed back through the snow to Geof's car and I got in and sat in the driver's seat and I stared out the window in the direction that was opposite of my parents' house.

He followed me out. He opened the door on the passenger's side and leaned in toward me.

"I'm all right," I said to the window.

"I don't think so."

"I don't think so either."

"You'll be cold if you wait here."

"I'll live."

"I'll have somebody take you back to my house."

"That would be good."

"Jenny . . ."

"Actually," I said to the window, "I'm too old to be living in my parents' house. Even if they're not home. And there's no need to pretend I'm keeping it safe for my mother's return."

"Darling . . ."

"It's time to move on." My breath frosted the window so that I couldn't see out of it. I said to the frost, "It's time for me to move on."

Geof closed the door gently as the police cars turned the corner of the street where I no longer lived.

Chapter **26**

There weren't any fingerprints, of course, except the ones that ought to have been there—mine, Michael's, Ginger's, etcetera. And whoever it was didn't just happen to drop a telltale matchbook or leave behind a cufflink with a type of rare stone that was owned by only five people in the world, three of them now in prison and the fourth paralyzed from the neck down by a freakish tobogganing accident in Switzerland. Whoever it was didn't leave any footprints, either. Whoever it was had either traipsed barefoot through the snow or had removed his shoes or boots at the door so as not to track traceable prints of mud on the rug.

Very clean, the one who hated me, and careful.

"I think we have to face that possibility," Geof said that afternoon in his office at the station. It was small, neat and functional, giving not a hint of the sensuous side of him. He had, on second thought, had me delivered there—like a perishable package—instead of to his house.

The possibility he thought we had to face was the one that ran along the lines of somebody out there hating me.

"So maybe the one they're out to ruin is Ms. Cain, here," Ailey Mason said. "Maybe they were after her all along, and not The Foundation."

"Oh, come on," I protested. "They didn't attack the others just so The Foundation would collapse and I'd lose my job!"

"Maybe," Geof mused, "maybe you're just a double victim, in a sense . . ."

"Just?" I said faintly. I'd wept for a solid hour in the women's john at the police station; now I felt drained, calm and capable of murder myself.

"What I mean," Geof said, "is that you're a potential victim, A, because you're one of the Big Five. But you're also a potential victim because, B, you're the obvious living symbol of The Foundation."

"I thought double jeopardy was illegal," I said, still more faintly.

"Or maybe he was just plain frustrated because he couldn't get at her to kill her at The Foundation," Mason suggested. "Because she was always there with other people and because you, uh, protected her at other times. So he goes to her house to kill her and when she's not there, he gets real pissed off. I can see that, yeah, I can see that."

I rolled my eyes at Geof.

"He can see that," I said. "He can understand how some homicidal maniac could get so angry at me for not having the courtesy to be home when he wants to kill me . . ."

"He didn't mean that, Jenny," Geof grinned. "Tell her you didn't mean it that way, Ailey."

Mason lit a cigarette and looked disgusted. He probably thought he looked blasé and sophisticated.

"What I want to know," Geof said, "is when he broke into your parents' house. Obviously, it had to be sometime between Tuesday night when you left and today when we got back from the hospital."

Mason lifted a quizzical eyebrow that Geof didn't answer. So Mason said, pompously, "I can determine that by the neighbors and the postman and the snowfall." If there's anything worse than a pompous ass, it's a young one. This particular sample of the species proceeded to lecture his elder. "You know— today's Sunday, so did the postman notice the door was ajar when he delivered the mail yesterday? I can narrow it down fast with easy stuff like that."

Geof nodded seriously, managing to control his grin. Then he said, "Then I want to know the alibis for that time period for the people who knew of the existence of the Big Five list."

For an instant, Mason looked like the young, over-worked kid he really was. "Jesus, Geof," he complained, "why don't you just ask me to get alibis for everybody in Poor Fred?"

"Don't make this harder than it is," Geof said mildly. "Concentrate on the primary possibilities— the staff of The Foundation, the trustees, the directors of the charities, the relatives of the victims, and don't worry about the secondary layer of people who might have known about the Big Five—spouses, friends, and so on. At least not yet."

Mason grunted, but there was a measure of respect to the sound, if that's possible.

Geof turned back to me.

"Now we need to talk about you, Jenny. Tell me who hates you, not that I believe for one minute that anyone could."

Mason grunted again.

"Hate?" I felt uncertain with the word, much less the idea. "Well. I suppose I've made some people angry if they didn't get the money they wanted from The Foundation, but I don't think I'd say they hated me."

"Okay," he said patiently, and smiled. "Let me phrase it another way. Whose blood pressure rises at the sound of your name? Who, if given the chance to invite you to dinner, would not? Who, upon hearing you'd had a run of bad luck, would smile?"

I glanced at Ailey Mason. He smiled.

But it was my sister who stood in the doorway behind us and said, "You called?"

Geof glanced up at her and his mouth visibly dropped. Mason and I swiveled at the sound of her voice, and when the young cop saw her he rushed to his feet, dropping cigarette ashes down the front of him in his hurry.

She was a knockout's knockout.

She'd tucked her silver-blond hair into a snug mink cap that matched her knee-length mink coat. Both were the color of bittersweet chocolate, a shade that dramatically framed her Swedish complexion. Her eyes were so big and blue you'd have sworn there were clouds passing through them.

She pulled off the cap, releasing a long loose swirl of fragrance and hair. Mason released a short, tight sigh.

She slipped off the coat, revealing a multi-hundred-dollar cashmere sweater in a gold as soft and pale as antique coins. It clung to her as if it were afraid she'd lose it. Her slacks were the color of rich, moist real estate and just about as expensive. Her tiny feet in their tiny boots had walked only on shoveled—if not hallowed—ground and did not drip snow upon the floor.

The vision parted her red wine lips to reveal beauty queen teeth. The vision smiled.

"You're Jennifer's sister, aren't you?" Geof managed to say. "The resemblance is amazing."

"You think so?" Mason said. I hoped some of the ashes that had spilled on his chest were still hot. He quickly stepped out of the vision's way and offered her his chair.

She offered him her cap and coat to hold.

He took them like a votive offering; she took the chair like a birthright.

The vision turned to me and spoke.

"Happy birthday, Jenny," it said. "How does it feel to be thirty years old?"

"Hello, Sherry. Right now, it feels about forty."

"Looks it, too," she said softly. "A policewoman called my home, Jenny, and asked me to come down here. What's going on?"

"Sherry, I'd like you to meet Detective Geoffrey Bushfield and Detective Ailey Mason."

"Bushfield?" She turned the sky-eyes on him. He managed, somehow, not to swoon. "Your name's familiar, have we met?"

"We went to the same high school," he smiled. "I think it's a little more likely that I'd remember you than that you'd remember me."

She nodded to indicate her acceptance of this probable truth. "Still," she said, managing in the most ladylike way to examine him from head to foot. "I'd have thought I'd remember you."

"Thank you." He grinned.

"Sherry," I said, having had enough of her irritating behavior, "someone broke into the house and destroyed almost everything in it."

"What house is that?"

"Our house." I clenched my jaw and tried to remember this wasn't a whole, three-dimensional person I was dealing with, but only a pathetic, cardboard caricature of a woman. Sherry hadn't yet learned how to be a real and fully developed adult— she was stuck somewhere in bitter adolescence—and so she, unconsciously, played grownup roles: This was her reigning princess act and she was very good at it.

"Why would somebody do that?" she said coolly.

"Don't you want to know what damage they did?" I said.

"Yes, tell me, I'd enjoy that."

Mason and Geof exchanged startled glances that she didn't see.

I told her.

She seemed to enjoy it.

"Well, I'm sure you'll take care of everything, Jenny," she said calmly at the end of my recital. "It's half mine, of course, so I'll expect half of the insurance money. You'll see that I get it, won't you, Sis?"

"It is not mine or yours, Sherry, not yet anyway. It seems somehow to have escaped your notice that Mother is not yet dead."

"No?" She rose gracefully and smiled at Mason as she held out her arms for her coat and cap. He stumbled with them toward her. I hoped he tripped on them. She said, "Well, with any luck, by the time you get the claim filed and the insurance company settles this thing, she will be."

Geof looked stunned.

"Mrs. Guthrie," he said, "the vandalism at your parents' house seems to have been an act of premeditated malice. Do you know anyone who hates your sister?"

"Hates Jenny?" Her lashes blinked once over the big blue guileless eyes. "How could anyone possibly hate my sister? She's as nearly perfect as anyone I know, Detective Bushfield. Everyone loves Jenny; everyone has always loved Jenny."

"And you?" he said softly. The silky down at the back of her neck should have prickled at his tone. "Do you love Jennifer?"

She smiled at him, the smile the Wicked Queen gave to Snow White along with the poisoned apple.

"She's my sister," Sherry said. "Of course, I love her."

There was a moment of appreciative silence after she had swept regally from the office.

"My sister is a . . ."

". . . knockout," Mason said.

". . . bitch," Geof said. "A-Number-One, USDA Prime Cut, Grand Champion, certified bitch."

"You," I said, "are so perceptive."

The day was beginning to intimidate me.

"I'd like to make a phone call, if that's all right," I said to Geof shortly after Sherry's departure.

"Suspects are only allowed one call. Victims get two." His smile was so gentle it left me awash in

223

gratitude for the one intelligent, compassionate, loving, six-foot-two-inch thing about my day.

"Use my extension," he added as he pushed Mason out the door with him. "My young friend and I have people to see and things to do. But please don't leave without me, Jenny."

I wasn't likely to do that. I didn't, in fact, particularly want to leave the security of the police station ever again. I thought I might just stay there forever and have my meals brought in.

I sat down in Geof's swivel chair behind his immaculate desk and pushed the buttons on his phone.

"Hello?" said the party I called.

"Michael," I said, then waited a beat for him to reply. When he didn't, I said, "It's Jenny."

"The voice is familiar," he said, "and I think I've heard the name somewhere before. Do you sell siding?"

"No, but we have a special today on full-color photographs of your entire family."

"Actually, miss, you've called at a bad time. My entire family has just sat down to dinner."

"We also take photographs of entire families eating dinner."

"I get the picture."

"We hope you will, for just $300, which includes two glossy eight-by-tens and one hundred wallet-sized photos of your dog or child, whichever you prefer. We'll throw in a genuine plastic frame for free."

"Let me tell you how I see the situation, miss, what did you say your name is?"

"Jenny."

"The way I see the situation, Jenny, is that you

wouldn't call me unless you had something pretty important on your mind. Because you know the sound of your voice is a twist in the heart for me and . . ."

"Michael."

". . . and you are basically a kind and loving person who wouldn't twist said heart unless she had a damned good reason to do so. Do you have a damned good reason, other than to ask me to wish you happy birthday, Jenny?"

"Would you, given the chance, wish me a happy birthday?"

"Happy birthday, my love," he said softly. Then, in a firmer voice: "Scratch that. Happy birthday, somebody else's love."

I took a deep, trembly breath.

"I shouldn't have called you," I said.

"First, tell me why you did; then we'll decide if it was the right thing to do."

"Michael, somebody broke into my parents' home. They've ruined almost everything. Mom's crystal and china, our clothes and the furniture. They broke the stereo and the records. They smashed the TV, they . . ."

"Jesus! Who, why?" he exclaimed. "My God, Swede, is there anything I can do to help you?"

"I don't know." Suddenly I was confused about my motives for calling him. "I thought there was, that's why I called you, but now I'm not sure what I thought you could do."

"Maybe just hold your hand," he said.

"Maybe," I whispered. "Yes, I guess so."

"Consider it held."

"I don't suppose this is fair, is it?"

"Neither was the son of a bitch who smashed your house."

"Are you moving, Michael?"

"Yep."

"Soon?"

"Yep."

"You're not going to tell me more?"

"I don't think so, no."

"You don't want me to be tempted to write to you, and thereby raise your hopes," I humbly suggested.

"That's pretty much it." He sounded sure of himself, older, more mature. "If I'm going, I'm going clean."

"Do you think," I said very, very hesitantly, "that I could take you out for a farewell dinner?"

"No." Then as if to ease the abruptness: "Thank you, Swede, but I don't think that's a good idea."

"Well." I felt suddenly bereft and I wondered if it was a temporary or a permanent bereft. "Well, I guess we'll see if I miss you."

He managed to laugh.

"Oh, Jen, I do love you," he said. "And yes, I guess we'll see."

We said goodbye and hung up.

Calling him was a stupid and cruel thing to have done, I told myself. And I shouldn't have wondered out loud if I would miss him. In the core of me, I knew I wouldn't—at least, not in the way he wanted to be missed.

Geof opened his office door and stuck his head in.

"We're sending out for hamburgers, Jenny. Want me to order something for you?"

"You're it," I said.

"I'm what?"

"You're what I would order right now if I could order anything I wanted in this world."

He leaned against the door frame as if he'd lost his strength. "How do you want that fixed?" he said in a low voice that turned my wrists to water. "Mayo, mustard, all the trimmings?"

"No," I said, "just bare. Do you deliver?"

"I don't know," he said, "do I?"

"You certainly do."

We smiled at each other.

Chapter **27**

Whoever had thrown the tantrum at my parents' house had somehow missed my pet—the little home computer. At my suggestion, Geof had it lugged over to his house that night. When we walked in, late, it was set up on the floor beside the empty hot tub in the living room.

"Hello, Fido," I said and gave its molded plastic top a fond pat. "I'm going to feed you tonight and then we'll see if you'll do tricks for us."

We could have used the police computer, but we'd have had to file time requests in quadruplicate, and this was to be only an informal effort, anyway, just to see if by any luck we came up with something new. So it was a lot simpler and more direct to use Fido.

I plugged him in and sat cross-legged on the floor in front of him. Geof set a glass of iced orange juice beside my left hand. He sat on the bare floor too, his back against the tub and his own glass of juice nearby.

"Why is there an empty hot tub in your living room?" I had to ask, having meant to ask from the first night.

"This is as far as we got when some friends helped me haul it up from the rec room in the basement," he said. "I wish it were full and hot and we could get in it right now."

"You and me both, pal."

"You're sure you're not too tired, Jenny?" He reached out a long arm so that the hand attached to it could massage the back of my neck.

"That's wonderful," I groaned. "Please stop, or I *will* fall asleep." I turned Fido on, inserted the disc I needed and tapped the keys. My body was exhausted, but my brain was perking on pure adrenaline; I could stay up all night if my body didn't fall apart.

I tapped and six words appeared: "WHO WHAT WHEN WHERE WHY HOW."

Behind me, Geof laughed and said, "Why do I get the feeling you're always one step ahead of me?"

"That's why your legs are longer," I said, "to compensate."

"Okay if I dictate?"

"Fire away, Mr. Executive, sir."

"We'll put some names under WHO . . ."

"They being the people who knew of the Big Five?"

"Right."

I tapped them in as he dictated them: Jennifer Cain, Derek Jones, Faye Basil, Marvin Lastelic, Edwin Ottilini, Jack Fenton, Pete Falwell, Roy Leland, Michael Laurence.

We paused over the name of the fifth Foundation trustee. Geof said, "He's the one who drove us to the church, isn't he?"

"Um hm."

"He looked intelligent; I therefore assume he's in love with you."

"Um." I kept my eyes straight ahead on the glowing screen and my fingers resting lightly on the keys.

"You haven't seen much of him lately, I would guess," Geof said casually. "How's he taking it?"

"He's leaving town." Then I added quickly, "But not because of me, because his father's come back to take over the family business and Michael is splitting to go out on his own."

"Where's he going?"

"I don't know exactly," I said to the keyboard. "Someplace in Colorado, I think."

"When's he leaving?"

"I don't know that either." I picked up my glass of juice, took a sip and turned to smile at him. "Who, what, when, where, why and how? I called Michael today, from your office, to tell him about my parents' house. He was shocked. He was concerned."

Geof seemed to take the information in, like a computer, and consider it. I waited for his next question, which was: "Okay, now please add to our list the names of the directors of the charities you serve, if you have reason to believe they know of the Big Five."

I tapped in Simon's name and Allison Parker's and five others, even adding Dr. Ian Priestly. Then we added the names of the immediate family members of the victims—Marvalene and Franklin Culverson, and Moshe's only son who lived in town, and Mr. Charles Withers Hatch and the three Hatchlings.

"Surely we can eliminate Minnie's husband," I said. "He's an invalid, after all. And I wouldn't think we'd need to bother with the relatives who live out of town."

"I agree. Does Ginger Culverson know of the list?"

"I wouldn't think so, unless Simon has told her."

"They're friends?"

"I introduced them about a week ago and they seemed to hit it off. I don't know if either of them has followed up on that meeting. I'll find out."

I stared at our lengthening list of names.

"Good grief, Geof, that's twenty-three names counting me!" It made me more tired just to look at the length of the list. "And I'll bet there are others who know of the Big Five."

"Twenty-three's not so many," said the only experienced cop in the room. "We can trace the movements of twenty-three people fairly easily, knock on wood. In fact, we've already done a lot of it this week. All it takes is time and patient policemen. And women. We won't concern ourselves with the secondary possibilities yet; I have a gut feeling the name we want is among those twenty-three."

I gazed at those names of twenty-three people I knew. While it was true that I didn't necessarily *like* each of them, I hated the thought that one of them might be a murderer.

"Jennifer," Geof said, "what about your sister?"

I almost spilled my juice on the computer.

"Oh, Geof!"

"Did she know about the Big Five?"

Reluctantly, I said, "Yes. About four months ago, I asked for a meeting with her in Mr. Ottilini's office— neutral ground—to discuss our trusts and wills. She was curious about my leaving so much money to The Foundation. I did a little pious preaching about the good I hoped it would do. I'm sure I mentioned the Big Five, heaven knows why, maybe I hoped she'd like to be the Big Sixth."

"So," he said gently, "we have twenty-four names."

I let out a whoosh of breath through my mouth and tapped in the name Sherry Cain Guthrie. Suddenly I felt a great deal more weary. My back hurt. My head hurt. My heart hurt.

"You sure you want to continue?" Geof asked.

I thought of the devastation at my mother's house. I thought of how Minnie looked when they carried her off in the ambulance. I nodded and gulped the last dregs of the juice; it was crisp and fruity like an afternoon in the sun in June, and it cleansed my palate of the bitter aftertaste of the day.

"Carry on," I said.

"Okay, now for WHAT." I could hear the strain of exhaustion in Geof's voice. "This one's easy—in each case, the murder weapon was an overdose of Soronal."

"The hypertension medicine that Arnie took."

"Right."

"Was it all from his prescription? I mean the drugs that killed Moshe and Mrs. Hatch and the one that was used on Minnie?"

"Maybe, but it's hard to say."

"It is? Why?"

"Well, you remember we found two pill bottles on Culverson—one of them was empty, but the other still had a few capsules in it. Unfortunately, we have no way of knowing how many of those pills he took legitimately in the days before he died. So we don't know if the killer doped Culverson and then stole some extra pills, or if he's been using some other prescription since then."

"Some *other* prescription? Whose?"

"You make it sound so simple," Geof laughed. "Whose? Well, for starters, think of all the Type A, hard driving, nervous people you know. Any of them could be candidates for migraines or hypertension and that means any of them might take Soronal."

"Oh," I said, chastened. "That describes half the people on our suspect list, doesn't it?"

"It certainly does," he agreed wearily. "And even if they don't take Soronal, they probably know people who do since those are common ailments and that's a popular drug. It'd be easy to get access to it."

"Why did he have two bottles of pills on him?"

"Because he'd had his prescription refilled that afternoon after he left Ottilini's office."

"Where'd he go after that?"

"First to the country club, where the waiter says he ate alone and only picked at his food. Then it looks as if he went directly to the museum."

"Well." I tapped my front teeth with a fingernail. "I suppose any one of the twenty-four of us could have met him at the Martha Paul that night, if we could have got past the guard."

"Maybe," Geof said cautiously.

"But if you can't prove he went anyplace else and you can't prove any of the rest of us met him at the museum, then things don't look too good for Simon."

"They shouldn't, no, especially since he admits he was there at the museum that night and that he met with Culverson. On the surface, that looks bad. And he was also at the cocktail party the night Cohen died, so he might have been the one who doped the old man. But we checked Simon out—he has two alibis that even I have to believe, one for the attack on Minnie and one for the attack on your home."

I was surprised. "You know when that happened?" I said. "You didn't tell me."

"I forgot." He was apologetic. "It was last night. The mailman says your door was not open and the glass was not broken when he delivered the mail yesterday. And a neighbor stopped by your house in the early evening yesterday to say hello and there was no sign of entry then, either. And it doesn't make sense that whoever broke in would do it in broad daylight today, so that leaves last night. On top of all of which is the fact that you haven't shoveled your walk."

"Huh?" I said brightly.

"It has snowed twice since yesterday," he explained. "The first time, it started after the postman made his rounds on your block. It snowed about an inch total. The second time, it started to snow about four-thirty this morning and accumulated another inch. Well, there are two inches of snow in the postman's footprints, but only about half that is those other slurred prints. So we know your visitor arrived between the end of the first snowfall yesterday and the start of the second one this morning."

"Well," I said, "that assuages my guilt for not having shoveled my walks."

"Your neighbors," he smiled, "might not agree."

"About Simon," I said quickly, "I know he has an alibi for the attack on Minnie, because that's the day he was in New York with us. There wasn't time for him to . . ."

"Sure there was," Geof said. "Simon could have called her from New York just as easily as someone else could have called her from here. And he had a good hour and a half from the time our plane landed to the time we arrived at the church. Unfortunately, the museum guard swears that Simon arrived at the museum straight from the airport, that he went to his office and stayed sequestered there all evening. In fact, that's where I located him."

"The guard actually saw Simon?"

"Yeah, on his outside rounds. Every time he walked by the window, there was Simon bent over his desk, working. And that's where he was all last night, too, and I mean literally all night. I guess he's got a special photographic show coming up and he spent the night there working on it. If he's the workaholic you say he is, I can believe he'd do that."

I was happy to hear it; at least that let one of my friends off the hook!

"Lucky for him, too," Geof said as he poured more juice from the pitcher. "Because if you gave me half a chance I could come up with a real good motive for dear old Simon."

"Tell me," I said, although I didn't really want to hear it at all.

"Well," he said a little too eagerly for my taste, "what if Culverson had a spasm of remorse when he went to the Martha Paul that night? Remorse about leaving the money to his daughter? And what if he worked up the courage to tell Simon the news?"

"This is pure conjecture, Geof," I said sternly.

"Sure." He raised an eyebrow in challenge. "Want to conject with me?"

I didn't, but I couldn't chicken out at that point.

"Okay," I said unwillingly, "we all know that Simon has the emotional control of a spoiled brat . . ."

". . . and he's a fanatic about his museum . . ."

". . . and we know he views the loss of Arnie's money as the death of his dreams. So you're thinking that maybe they got in an argument and Simon was furious and hurt—he would be, of course—and, and what?"

"Well, by this time, Culverson's pretty upset, too, right? So maybe he starts getting one of those migraines he used to get . . ."

"So he pulls out his pill bottle and takes a couple . . ."

"And Simon sees his chance for revenge against the old man who was cheating him."

"I don't know, Geof," I said doubtfully. "That's pretty cold-blooded. I mean, I can see Simon grabbing a lamp and bringing it down over Arnie's head in pure rage, but I can't see him cold-bloodedly taking the time to get hold of Arnie's pills, dump them in whatever Arnie was drinking . . ."

"Wine, from a bottle in Simon's office."

"So Arnie would have to drink the drugged wine. And then maybe before it knocks him completely out, Simon suggests they take a stroll around the Chinese Gallery . . ."

"You're very good at this," Geof grinned. "And when Culverson finally keels over, all Simon has to do is lift him onto the testered bed, run down for the comforter and then tuck the old man in."

"Simon's little joke."

"Ha ha."

I shook my head violently. "But he didn't do it,

Geof! This is cruel and absurd to pretend he did! Simon is the one with the alibis, you said so yourself. And it doesn't sound like him anyway—if Simon got mad enough at you to kill you, you'd be dead in a minute because he'd act impulsively, and not so coolly as we've imagined.

"I don't like this exercise," I said petulantly. "Let's stop now, please."

"Yeah," Geof said with regret in his voice and face. He slid his back down the side of the hot tub until he was flat on the floor. "Damn."

"Who else has alibis?" I said to change the subject and relieve my sense of disloyalty to Simon.

"Okay," he sighed, "call up your WHEN category." I did that.

"Now," he directed, "we'll enter the names of those people who cannot adequately account for any one of the time frames of the attacks, excluding the one today on your house, since we haven't talked to everyone about that yet."

"What do you call adequately?" I wanted to know.

"Two reliable witnesses who are not alcoholics, drug addicts, felons, devoted wives or mothers or boyfriends."

"Is that the official way?" I was curious to know how the official police mind operated.

"No," he laughed, "that's the Bushfield way. This *is* a small town, Jen, and I am *not* the FBI. We catch more crooks by using common sense than by the application of criminology, to tell you the truth."

"I won't tell anyone," I promised. "I do believe I like your style, Detective Bushfield."

He laughed again. It took all my willpower to keep my body seated and upright and not let it tumble to the floor where my weary head could rest so snugly in the crook of his shoulder.

Abruptly, he got up to pull a thick notepad from the inside pocket of his sport coat. He flipped through it until he came to the pages he wanted, then dictated names while I entered them in the computer.

When we were through, I looked at the screen.

"Well, that's a mixed bag of nuts," I said. Maybe Geof could make sense of it, but it looked to me as if we had plenty of nothing. There weren't many holes, the holes that existed were not very big and there wasn't a single person among the twenty-four who could not account for more than two of the time periods. Plus, since so many of us knew each other—served on the same committees, attended the same parties, etcetera—a lot of us alibied for each other.

"Chummy lot," Geof said, halfway through.

"You're the one who said it's a small town," I countered.

Derek Jones had alibis for three of the pertinent time frames—"I think he was with a woman he'd prefer not to name," Geof smiled; Faye was quoted as saying she "couldn't for the life" of her recall what she was doing the night Arnie died—it was, after all, several days later before anyone thought to call it murder and begin inquiries; Marvin, of course, had everything but an annotated diary and five notarized witnesses to account for his well and constructively spent time.

Like Simon, all the other directors of the charities had alibis for one, two or even all of the times in question. That held true for the relatives of the victims too. As for my trustees, they were well alibied, mostly by each other. Michael had been at the cocktail party along with most of the other suspects the night Moshe died, but he could account for the other times, having spent them on dates with women who were not me.

"Hmm," I said to that information. "That's interesting, not that it matters to me of course."

"You didn't expect him to be celibate, did you?" Geof sounded amused.

"Don't be so bloody fair-minded," I said huffily.

"Having known you, shall we say, intimately, for a time, Ms. Cain, it surprises me that *you* were chaste for all those months you dated him."

"I don't recall saying I was."

"Oh." He sat up and took a drink of juice. "Well, I guess that just because you never slept with him doesn't automatically mean you never slept with anyone."

"I don't recall saying that I never, to coin a euphemism, slept with him."

"God damn it, Jennifer, don't be so bloody honest."

"It's not supposed to matter in this day and age," I said and smiled at him. I wasn't talking about honesty.

"Do you like to think of me sleeping with other women?"

"Not on your life, buster," I said, widening my grin. "But neither do I blame you for having done so. Heck, if they contributed to your present level of expertise, I'm grateful to them!"

"I don't blame you either," he said crossly. "I just don't want to have to hear about it."

"You brought it up," I said gently. "Sexist porker."

He grinned back at me.

I leaned over and kissed him.

"You're a sweet old hypocrite," I said.

"Let's go to bed," he murmured. He held up his wrist so he could see his watch, but he seemed to have some difficulty in focusing on what it told him. "Good grief, Jenny, do you know what time it is? Let's get some sleep and start fresh in the morning."

"That's easy for you to say," I huffed. "Your life doesn't depend on what we might be able to find out tonight."

His eyes focused and he sat straight up.

"Right," he said dutifully, but a good deal more alertly. "Where are we?"

"WHY."

"Why what?"

I started to giggle. "Not WHAT," I said, "WHY?" The silliness was contagious.

"When?" he, I swear, giggled back at me, "Now?"

"Not WHEN, dummy, I said WHY!"

"Why not?" he said and we fell on each other in hysterical, after-midnight, tears-rolling, helpless laughter. It felt wonderful. We let it roll over us until the last guffaw died and the final giggle trickled down and out.

"Oh, Abbott," I gasped, "my stomach hurts."

"Me too, Costello."

We lay like that for several more minutes and then—by another of those silent accords—sat up again and began to discuss motives. It didn't take much time because there weren't any to speak of. We couldn't figure out why any of my staff or the trustees might wish to harm The Foundation; we didn't think my sister hated me enough to kill several other people just to establish a camouflage for killing me; I doubted that Michael wanted to ruin The Foundation just so I'd lose my job and be persuaded to leave town with him; and none of the victim's relatives had anything to gain from the other deaths.

We agreed it was *theoretically* possible that Simon might have killed Arnie in a fit of fury; that Allison might have slain Mrs. Hatch to get funds for the Welcome Home; that the manager of the theater might have murdered Moshe to aid *that* charity; and that the Reverend Dr. Ian Priestly might have . . .

"Ridiculous," I said in disgust. "And what's more, none of *them* has any reason to kill the rest of us."

"More's the pity," Geof said wearily.

He reached over me toward Fido.

"May I turn this thing off?" he said. When I nodded, he flicked the switch. "We're no smarter than we were, are we Jennifer?"

"Ugh," I said, "and arrgh."

"Enough scintillating repartee," he said and yawned. "To bed, woman."

Chapter 28

I woke when Geof did, but I didn't get up and get dressed and drive in to work with him. Instead, I pulled the phone down beside my head on the pillow and called Faye to tell her I'd be late. She didn't seem to know about the vandalism of my parents' house, and I didn't tell her. Then I phoned Ginger Culverson to ask her to a late lunch at the Buoy. After that, I called my friendly neighborhood Standard station to ask them to tow my car away and *fix* it. Then I called Avis and Budget to reserve a rental car. But because of the bad weather, other drivers had beat me to the available inventory. Those agencies didn't have an engine to offer.

I decided to take a chance and call our local version of Rent-A-Wreck. Bless their battered hearts, they had a '67 Ford Galaxie with only 150,000 miles, maximum rust, minimum chrome. I could have it, they said, if I picked it up that afternoon. What the hell, I thought, as long as it runs.

Then I rolled over and slept some more. What's the use of having executive privilege if you don't abuse it now and then?

The Buoy was crowded when I got there at one-thirty. I hung my coat in the ancient cloakroom, hooked my lady executive hat on top of it and squeezed my way through the drinkers at the bar to the eaters in the deli at the back. I have a passion for the Buoy's lobster sandwiches and homemade cole slaw and fries.

I looked along the west wall where the tables for two are lined up, but I didn't see Ginger there.

"Jenny!"

I turned at her voice. My smile of greeting must have wavered a bit when I saw that she was seated at a table for four and that mine was the only empty chair.

I walked resignedly over and sat down.

"Surprise," Franklin Culverson said with a smirk.

"Jennifer, dear," his mother added.

I gave them my best gracious-loser smile and said weakly, "Well. How nice."

Franklin snorted delicately through his nose. His sister scowled at him and then smiled apologetically at me.

"I can explain," she said quickly, causing Franklin to exchange arch glances with his mother. "When I told *them* I was meeting you for lunch, which was obviously my first mistake—not meeting you, but telling them—they insisted on coming along. I tried to talk them out of it . . ."

I was beginning to feel embarrassed. I needn't have bothered though; neither Franklin nor Marvalene appeared to be in the least offended, at least not by Ginger's attitude. They *were,* I would learn, deeply offended by something else she'd done.

"Go ahead and order your lunch, Jennifer, dear," Marvalene instructed. She was chic in pale yellow Ultra Suede, with not a drop of dirty slush on her pale yellow high-heeled shoes. I wondered how she did it: boots, maybe, that she took off in the cloakroom? She pushed a menu away from her. "I'm too upset to eat," she said. "Franklin is too upset to eat. Ginger is upset, but never too much to eat."

Her daughter's mouth, which was closed over a forkful of potato salad, curled into a grin. Obviously hers was a duck's back and her mother's insults were only water.

I ordered the lobster, slaw and fries I'd been salivating for and a diet cola. The four of us made banal and tense conversation until my food arrived. My sandwich was a glorious three-inch high creation of hard bun, pink meat, mayonnaise and secret seasoning. I sank my teeth into it and tried to keep the innards from dripping out the far end of the bun, under Franklin's fastidious and amused eye.

"Don't ever order one of those on a first date," he said. I had to laugh, and that caused one of those now-and-then moments of genuine warmth that I had been known to experience with him. It didn't last long.

Marvalene lit a Virginia Slim and blew a thin cloud of smoke toward her daughter. "Ginger, dear," she said, "tell Jennifer what you told us this morning."

"Yes, Mother." Ginger's voice was full of wry. But her

father's eyes were dancing with eagerness and happiness.

"Jenny," she blurted, "I think I'm going to give some money to Simon—I mean to the Martha Paul."

"Some money!" Franklin practiced his snort; it was already nearly perfect. *"Some* money!"

"Well," Ginger amended, "what I think I'll do is give him enough money to hire the lawyers and go to court to overturn Martha Paul's will. What do you think?"

I washed down a chunk of lobster with a gulp of cola.

"I think that's wonderfully generous of you," I said with what I hoped was not a noticeable lack of enthusiasm. She had said she would give "him" the money—no mention of The Foundation as intermediary. Well, that was her choice and her right, but I was instantly concerned about Simon's ability to manage the funds wisely. It also occurred to me that Ginger had just very clearly answered Geof's question about whether or not she and Simon had become friends.

Ginger beamed at my praise; her relatives glared.

"That's not all," Ginger said excitedly. "I've also decided to give them the seed money they need to build a new museum! I'm not going to give them as much as my father was, obviously, or I'd have to donate my whole inheritance. But I'll make it a nice healthy sum—maybe a quarter million—and I'll call it a challenge grant."

"Terrific idea," I said and wondered if perhaps I should take some lessons from Simon on fund raising. He must have put her up to the challenge grant idea, and it was a good one; I doubted that she'd have thought of it on her own, inexperienced as she was in the field of fund raising. A challenge grant acts as a spur to other donors; in effect, it means the original donor is saying, "Okay, for every dollar you raise, I'll match you one, up to X amount of money." As a fund raising device, it's dynamite. But it's also one that required the leadership of a superb fund raiser to direct the campaign. Did Ginger know that Simon was probably not that man? I wanted to warn her, but any way I approached the subject it would look like sour grapes and envy. Hell, maybe it was. Maybe Simon could do the job—God knows he was a driven demon when it came to the preservation of his beloved museum.

I tried to look wholeheartedly instead of halfheartedly delighted. Ginger may have wondered why I didn't have more to say about her momentous decisions, but she'd just have to be satisfied with a "terrific" and a smile. Too many things had been happening to me lately—and too many dramatic bombs had been dropped in my lap. My internal computer was near overload.

I wondered why Marvalene and Franklin were so upset by the news; it wasn't ever going to be *their* money, so why did they care what Ginger did with it? And why had they trotted along to lunch with her?

"Jennifer says that's terrific news, Mother," Franklin said. His eyebrows made twin St. Louis arches over his cynical eyes. "Do you want to tell her the rest of it, or shall I?"

"I'll tell her," Ginger said firmly.

I waited, as I seemed to have been doing so often in the recent past, for someone to hand me what was sure to be more bad news. But, as with the Degas painting from the little old man, I was wrong.

"Jenny," Ginger said and smiled her father's most mischievous smile at me. "Mr. Ottilini has persuaded me that with so much money at stake, I ought to draw up a will immediately. And that means I've had to figure out who to leave the money to. Well, I don't have any family but these two charmers, and they're *not* rotten *clear* to the core, so I'm going to leave half of it to them . . ."

"Them" smiled benevolently upon the prodigal daughter.

"I don't know why you're so pleased," she laughed at them. "I *am* the youngest, you know. I'll outlive you by decades."

"There's always the long shot," Franklin said pleasantly, and Ginger guffawed. Obviously *she* didn't take their nastiness at all seriously.

"As for the rest of the money," she continued, "well, my father was a good businessman, whatever else he might have been. I trust his judgment in matters of money. So I'm going to leave the rest of it to The Foundation."

I was stunned. Grateful. With any luck, she'd live another sixty years and it would be that long before The Foundation saw a penny of her gift. By then, I'd be too old or too dead to administer it. But her decision was enormously gratifying all the same, because it was a sign of renewed faith in The Foundation, and in me, I suppose. Perhaps it was a sunny omen that portended change in our drooping fortunes. I nearly cried in my cole slaw.

"That's wonderful," I said inadequately. "I'm really grateful, and the trustees will be, too. I don't know how to tell you what this means to us, Ginger, how very much."

She looked gratified and proud, as well she should. She excused herself to go to the restroom. Her mother waited until Ginger was out of earshot.

"Well, now you see why *we're* here," she said.

"No, I don't," I said.

"Come *on,* Jennifer," Franklin said impatiently. "You've got to help us talk Ginger out of dumping all that money on the museum. Everything she spends on it will be that much less for the rest of us."

"Dear God." I didn't know whether to laugh or cry. "Maybe honesty is not the best policy after all. I think I wish you'd be a little less open in your greed."

"Don't try to tell us you think it's a good idea for her to give all that loot to Simon," he countered. *"You* know Simon, you *know* how he *is."*

"Why does it matter to you, Franklin?" I was really irritated. "Odds are you won't outlive Ginger, so you won't get the money anyway. What do you care?"

"What do we *care?"* Marvalene was shocked to the core of her stainless steel heart. "My dear Jennifer, one always cares about money. Every little bitty *penny,* one cares about."

By the time Ginger returned, her relatives and I were past speech. Well, I was past speech; they were past believing. And the awful, ironic truth was that I *did* want to talk Ginger out of giving money directly to the museum. Only now I couldn't do it without arousing smug suspicions on the part of *mère* and *frère* that my motive was identical to theirs.

I avoided further discussion by looking at my watch.

"Ginger," I said, "can you drop me off at Twelfth and Central? My car's still out of commission. I've ordered a Lease-A-Lump."

The happy family made room for me in Marvalene's Seville. They dropped me off a few minutes later.

"Beauty is only skin deep," the young woman at Lease-A-Lump pontificated. We stood in the cold slush beside the pitiful heap I had just leased against my better judgment.

"True," I said and kicked a tire to fool her into thinking I knew what I was doing, "but ugly goes clear to the bone." She looked confused. "Or," I amended, "clear to the U-joint, as it were. Are you sure this piece of junk will run?"

I had offended her. She patted a broken headlight as if to console the car. "We guarantee all our babies to within one hundred and fifty miles of town," she said reprovingly. "In the unlikely event that this car breaks down, we will drive out and pick you up and provide you with alternate transport."

"Ation," I said irritably, under my breath. "Transport*ation.*" Aloud, I whined, "You don't have anything else? Something with fewer miles on it? A '39 Hudson, perhaps?"

I wrested open the door. It fought back, but I won.

"My God, who had this car last?" I said. It was a mess of dirt and salt from the streets and sidewalks.

She looked mortified.

"I really am sorry," she said and became, at once, human, "but we've been so busy we haven't had time to clean our cars as well as we should. Really, though, I know the last driver took good care of it."

"Only driven by a little old lady on Sundays," I muttered. "Listen, I've seen some of those Sunday drivers and what they can do to a car you wouldn't do in a demolition derby." Car dealerships of any kind bring out the worst in me; it's because I feel so ignorant.

"No," she said seriously, "by a museum director, which is probably just as good."

"Not Simon Church by any chance?"

"Yes!" She was pleased as punch to find some area of rapport with this difficult customer. "He just brought it back in this morning. Such a nice man, and so funny! Do you know him?"

I nodded. "Poor Simon. I didn't know he'd been having car troubles, too."

"He said he had a fender bender a couple of weeks ago and his car's been in the shop ever since." She handed me the keys to the ruined beauty and said, "If you talk nicely to her, she'll follow you anywhere."

I laughed and felt better about the whole dubious transaction. I climbed in the driver's seat, turned the rusty key in the rusty ignition and backed jerkily out. The young woman and I waved at each other. She looked like a proud but nervous mother who's never quite sure when she sends her kid off to school if the principal will call and say the kid's in trouble again and will she please come pick him up and take him home.

"Behave yourself," I said to the car, "or I'll tell your mother."

The massive auto and I rolled heavily if not merrily along to my office. "Baby" didn't have power steering, but I muscled her into the parking lot. As I drove past the corner where Geof had been dropping me off of a morning, I thought of the morning after the night of the attack at the church on Minnie Mimbs, the morning when Simon and Derek "caught" us together. I grinned at the memory of their ribald kidding. I could still clearly see the utterly surprised expressions on their faces, Derek staring at me from the passenger's seat and Simon from the . . .

My heart skipped a funny beat.

Derek had hitched a ride with Simon that day because *Derek's* car was in the shop, not Simon's. And yet the young woman at Lease-A-Lump said that Simon told her he wanted to rent a car because his own was being fixed.

Why would he lie to a Lease-A-Lump lady?

Why would he need two cars, one of them an old dump that nobody would recognize as his?

I stopped grinning.

Chapter 29

The car seemed to swing of its own accord around the perimeter of the parking lot and back onto the street again, as if it were a dowsing rod and I the dowser. Its long blunt nose pointed aggressively in the direction of the Martha Paul. I felt as I had on the day when Edwin Ottilini and I had met at the Welcome Home because our feelings of unease spurred us into intuitive rather than rational action. Those same queasy feelings propelled me toward the museum.

What did I think I was going to ask Simon? I didn't know. What was I looking for? Didn't know that, either. I had a feeling I was taking a risk, but I couldn't have admitted, much less articulated, its specifics.

I just went, sweating palms, jumping heart, terrible sensation in the pit of my stomach and all.

The parking spot with the label "Director" was empty of Simon's vintage Mustang. I stashed "Baby" a couple of slots down the row and walked in the staff entrance on the north side of the museum.

"Good afternoon, Miss Cain," the old guard smiled, though "old" is, I suppose, redundant in describing the guards at the Martha Paul. He pushed the buzzer that allowed me to open the security door; then he pointed out the empty line on the security log where I was to write my name, time in and the name of the person I wanted to see. I wrote in the name of an assistant curator whose car I'd seen in the lot.

"I'd like to see Simon, too," I said casually, as if it were an afterthought. "When do you think he'll be back?"

"Oh, not for an hour at least," the guard said. "He's off to some meeting or other."

"Okay, thanks." With my heart beating preposterously fast, I walked down the hall toward the cramped suite of closets that passed for staff offices. Some other visitor came in behind me, distracting the guard's attention so I was able quietly to try the door to Simon's office. I knew it would be unlocked because none of the locks in the building worked anymore—they were old, rusted, useless.

I breached Simon's cubicle and silently shut the door behind me. I decided not to consider how mortified I would feel if someone opened the door and saw me standing there, alone, in the thin light from the window. If Simon walked in, well, I'd just cover my presence with a perfectly logical excuse like, "Oh golly, I thought this was the ladies' room," or else I'd proceed to feign amnesia, grand mal or, possibly, death. I felt like a spy in one of those movie scenes I've always hated—where the spy sneaks into an office and rifles the files while the audience squirms, just *knowing* someone's going to walk in on him.

I squirmed for a long moment until my brain clicked back into gear. "Look," it commanded, "Think Fast So You Can Get the Hell Out Of Here!"

An office supposedly tells a lot about the person who inhabits it. This one told only partial truths about Simon. Here was his public persona—the serious and respectable museum director, holder of advanced degrees and recipient of multitudinous honors. I knew that his apartment, however, displayed a rather different personality; his bookcases there held an eye-popping—and valuable—potpourri of pornography through the ages; the original paintings on the walls of his home and the sculptures on their stands pursued the same unnerving interest. Long ago, when he was an adolescent, Simon's first porno-graphic purchases had undoubtedly been purely, so to speak, prurient. As he matured, however slightly, his devotion had changed to the more detached attitude of a collector. Simon's apartment might be X-rated, but because of the quality of the art within it, it was not without its socially redeeming qualities.

The only painting on the walls of Simon's office, however, was a superbly executed and incredibly boring nineteenth-century still life with nary a phallic symbol to its name. The floor-to-ceiling books in this room had never required discreet brown wrappers; they were volumes on art history, museum management, photography, philanthropy; they were trade magazines and catalogs. The office was cluttered, but that was more an effect of space than personality. One advantage to its being small was that I didn't have much to search.

I started with the file cabinets and flipped through the folders. They only proved the enormity and difficulty of a museum director's job, especially in a museum that was shamefully understaffed and underfunded. At the Martha Paul, Simon was jack-of-all-trades, but unlike the cliché, he was master of some of them. His expertise and love of his work shone from the full, professional and well-organized files. Holding them, I felt as though I had Simon's heart in my hands. I hoped I wouldn't do something stupid to hurt it.

Like a proper television-trained spy, I invaded his desk next. Nothing was locked. More files. More art catalogs. Personnel files on museum staff members. A file on The Foundation which contained nothing more incriminating than an obscenely funny sketch beside my name. Pens, pencils, film. The same tourist magazine guide to New York that I had saved from our trip the previous week. Stuck inside was a paper napkin from an Italian cafe just off the Bowery, near Soho, with a woman's name and phone number scribbled in the corner. Proofs of payment for tax purposes, and expense vouchers. Other paper napkins from other cafes and bars with other women's names and phone numbers. Simon's version of the little black book, I supposed. Loose paper clips, drafts of memos, two out-of-date calendars.

I had a bad moment when there was a knock on Simon's door. I ducked behind his desk, held my breath and waited. Whoever it was called "Simon?" once, then went away. I let my breath whoosh out, but it took a while longer for my heart to beat again.

I commanded myself to finish the job; there wasn't much left to search. I carefully moved an expensive-looking camera off a straight-backed chair and leafed through the magazines underneath. Nothing. I put the camera back.

Simon's trenchcoat, left over from the last day of fall, hung on a hook on the back side of the door. I fumbled through its pockets, coming up only with lint, matches and a couple more napkins with the requisite phone numbers. I wondered if he ever followed through. What in heaven's name did these women think when he took them back to his apartment for the first time? They felt paralyzing shock, probably. Maybe that accounted for the fact that I'd never known Simon to have a steady girl. They probably took one look at those paintings and sculptures, screamed "pervert" and ran back out the door without stopping to discuss redeeming social values. I had a feeling that Ginger Culverson would probably at least give Simon a chance to explain himself.

There was nothing more to search except my own brain. And something very definitely was nudging me from in there. Something to do with what I'd just seen in the bookcases or the desk, something about a magazine, a napkin, an alibi. I didn't know what it was yet, but I had a feeling that whenever it dawned on me, I wouldn't like it one bit.

And then suddenly, I had it.

With fumbling fingers, I dug back into Simon's desk drawer until I found the New York City tourist magazine with its advertisements for current attractions. I called a phone number in one of those ads and got an answer that put a name and face to the vague picture that had been ominously building in my mind.

"Thank you," I said to the helpful person who answered my call, "thank you very much." But, in truth, I wasn't grateful at all—I was shaken, appalled.

And oddly, still puzzled.

It made sense now, at least some of it.

But not all of it.

I called Geof at the police station and told him what I had found out and deduced. "Get out of there," he said harshly, "and call me when you reach your office."

I got out.

"Jennifer Cain!" The curator of Oriental art almost trod on my foot as he rounded the corner. I still had my hand on the doorknob of Simon's office.

"Simon's not there," I said inanely and pointed back over my shoulder at the empty room. "I missed him."

"Ah," he said Orientally.

"Nice to see you," I lied. I turned quickly toward the exit and escape.

"I'll tell Simon you dropped by," the curator said.

"Don't bother!" I said, equally bright and cheery. I signed out, flashed my teeth at the guard and steered my shaky legs toward Baby.

I finally made it to the office, where the mystical grapevine had been twining, telling wild tales of the previous day.

"Jennifer!" Faye's eyes were big with sympathy. "I can't *believe* somebody would try to burn your house down!"

"Don't believe it," I assured her. "Nobody tried to burn it down, they just made a mess of it."

"Is it related to the murders?" Marvin asked.

"Probably," I said. "Where's Derek?"

"Late from lunch." Marv was disapproving. It was obvious that murders and mayhem were having serious effects on the discipline and morale of my staff. If the murderer wished to harm The Foundation, he was well on his way to success. I resolved not to be late or absent in the near future, no matter what.

"Phone for you, Jenny." Faye held out the receiver to me. The look on her face gave me a feeling that "no matter what" was about to be tested severely.

"Miss Cain?" The voice was vaguely familiar. Whoever it was had an awful cold.

"Speaking."

"Hampshire Hospital calling."

Oh God.

"Do you think you could come out here as soon as possible?"

Oh dear God.

"What's wrong with my mother?"

"I don't want to alarm you, Miss Cain, but the doctors feel you might want to, well, I'm afraid your mother is, uh . . ."

I experienced a terrible, traitorous moment of thinking: Please, not yet, not now.

I said, "Is she dying?"

"Yes, I'm afraid so. I'm so sorry. Can you come out?"

Mother, don't die yet, I'm coming.

"Thank you," I remembered to say. "I'm sorry, I didn't get your name."

"You're welcome, Miss Cain."

I heard the dial tone.

The office behind me was repressively quiet.

I dialed my sister's home, but had to settle for leaving a message with the maid: "Please tell Mrs.

Guthrie her mother is dying. Dying. D-y-i-n-g. Yes, that's right. Thank you. I'm sorry, too."

I debated as to whether or not I should call my father in Los Angeles and decided to wait until after the fact. There was nothing he could do but wring his hands and feel guilty. He'd be as helpless now as he'd always been.

I said to Faye, "Call Geof Bushfield at the police station, will you please, and tell him where I've gone and why. As for anybody else, it's none of their business."

"Michael Laurence?" inquired Faye, ever hopeful.

"He won't call," I said. "I think he may have left town already."

She looked as I imagined Cinderella might have looked if the Prince had not shown up with the slipper.

I didn't have to put my coat back on because I hadn't been in the office long enough to take it off. I had my hand on the doorknob when the phone buzzed again. I waited long enough for Faye to silently mouth a name at me.

"Simon Church," her lips informed me. Her hand covered the mouthpiece.

"Tell him I'll call him back," I said shakily. His call was a reminder of that other grim reality—the one in which death arrived via murder, not nature. Was I foolish to drive alone to the hospital? Geof might say I was and he might insist on a police escort—which is why I had asked Faye to call him for me. I couldn't take the time to wait or to argue with him because minutes might make the difference between whether or not I got to see my mother before she died. Anyway, there wasn't any risk. I knew I'd be safe:

According to the pattern established by the killer, the danger to me lay within The Foundation, just as it had lain in wait at the museum for Arnie, the theater for Moshe, the Welcome Home for Mrs. Hatch and the church for Minnie Mimbs. Death might be waiting for me at the hospital, but it wouldn't be my own.

When I stepped outside, I was shocked to see how late in the day it was. It didn't seem possible. Time should have been standing still instead of racing toward four-thirty already. By the time I got through rush hour traffic and reached the hospital, it would be dark. I hated to make the drive back alone at night even under the best of circumstances. Of course, there was no guarantee I'd be back before morning— Mother might linger so that I'd need to spend the night or even the next day at the hospital. I wished I had a toothbrush with me. I wished I had Geof with me. I wished I felt less drained from the emotional traumas of the last two days. I wished I was driving my own car and I wished I didn't know the terrible things I knew.

I switched on Baby's radio to a classical station, more for its calming than its cultural effects. But the selection on the air was a cacophonous screech of hyperactive violins. I fiddled with the dial, but couldn't find anything more soothing than a winter storm forecast on one station and a jazz trumpet on another. I turned the damned thing off.

"Well," I said to the car, "it's just you and me and the night, Baby." If it snowed hard, I would particularly miss my front-wheel drive. But if the storm came in off the ocean, as forecast, it would bring humidity that might turn to ice, and there's no car in the world that can handle our ice storms.

"How about a hurricane, God?" I muttered. "Just to top things off, put some icing on this miserable cake."

I was delayed by rush hour fender-benders and a malfunctioning stoplight. By the time I finally pulled through the stone gates of Hampshire Hospital, it had started to snow. The yellow that glowed from the windows of the hospital should have been the archetypal warm beacons in the night; they looked sallow and cool instead, and anything but welcoming.

I walked quickly past the volunteer on duty at the information desk and onto the elevator. The hospital had that busy, purposeful air that hospitals get around feeding time. Nurses' aides rolled food carts clatteringly down the long halls. Somewhere, from some room, an old man yelled that he was "hungry, dad blame it!" There is, at least, that sort of freedom within the prison of senility. A male attendant pushed "4" for me and then proceeded to stare fixedly at my feet all the way up. "It's a perfect day for bananafish," I said to him in parting. As the elevator doors closed on him again, he was still working it out in his mind, having evidently never read Salinger. I glanced down at my feet. They were cold and drippy from the snow, but they looked all right to me.

Sometimes, I thought, it is certainly hard to tell the players from the fans.

I waved a small hello to the nurses on duty at the desk. They looked surprised that I'd got there so fast, though I thought I'd been fearfully slow.

The door of my mother's room was closed.

I stood in front of it for a moment and stared at it

much as the attendant had stared, probably unseeingly, at my feet.

"Are you Mrs. Cain's daughter?"

A young male patient appeared at my shoulder and companionably stared at the door with me. He couldn't have been more than twenty; he might have been the young shuffler I'd seen on one of my earlier Sunday visits. He had brown hair that someone had neatly brushed for him and body odor. He looked as thoughtful as Einstein.

"You do not usually come to visit during the week," he observed.

"No," I said.

"Usually you come on Sundays and you do not often arrive this late at night."

"That's true. She's dying." I had a feeling he'd understand better than some people.

"That is true," he agreed seriously. My words sounded odd coming out of his mouth. "As are we all. Do you know, I have noticed that very many of the people I know tend to die. I wonder sometimes if it has anything to do with me."

"I don't think so," I said gently. "No, I definitely think that is not the case." I could have told him that very many of the people *I* knew tended to die, too, but that it didn't have anything to do with me.

He nodded his chin deep into his chest.

"Well, at least that is one good thing," he said with great dignity. He shuffled off. I opened the door of my mother's room. Someone had turned off the lights. That made me angry. I didn't think she should die in the dark.

I flipped the light switch.

Chapter 30

od damn you to hell!"

The curse hit me just as the lights came on. My nerves were already pretty well shot, so it didn't take much more than those hissed words to throw me back against the wall. But the shock to my eyes was greater even than the shock to my ears.

As I had expected, my mother lay like death on the bed.

As I had not expected, someone sat in a chair pulled up to the far side of the bed. That someone had jerked her head violently when I entered the room. Now her platinum hair lay tangled on her shoulders; her blue eyes were rimmed in ugly red and they stared at me with the hopeless, dreadful stare of someone who had just glimpsed the black hole of her own soul.

My sister.

She repeated the curse. It occurred to me that I'd never before had the experience of someone saying

"God damn you" and meaning it. It was chilling. Before I could react with anything more than a shudder of surprise, she bowed her pale head on the bed and took up where she had obviously just left off—sobbing.

"Is she dead?"

The pale head rose again and the haunted eyes glared at me over the covers. "Cut it out, Jennifer, you don't have to play your little game anymore."

"What the hell are you talking about?" I was getting fairly angry myself. Our mother lay dead or dying, and Sherry wanted to play hate-your-sibling games. I walked quickly into the room, past the door of the private bath, toward the bed to see for myself.

Mother was breathing softly and easily.

Perhaps, out of compassion, I should have been sorry to see that she lived. But I wasn't. I was overwhelmingly, selfishly overjoyed. Her death was one blow I wasn't prepared to absorb that day. "She's alive," I think I whispered, awed and grateful. "Oh, Sherry, Mother's alive!"

My sister stood up so abruptly she knocked her chair over backward. "Of course she's alive!" she hissed. "You call my house and you say she's dying, just to get me out here because you knew what it would do to me . . ."

"Sherry, I didn't . . ."

"Well, I don't care if she dies, do you hear that, I don't care! Why should I care! Who ever cared about me? You don't know, you don't know what it was like. You went off to college and left me alone with a crazy mother. Dad left me, you left me, she left me. And they hated us, people hated us. You don't know, you don't know what it's like to go to high school with kids whose fathers are out of work because of your own dad. You weren't there, you don't know . . ."

She was, without one single doubt, as hysterical as they come, but also as close as I'd ever seen her to getting down to bedrock. I stood paralyzed, waiting for her hysteria to wind down.

It never had a chance. As her voice rose to a scream of anger and anguish, nurses came running to calm her down. They couldn't have this kind of behavior in their hospital, though I wanted to tell them it was more healing than many pills they dispensed. In the best melodramatic tradition, two attendants held her while a nurse shot her with something that knocked her to her knees in a split second. I'd always wondered if hypos could really work that fast. For a tempting second I wondered if they had a second dose handy for me.

"We'll take her to a private room, Miss Cain," a nurse informed me disapprovingly. "Does she have a husband we should call?"

Numbly, I gave them the information they wanted and I watched the attendants lift my sister and carry her gently from the room.

I also told the nurses that I had received a phone call from the hospital telling me my mother was dying.

They said in shocked tones that it wasn't true and wasn't it simply awful how some people could play such cruel practical jokes? Would I like them to call the police and lodge a complaint?

I turned away from them and gazed out the window of my mother's room and saw that the night was very much upon us, as well as the blowing snow that pinged like sleet against the glass.

Then I looked down at my peaceful mother and realized that I had been wrong about what I'd told Geof that day in the carriage in the park in New York. What's *your* passion? he'd said and I had told him it was The Foundation. But it wasn't. If I had a passion in life, it was caring for and about this woman who had loved me until her body had betrayed her mind into forgetting such abstractions as love—and daughter.

"Yes," I said to the nurses, "it might be a good idea to call the police in Port Frederick. Ask for Detective Bushfield, would you please?"

They left me alone in the room.

It took me a slow-witted minute to comprehend that being alone in that hospital was probably not a very smart idea, not smart at all. A thrill of fear propelled me quickly toward the door the nurses had left slightly ajar behind them. I ran toward the comfort and safety of the lighted, populated hallway.

As I passed the closed door of the private bath in my mother's room, it opened quietly, swiftly.

Before I could react, I saw the warning of the absurdly tiny barrel of the absurdly tiny handgun. It looked for all the world like a child's toy, but it wasn't.

"Shut the door," said Allison Parker, the esteemed director of the Welcome Home for Girls, "and turn off the lights."

She pointed the gun in the direction of my mother's head. I did as I was told.

Chapter 31

Allison Parker? I was stupefied. It was so unlikely, impossible, unbelievable that I wanted to laugh. I wanted to reach out my hands and say "Very funny, Allison, now give me the toy gun."

For a moment, we just stood and stared at each other in the faint glow of a night light, installed for the safety of patients whose bladders called to them in the night.

She smiled. I didn't.

"How nice of you to come when you're called," she said, just as if I'd responded to a request for a pound of tomatoes and a gallon of milk for "her girls." As always, she looked about twelve years old, but a mean twelve. It *couldn't* be Allison Parker; I *knew* who the murderer was and it wasn't she!

"Did you kill them?" I said. I was damned if she'd hear my voice shake.

Her smile was a nasty parody of the one with which

she welcomed gifts and visitors to the Welcome Home. "I'll tell you what we're going to do," she said. I'd heard her say that very thing any number of times to her teenage charges, but never with so much steel behind it. "We're going to leave this hospital separately. You will walk out first. If anyone asks, you will say you are going to the cafeteria. You will not mention me because I will have this gun pointed at your mother until I see you drive around and flash your lights twice.

"You will wait for me in your car. You will not try to escape because if you do, I will immediately come back up here and kill her. I'm afraid I took a bus out, so I'll have to ride with you, Jennifer."

"Where are we going?"

She laughed.

"Your sister made it plain where you're going," she said, "but that's for later. First, you're going to your car. I'll give you two minutes to do it. Any longer and *she's* dead."

One hundred and twenty seconds gave me barely enough time to walk quickly down the hall, run down the stairs rather than wait for an elevator, open and start my car, drive around and flash my lights. It didn't give me enough time to write a note, whisper for help, call the police or fumble my keys.

She opened the door for me.

My muscles tensed with the knowledge that I could throw myself at her and her gun. But she anticipated my martyrdom.

"No, no, no," she simpered and leveled the gun once more in the single direction where I was most vulnerable: at my mother. "Your time starts now, Jennifer."

I stepped into the bright hallway, quickened my pace and didn't look back. I could almost appreciate the irony of the fact that I might, after all, never see my mother alive again. It also occurred to me that the situation had the makings of a good news/bad news joke.

The good news was that it wasn't Simon after all.

The snow that had sounded like sleet was sleet. Baby was already lightly iced, causing the door to jam for a heart-stopping moment until I finally and frantically jerked it open. There weren't enough of my one hundred and twenty seconds left to scrape off the windshield, so I had to drive blindly to the side of the hospital where I knew my mother's room was. I flashed the headlights.

In the time it took Allison to join me, Baby's massive heating system had warmed the interior of the car and melted the outer ice sufficiently for me to see to drive.

I knew the winding two-lane highway would be a slick sheet of danger. With any luck, I thought grimly, maybe we'd slide off the road into a tree, conveniently killing her without harming me. Such is the stuff of futile fantasy. I did not dare to instigate a crash because, on the ice, there was no guarantee the car would land where I wanted it to. If we plowed into a ditch—and I *did* survive the crash—I could freeze to death before the road crews discovered us in the morning.

I decided to try to navigate the roads so that we got wherever it was that Allison wanted us to go alive, and *then* I'd figure out my escape. I'd always wondered how I'd react if a rapist, say, kidnapped me and forced

me at gun or knife point to drive him somewhere—
would I acquiesce and hope for the best or would I
fight?

Well, I had the answer to that question if not to
some others. I wasn't about to *let* her kill me. She'd
have to claw for the opportunity. As she and her
deadly little friend climbed into the car, I was no
longer merely frightened. I was also mad as hell.

How *dare* she.

"Which direction?"

"Port Frederick. You're going home for the last
time, Jennifer Cain."

"Screw you." My peripheral vision told me she
looked a little surprised; she must have expected me
to be more intimidated. It was a stupid thing to say, of
course, though it felt wonderful to say it. I knew I
shouldn't put her on her guard by acting aggressive; I
should play the meek victim so she'd be surprised by
my attack when I finally made one. I was starting to
feel sure of myself, as if all future surprises would be
on my side.

More fool I.

However, my delusions of power steadied me during the hazardous, half-blind drive back to town.
Maybe I should have tried to get her to talk, to
establish a rapport with her, as they say, but I'm no
psychologist.

I just drove.

She just silently pointed the gun, and smiled that
dreadful parody of her Welcome Home smile.

I surmised that Allison had killed Florence Hatch
to get the bequest for the home and secure her own
job . . . the other killings must have been a cover for
that sole intent. There was probably some simple

explanation for how she lured Mrs. Hatch to her death, but I couldn't figure out how Allison managed to kill Arnie Culverson at the museum or how she—wiry but tiny—had the brute strength to manhandle Minnie Mimbs at the church.

But what puzzled me most was the feeling of, well, overkill. Surely she didn't *have* to kill four people just to camouflage one murder. It seemed like a lot of unnecessary trouble and danger to me—even given Allison's reputation as a workaholic. Maybe, in the best classic tradition of last-minute braggadocio, she'd tell me all about it before she shot me: The good news is I'll tell you how and why I did it, the bad news is these are the last words you'll ever hear.

"Turn left."

We'd reached the outskirts of Poor Fred. My shoulders ached from the effort of keeping Baby on the road, my eyes stung from the strain of squinting through the falling snow. But I did as I was told through several left and right turns. She was clever to keep me guessing block by block—I couldn't devise a plan of escape if I couldn't think more than half a block ahead at a time.

My worst moment was the one when I realized that Geof didn't know I had rented a wreck, much less what make or model. If he sent the police out for me, as he surely would, he wouldn't know where to look or what kind of car to look for. That moment of dreadful awareness was so bad I lost my concentration and very nearly drove us into a ditch after all.

All things considered, I wish I had.

We reached our destination.

As directed, I rolled Baby over the snow into the

dark parking lot, stopped the car near the door and turned off the motor. I stared straight ahead at the building to which Allison had brought me—the Martha Paul Frederick Museum of Fine Art.

What in the *world?*

Maybe she was going to duplicate her murder of Arnie Culverson, using me as leading lady? Like hell she was. I knew this building as well as I knew The Foundation offices and that was one small fact to my advantage. I intended to use it for all it was worth.

"I'll tell you what we're going to do," she said once more. I stared at the building. The only lights shone from the south entrance—the staff door—where the night guard kept watch. At intervals he would roam the building—inside and out—looking for just such intruders as we. I certainly hoped he found us.

"Look at me."

I made my movements calm and deliberate.

"My, aren't we displaying grace under pressure," she sneered. "I'll enjoy seeing that famous poise crumble. And it will." She laughed. "Oh, it most certainly will."

"Please . . ." I made the mistake of saying.

"Please?" Her eyes glowed as if I'd said the magic word and won the money. "Oh no, Jennifer, I'm the one who always says please, aren't I? Please and thank you and oh, I'm just so very grateful and oh, aren't you sweet to be so generous and thank you, thank you, thank you!" Her small, high voice rose in pitch and volume with each bitter, sneering phrase until it filled the car with bile.

"Do you know, Jennifer," she said, "that in the Far East, if a Buddhist wants to comprehend the American psyche, he sets himself the task of saying a certain mantra over and over. And do you know what that mantra is? It consists of the words 'thank you, please, excuse me.' Over and over again, the Buddhist repeats that American catechism. And thus he enters the soul of America.

"That makes me the archetypal American, wouldn't you say? I've been saying please and thank you all my goddamn life. And of course, I'm always saying excuse me in case I happen to offend the delicate sensibilities of the rich. You know the rules of charity, Jennifer—never say what you think, never say what you feel. Just smile and smile and say please and thank you and oh, I'm so very sorry, I didn't mean to offend."

She smiled that terrible smile again.

"Excuse me, Miss Cain, but won't you please get out of the car? Thank you so very much."

She was full to sickness with the bitter taste of begging. It didn't, somehow, seem the appropriate moment to point out to her that she had chosen her profession, that other more healthy personalities knew how to ask without begging, that for every donor who demanded eternal gratitude there were others who gave willingly from the heart, sometimes without even being asked. Nor did I suggest that she stop to consider the lack of proven and workable alternatives to our social and economic systems.

Perceptive as I am, I sensed she was not in the mood.

She continued to issue her instructions only one step ahead at a time. It was unnerving, effective.

"We'll walk to the staff entrance now."

When we stood there, with her so close I could feel the gun in my spine, she said, "Ring the bell."

"Why, Miss Cain!" the old guard exclaimed when he answered my summons. "Whatever brings you out to see us on such a night?" He glanced curiously at my companion.

"I'm Allison Parker," she surprised me by saying, "the director of the Welcome Home for Girls." I could hear in her voice the deceiving smile on her face. "Do you think we could come in? It's awfully cold out here."

"Of course, of course." He shuffled out of our way. As we followed him into the anteroom, he turned his back on us in order to open the inner door.

We followed him past that barrier. I automatically started to walk toward the log book where visitors always sign in. But that unthinking movement on my part separated me from Allison, who stood behind me, so that when the old man turned around he saw the gun.

She shot him.

Just like that. Bang, you're dead.

He hadn't even had time to change the expression on his face from startled to afraid. No wonder she hadn't cared whether he knew her name. No wonder she'd marched so boldly into the museum. It was easy to get past a guard; all one had to do was kill him.

She got one of her wishes, too: My poise collapsed into a horrified, craven puddle of terror and shock. "No!" I screamed, and it was only the sight of the little gun pointed once more at me that shut my mouth on hysteria.

"Simon's office," she said.

The corridor was black. I made my way by memory and feel. It was childhood's worst fears come to life—fumbling down blind hallways, scared of the bogeyman who will grab you in the dark.

The bogeyman walked behind me with her left hand on my shoulder and her gun in my spine again. I understood then how mesmerizing and controlling even the smallest barrel of a gun can be. I cursed myself for a fool, knowing that by safely driving us here I had probably squandered my only chances for escape.

In addition to all of which I had suddenly begun to take Allison Parker very seriously indeed. Excuse me if I have ever offended you, I wanted to beg of her, please don't kill me, thank you very much.

A faint light shone around the edges of Simon's closed office door on the north side of the building. How typical of him, I thought irrelevantly. Childishly, irresponsibly, he seldom remembered to turn off the lights when he left a room.

"Go in."

I threw open the door.

Simon Church raised his head from where it had been lying on top of his crossed arms on top of his desk and sleepily rubbed his eyes.

"Jenny!" he said and yawned. "You're late."

Chapter 32

Just in case he had some innocent reason for being there and for expecting me, I acted quickly to prevent a repeat of the tragedy at the staff entrance.

"She has a gun!" I shouted at him. "She killed Max!" I was still standing right in front of her; she'd have to shoot through me to get Simon.

Behind me, she took the steam out of my drama by laughing—possibly as much at my bravado as at the bewildered look on Simon's face. She said contemptuously, "I'm not going to shoot him, Jennifer. You can go in." With a sharp nudge of the gun on the back side of my ribs, she suggested I get a move on.

Finally he saw who she was and what she held.

"Allison Parker?" He was all incredulous disbelief, just as I had been, and it looked as real as mine. But he didn't look nearly so sleepy now. "Is this a joke, Allison? No, it can't be a joke. You don't have a sense of humor."

"She killed them," I said shrilly, panicky. My knees gave way and dropped me into the only other chair. "Arnie, Moshe, Mrs. Hatch . . ."

His eyes filled with comprehension and astonishment.

"I'll be damned," he breathed, "so you're the one. Oh, that's wicked, Allison, you are a nasty, wicked bitch."

She grinned as if she were quite enjoying herself. And I—I was filled with remorse for ever having suspected my friend Simon. Because that's exactly who I *had* suspected after my search of his office and it was Simon's name that I had presented to Geof on an incriminatory platter. What had I done to Simon's good name and reputation? How could I have been so stupid as to add two and two and come up with five?

He never took his eyes off her as he said, "I got a call from your office, Jenny, about four-thirty. I thought it was Faye with a cold. She said you had something important to tell me about Arnie Culverson's death and you wanted to meet me here at eight. I don't suppose you know anything about that call?"

"No," I said angrily, "but you might be interested to know that I got a similar call, supposedly from the hospital. My mother was dying, they said; would I come at once, they said."

His eyes flicked to me and then back to her.

"Pull the wings off flies, do you, Allison? I suppose you drown puppies and kitties, too?"

"Self-righteous, aren't we?" she purred. Then, viciously: "You want to compare sins, Simon? Then we'll see who gets to throw the first stone!"

This was too much for me.

"For God's sake, don't pretend you're no worse than anyone else, Allison!" I was thoroughly sickened by her murderous, self-deceiving egotism. "You—you've killed three people and you tried to kill Minnie . . ."

Silence grew large and heavy in the small room. She didn't respond to my outburst—I might as well not have been there and certainly I wished I weren't—but only smirked infuriatingly at Simon.

"You wanted the bequest from the will," he said accusingly, petulantly.

"Of course," she said. "She strung us along for years with hints of all the money she'd leave us if we were good little Christian girls. I did everything but get down on my knees and beg for that money. I curtseyed, I wagged my tail, I debased myself to that stupid woman." Allison's face darkened, suffused by the ugly red hate that ran through her like thick blood. "One week she'd say she would leave it all to us; the next week she'd get mad about some slight and she'd threaten to cut us off . . ."

I could well imagine it. As I'd told Geof, Florence Hatch was a wonderful woman, but . . .

"So when she finally, actually wrote a will," Simon said slowly, obviously thinking out loud, "you didn't want to miss your chance at last."

"She could have changed her mind," Allison said defensively. "And she *would* have, again and again!"

"And," Simon drawled, "you couldn't take the chance that she might die during one of those weeks when she'd decided to cut you off without the proverbial cent." He seemed almost to empathize with her while also loathing her.

"Well, you know how it is with philanthropists, Simon," she smirked. "We live for the day they die, don't we!"

A look of sheer disgust crossed his face.

"But the others!" I burst out against all known better judgment. "Why did you have to kill the others? And why me, why my parents' house?"

The loaded, threatening silence descended for a heartbeat. I thought I'd pushed her too far.

"But Jenny," she said finally. Quietly. Horribly sweet and unctuous. "I didn't . . . "

Simon seized the opportunity of her looking away from him to lunge violently across his desk. She stopped him with a single bullet that creased the back of his chair and missed his neck by millimeters.

"Down," she said as to a dog.

Wisely, he obeyed.

Her glance at me was briefer this time. She wouldn't make that mistake again; if we wanted to distract her, we'd have to do a smarter job of it.

"As I was saying," she continued smoothly, "I killed dear generous Mrs. Charles Withers Hatch, yes. And I killed Moshe Cohen, by dropping the drug in his wine at the cocktail party before the premiere. It was so easy! And there was such a crowd, nobody saw me slip the verse in his pocket."

"But he might not have died," I said. "What if the medicine hadn't worked the way you thought it would? What if he hadn't died, or he hadn't died at the theater?"

"That wasn't important," she surprised me by saying. "If he died, fine. If not, at least it would look as if somebody had tried to kill him. And when the cops found the verse I hid in the bed where Arnie Culverson's body was found, they'd think somebody killed him, too."

Simon looked suddenly as if he might be sick. I felt like gagging myself.

"And all that was only prelude to the murder of Mrs. Hatch?" I tried to keep my voice calm and nonjudgmental as if we were only discussing some clever thing she'd done. I was trying to fit all the pieces together. I was also trying to figure out some plan of attack and escape. And I wasn't yet succeeding at either effort.

"She had to die," Allison agreed as if it were the most reasonable conclusion in the world. "And quickly, before she changed her stupid mind again."

"How?" Simon sounded strangled.

"How did I do it?" The smirk was back, that insufferable, maddening, terrifying smirk. She was so proud of herself. "I'm certainly glad you asked that question." She giggled. "See? You're wrong, Simon, I do have a sense of humor."

She told us—with great pleasure—how she and the house parents had taken the girls to their regular Sunday night movie. Allison made sure they arrived late at a popular show so they'd have to split up their group and take separate seats in different parts of the theater. No one noticed as she sat down on the aisle in the rear. When the lights went off, she walked out. She knew Mrs. Hatch was attending a meeting that night, so she called and got her patron summoned to the phone. They must talk immediately, Allison said, about an urgent and confidential crisis at the home. She convinced the older woman to let Allison pick her up, promising to get her back to her meeting as soon as possible. Allison drove her to a secluded street where nobody would notice or remember the car, and fed her lies and doped coffee until Mrs. Hatch fell heavily asleep. Then Allison drove back to the theater, left Mrs. Hatch lying on the front seat under a blanket, and returned to her seat in time to leave with the others. The usher thought she'd only been to the restroom, if in fact he noticed little Allison at all. The girls all rode back in the van—as she knew they'd want to do—while Allison followed behind with her doomed cargo.

Later that same night she crept out of the home, woke Mrs. Hatch sufficiently to get the poor woman to stumble to the abandoned refrigerator, opened its door, sat Mrs. Hatch down, shoved the rest of her in and closed the door. Sleep turned to suffocation and then to death.

"She'd been in my car dozens of times," Allison said, "so I didn't care if she left strands of hair or fabric behind her."

So easy, neat and horrible.

"That explains Florence Hatch and Moshe Cohen," I said hoarsely. "But what about Arnie Culverson . . . and Minnie Mimbs . . . and me?"

"Good question," she said softly. "Maybe one of *you* would like to make a dying man's confession. Jenny? Or Simon, how about you?"

He laughed at her, but not convincingly. His normal ruddy complexion had paled beneath the black, late-night stubble on his cheeks, neck and chin.

"Am I a dying man?" he said.

"Oh yes," she murmured, "yes, of course you are."

"Are you going to shoot me?"

"Heavens no, Simon."

"How then?" he insisted.

"Well," she drawled, "let's just say it will be different from the way I'll kill Jenny."

My heart lurched out of control.

"And how will you do that, Allison?" Simon's voice and eyes were watchful now, alert for another opportunity to disarm her.

"By giving you your fondest wish, Simon," she said sweetly. "Of course the shame of it is that you won't be here to enjoy its fulfillment."

I had a hideous feeling I knew what she meant.

"I'm going to give you a new museum, Simon," she said. "I know how desperately you want one, everybody knows that, so I'm going to do you a favor and burn this old place down . . ."

"No!" Simon and I were on our feet at once, together.

"Sit down, children."

We fell back into our chairs.

"When they find what remains of you," she continued, "they'll say you tried to start a little fire, Simon, just a little arson that would damage this place just enough so there'd be no choice but to build a new museum. Unfortunately, the fire got away from you and—well, it's a pity, they'll say."

"My paintings!" His anguish was painful to hear. I felt its echo deep in my own soul. "My sculpture! You'll destroy centuries of art—no!"

"How will they account for *my* body?" I said.

"Oh, easily." Her smile was sugared ice. "You see, they'll guess that Simon lured you over here and then killed you, leaving your body in the fire where he could later claim you died accidentally."

"That doesn't make sense, Allison," I objected. "Why would anyone think that Simon would want to kill me?"

She gazed almost kindly upon him.

And he—that great, handsome, infuriating, childish, brilliant bear of a man—began to cry. Violently. Appallingly. Revealingly.

Chapter **33**

When he finally spoke, it was in the dull dead monotone of the defeated. His body, even the flesh of his heavy face, slumped.

"How did you know?" he begged piteously, though there was no pity in that room. "How'd you know I killed Arnie?"

I bent over and buried my face in my hands.

"I didn't at first," she told him. "The newspapers said it was suicide and the police said so too. But then I began to hear people gossip about how strange it was that he, of all people, would do that. At the time, it just sort of passed through my mind that maybe he'd been murdered.

"But I didn't give it another thought—until dear Mrs. Hatch told me she'd finally written her will. I knew I'd have to kill her if I wanted to be sure of getting that money, but I'd need a good cover. That's when I really began to think about Arnie Culverson's death and how easily it could be made to look like murder."

"You still didn't know?" he said in horrified disbelief. "You mean you just decided to make it look like murder?"

"Bad luck for you, Simon," she laughed. "I decided that what I had to do was plant an obvious clue—like a note—to point toward murder. Then, I thought, what if a second philanthropist were to die in a similar way . . . same drug, a note. And then I could kill Florence Hatch and it would just look like one of a series of related murders of philanthropists."

"The hypertension pills," Simon said dully.

"My aunt takes them," Allison smirked. "I used hers."

"And the notes," he moaned, "those goddamn stupid poems."

"In the best classic tradition, wouldn't you say?" She was highly amused. "Well, I had to think of some obvious gimmick, didn't I?"

"You planted that note in the testered bed where I left Arnie." Simon was barely audible.

"I wish I could have seen your face when that janitor brought it in to you! Oh my that's so funny! If I'd only known what I was doing to you! And you *had* to call the police, didn't you, because the janitor had seen that poem."

"They didn't know!" he suddenly cried out, wringing his hands in futile anguish. "They'd never have proved it was murder if it hadn't been for you!"

"And I still didn't know you'd really killed him," she said wonderingly. "Don't you think that's funny, Simon? Even then, I didn't know you'd killed him."

It was very hot in that awful room and suddenly I grew aware of the fact that I'd never removed my coat. Moving slowly so as not to alarm Allison, I unwound the scarf at my neck and then shrugged out of my coat and jacket. She supervised my every move as if she suspected I might have a submachine gun hidden in a pocket.

"Comfy now?" she cooed.

I looked uneasily from murderer number one to murderer number two; all it needed was a third and we'd have set the scene for *Macbeth*.

"Arnie Culverson, Moshe Cohen, Florence Hatch," I murmured. "Three of the Big Five . . ."

"Well, yes," she said modestly, "it had occurred to me that would make a lovely pattern."

Simon lifted his body heavily out of his chair and leaned his weight on his knuckles on his desk top. For the first time a glimmer of fight showed in his eyes. "You screwed things up for me, Allison!" he said loudly. "Everything would have been all right if you hadn't got them thinking murder!"

"Well you didn't exactly make life easy for me either, you bastard!" she screamed at him, shocking me out of my fog.

It was his turn for mocking laughter and he threw it at her enraged little face.

"You didn't like it when I played your game, did you, Allison love? I don't see why you should mind, dear . . . I played by your rules, didn't I?"

"Why couldn't you leave it alone?" she screamed at him. "Why'd you have to try to kill Minnie Mimbs?"

They didn't even hear me moan. I might as well not have been there; this was a killer duet.

Simon managed a crooked grin.

"You put me behind the eight ball, Allison. When I heard how Moshe Cohen and Florence Hatch died, it was real clear to me that somebody was using Arnie's death to cover another purpose. And that put me in real danger because if the cops tried hard enough, they might prove I killed Arnie. I didn't have an alibi for that night . . . and I was at the cocktail party when you doped Moshe. So it was obvious to me that I had to take matters into my own hands again. If somebody was killing the Big Five, I was going to have to have perfect alibis for the last two deaths. And the only way to manage that was to kill Minnie and Jenny myself."

"Oh, Simon," I choked. "Oh, Simon."

He turned his face toward me but he didn't seem to recognize me as anyone he knew.

"The holograph," I stuttered, "and the rental car."

"How the hell did you figure *that* out?" he said harshly.

"I was here this afternoon, Simon," I said weakly. "See, my car's in the shop and the only place I could find a rental car was at Lease-A-Lump." He closed his eyes and shook his head as if he couldn't believe his own bad luck. Allison had a most interested expression on her face. I said, "And the car they gave me is the one you had leased. The woman told me you'd said you needed a car because your own was being fixed, but I'd seen you driving your car that day you brought Derek to work . . ."

His eyes still closed, he smiled slightly.

"I thought you might know whether Minnie was supposed to live or die," he said, "and I wanted to know if she was under guard . . ."

"Which information I helpfully volunteered," I said in disgust. "Well, when I realized you had lied about your car, I got a funny feeling—I don't know, I just got worried because I'd known all along that you *could* have killed Arnie, and I—well, I drove right over here."

Where I had noticed the books on photography, including several on the subject of holography. And a napkin from a cafe near Soho where the Museum of Holography happens to be located. And a tourist magazine where I had noticed an ad listing the hours the museum was open. And a camera that reminded me of the photography show Simon had been putting together for the museum.

"What the hell is holography?" Allison said.

"It's a three-dimensional image," I said tiredly, "projected into space by means of laser light waves. Ever been to Disney World, Allison?" She nodded, but suspiciously, as if she thought I was making fun of her. "Did you visit the haunted house?" I said, while Simon folded his hands on his stomach and smiled smugly. She nodded again. "Well, then," I said, "you probably remember the 'ghosts,' don't you?"

"That's a holo . . . hoga . . ."

"Hologram," Simon pedantically corrected her. "Yes, as Jennifer said, it's a three-dimensional image that can be projected into space so it looks like a real person. Holograms can be made into, well, movies, so the images look for all the world like real people moving about the room. I've been working with the people at the Holography Museum in New York City, putting together a demonstration of the art for my photography show."

"And I'll bet," I said, "that one of the holograms you put together just happened to be a three-dimensional movie of you working at your desk in your office. So if a guard just happened to walk by outside, he'd see you—or what looked like you—bent over your desk. Really, Simon," I said wryly, "I'll bet it's brilliant. I'd love to see it sometime."

"Do come to the show," he said and grinned at me, seeming to forget for the moment that he and I had a new, as it were, relationship.

"Gee, you'll have to miss it, Jenny," Allison said, and Simon's face turned ashen again. "You, too, Simon. But while you're boasting, do tell us why you needed a rental car."

He slumped back in his chair again, the spark of defiance having slipped away with the reminder of what she planned for him and his beloved museum.

"I had to get to and from the Episcopal church," he said, "without being recognized. And I had to leave my car in the parking lot here so the guard would think I was still here. I fixed the burglar alarm on one of the windows and just climbed in and out as I pleased."

"So you finally had a perfect alibi," Allison smirked, "but hardly a perfect murder. Minnie Mimbs is going to live, you know. Who knows? Maybe right this very minute, she's telling how you tried to kill her. And won't *that* fit in nicely with my plans for you."

Defeat settled deeper and more visibly into Simon's body, his face, eyes, voice. Plainly, she enjoyed his misery and was in no hurry to end it. But then why should she? No one in the world knew we were there or for what deadly purpose.

"Why didn't you leave a note with Minnie's body?" she asked. They seemed so interested in each other's technique; but then experts in a given field do like to exchange trade secrets. "You knew about my little rhymes."

Wearily, he told her how he knew he couldn't have duplicated the typewriting or style of thought. And rather than take the chance that the police might begin to suspect the existence of two murderers, he omitted that one part of her pattern.

"The verse in my car," I blurted out, "did you leave it there, Simon? Did you mean to kill me the same night you tried to kill Minnie?"

"What verse?" His eyes slid a surprised look toward me before they skittered quickly away again. He didn't seem to be able to look at me anymore. "No! I didn't try to kill you, Jenny, I couldn't, I . . ."

"I left that note," Allison cut in coldly. "Actually, I hadn't planned to kill anybody else after I killed Moshe Cohen and Mrs. Hatch. I thought that would be sufficient to confuse the police. But I did want the police to be sure to keep looking to all of the Big Five for a motive, rather than to any single victim for a specific motive. So I decided I'd make it look as if Jenny and Minnie were threatened. I thought that would be enough, I thought that then my job would be done and that would be all I'd have to do." Momentarily, she looked furious with him and for a terrible instant I was sure it was all over. But she must have wanted to prolong her triumph, because she swallowed her fury. The smirk returned.

"Don't you want to know how I figured it was you, Simon?" she taunted him. "When I read that somebody had attacked Minnie, I knew somebody was trying to use my pattern. I had to get control of things again before whoever it was inadvertently incriminated me. So I decided I'd have to kill Jenny." If there was regret in her voice, I didn't hear it. "I started looking for an opportunity," she explained coolly. "I knew I'd never get her alone at The Foundation, so I drove by her house every night, but she was never there."

I'd been at Geof's, of course, thank goodness.

"Well, when I was driving by one Saturday night, I saw that dear Jenny had a visitor . . ."

"Oh shit," Simon said, almost like his old self.

"There was enough light reflected from the snow that I was able to recognize you," she said. "I was curious. It was obvious that Jenny wasn't home, and yet you went up to the door and didn't come back down the walk for a long time . . ."

"Simon, how could you do that to me?" My voice shook as I confronted him with my memory of his sadistic labors. "How could you . . ."

Still, he wouldn't look at me.

"Consider the alternative, Jenny," he said. "I might have killed you, you know. I couldn't bring myself to do that, but I had to make it look as if there'd been some sort of attack on you or your property. Nothing personal, you understand, love."

"Nothing personal!" I flew out of my chair toward him and screamed at his averted face. "Nothing personal, you rotten son of a bitch! What about my mother's china, what about her clothes and her rug that you unraveled, what about the clam sculpture, what about the baby shoes you, oh Jesus, Simon, you . . ."

He did look at me then. His expression was one of bewildered, wounded innocence.

"Huh?" he said and then we saw awareness in each other's eyes and we turned as one toward Allison.

"So I finished the job for him," she shrugged. "So what?"

"Why?" I screamed and Simon grabbed my wrists to keep me from lunging at her and bringing instant death down upon both of us. "What have I done to you? Why, why?"

The little hand holding the little gun began to shake. I watched, mesmerized, as the trembling crept from her hand through her entire arm, into her shoulders, down her body. She shook as if she were in the grip of a fever, she shook as if she were convulsing and the gun began to slide around in the air, pointing wildly now at Simon, now at me, now at nothing.

"Stop!" Simon howled at her, terrified the gun would go off in her shaking hand. "For God's sake, stop!"

As abruptly as it started, the violent shaking stopped, leaving her coated in sweat and staring wildly at us—no, not at us, at me.

"My father," she whispered. "My father's name was Charles Parker, but you wouldn't know that, would you, Jennifer? He was just another little man canning clams."

"Oh my dear lord." I sank into the chair again. Instantly, I understood the source of her hatred.

"He worked for Cain Clams for thirty-two years, Jennifer, but you wouldn't know that, would you? And he was going to retire, but when your father took the money and ran there wasn't even any pension fund left, was there, but you wouldn't know that, would you?"

"I know! I'm so sorry, I . . ."

"Sorry! You don't know sorry yet, you don't know it at all! My mother died that year, you *do* know that, I

292

put that much on my résumé. And then Dad lost his job and his pension and he left us and they split up us kids and I had to start begging, Jennifer, just like I always had to beg from The Foundation. Just like I had to beg from Mrs. Hatch. Thank you, please, excuse me, thank you, please, excuse me . . ."

"Allison . . ." But there was absolutely nothing I could say; what had happened to her father and her family was a terrible thing and it was my father's fault. And no amount of good works on my part would satisfy her lust for revenge. It didn't matter that it wasn't my fault. I was a Cain. And worse than that, I was someone else to whom she'd debased herself with hypocritical gratitude.

Somehow, from some inner source of bitter strength, she pulled herself together. With one last look of vengeful triumph, she turned away from me and leveled her eyes and her gun at Simon once again.

"This morning," she said curtly, "I learned that you were said to have been at the museum all Saturday night and I was the only person in the world who knew that wasn't true. That's when I figured it out, Simon, that's when I knew you were the one who'd attacked Minnie because you had the same alibi for that night, too. And the only possible reason for you to follow my pattern was if you had killed Arnie Culverson here at the museum that night. You had something to cover up, and that was it."

"He came to me in my office that night," Simon said, looking off into a painful space of memories. "And he told me he was going to write the museum out of his will. I didn't know he'd already done it; I guess he didn't have the nerve to tell me that much. I thought my only chance was for him to die before he could write the new will. So I killed him. We got in an argument. He got a migraine. He took some of his pills and when I saw the bottle, I knew that's how I could kill him. He took off his coat because he was hot and he went to the bathroom. I emptied the pills out into my hand and I dropped them in a glass of wine. They'd dissolved by the time he came back. I said to him, I said, It's okay, Arnie, let's be friends again, let's have a drink on it. And we did. And all I had to do was wait for him to get drowsy. So I said, Let's take a walk, Arnie, I want to show you something in the Chinese Wing. And we sat on the testered bed and talked until he got drowsy and then he went into a stupor. And I put him on the bed and I went back down and got that damn comforter and pillow and I fixed him up on the bed and I wiped my fingerprints off the pill bottles and put the bottles in his hand so his prints would be on them again. And I thought I'd saved the museum."

Simon smiled gently into space.

"I've received a fair number of shocks recently, ladies," he said. "But I suppose the worst was that morning Jenny came to my office and told me there was a new will and we weren't in it."

Quietly, he crossed his arms on his desk top, lay his head on them and gave up.

"Don't go to sleep, Simon," Allison chided him. "I'll tell you what we're going to do. Get up."

He did, in slow motion.

I wondered if he could—would—help me if I made a move to escape. I was not so stupid that I failed to appreciate the danger to myself now from him as well as from her. If we got rid of Allison, we'd still face each other, Simon and I, he with his guilt and I with my knowledge of his guilt. Would his meager supply of scruples survive a second test with my life? Or would I have another killer from whom to run—my good friend, Simon Church?

"You too." She was beginning to treat me cavalierly, like the dispensable commodity I was to her. "Up."

She directed us, step by excruciatingly terrifying step, into the guard room.

Simon saw the dead guard.

He didn't speak, but just sagged further into his bones. I knew then he would be useless to me; the enormity of the chain of events he had triggered had caught up with him and overwhelmed him. I didn't think he consciously wanted to die, but I couldn't think of a single reason why Simon might want to live.

While those thoughts skittered around my brain, Allison lit a cigarette. I had a wild image of her blindfolding us, tying our hands behind our backs and giving us one last puff before she blew our brains out. But she was not so fanciful; simple arson was her plan. On the floor, there was a small pile of trash which the guard had evidently been in the act of sweeping into a dustpan when we interrupted him permanently. She dropped the lit cigarette and the burning match onto the trash. Then she lit the other matches in the book and tossed them into a wastebasket close by a neat stack of old newspapers. She didn't care if it looked like arson; she *wanted* it to look deliberately set.

"I'll tell you what we're going to do," she said calmly. "I'm going to shoot Jennifer. Or, would you rather do it, Simon? No? Oh, that's right, you don't have the stomach for killing dear Jenny. Well, that's all right, I'll do it. And then, Simon, I'm awfully sorry but I'm afraid that for this plan of mine to work, you're simply going to have to burn to death." He stared at the dead guard; he didn't seem to hear her sentence of death. "Or," she smiled, "if you're lucky, maybe smoke inhalation will get you. Either way, when they find you, they'll think you got hoist by your own petard."

I wondered—in the middle of my own sudden desperation—how she thought she'd get him to submit to such horror; maybe she'd knock him out before she escaped, put his fingerprints on the gun, toss it beside his body and leave him to the flames. It wouldn't be hard for her to do, not in the mesmerized, submissive state to which she had reduced him.

Her gun, which had been leveled at a midway point between Simon and me, moved slightly in my direction. On the floor, the trash threw off burning sparks; the flames in the wastebasket tickled the newspapers which caught fire and warmed the old wood walls. I had a fleeting, futile thought of the smoke detectors that had never been purchased for this room. It was, in fact, the *only* room without them—one of the many absurd little economies to which we'd resorted to save a penny here, there. Surely, everyone had said, in the guard room of all places a fire will be quickly seen and extinguished. There'd even been a little article about it in the local newspaper, an article that Allison had undoubtedly seen.

The flames from the floor were now waist high. I didn't have much time left; she'd have to make her move soon if she was going to get out unnoticed and alive herself. Smoke made my nose sting and my eyes water. Fire crept toward the outstretched arm of the dead guard. I knew I couldn't bear to watch his cremation. I'd have to make a move before that happened.

"Simon," Allison said suddenly, and she laughed at her own cleverness. "Tell me—is there any last work of art that the dying museum director wishes to see?"

Of all the millions of words she could have strung together in a sentence to say to him, those were the cruelest. Of all the ways to rub it in, that was the worst.

It was also the dumbest mistake she could possibly have made.

Chapter **34**

She had underestimated not his love of life, but his love of art. He might have let her kill him, but not his treasures. It was not for himself, but for El Greco and Rodin and even Andy Warhol that he leaped at her—through the flames, over the guard's body, past me—with a great outraged roar. She, having felt so confident of his slumping defeat, was taken shockingly off guard. The gun went off, but wildly, because her shot was reflexive rather than aimed. Still, the bullet hit him, piercing the palm of one of his outstretched hands so that when he wrapped them around her neck he bloodied her. Over and over as he strangled her, as they struggled on the floor, he yelled, No! No! No! She never let go of the gun, but beat it frantically against his skull and against the torturing hands that gripped her neck and would not let go. Her feet and knees kicked up convulsively at him; her back arched; her body twisted in its futile effort to wrench free; her round blue eyes bulged. But in the end it came down to this: His strength was greater than hers; his passion for art was greater than hers for living.

I didn't stick around to watch her last kick or to see him toss her body onto the flames. It wasn't possible for me to get past them to the exit and fire blocked my path to the telephone with its button that automatically summoned the police. So I bent down and unzipped my boots as quickly as my shaking fingers allowed and then slipped the boots off so I could run quietly if I had to. I turned from the wrestlers and ran away from them, back down the long dark corridor toward the museum offices. I'd break a window in one of those offices and yell for help, I'd find another door and run for help, I'd . . .

"Jenny!" It was Simon, free of Allison, shouting at me. "Come back! Help me put out the fire! Please! Jenny!"

Then came his pounding footsteps after me. I wouldn't be able to crash a window or find a door in time, not before he caught up with me. I'd have to hide somewhere in the museum, then wait for a chance to sneak back downstairs to some route of escape.

He, who knew the building even better than I, found a light switch. And for a blinding moment, predator and prey were illuminated so that when I whirled around he could surely see the fear in my eyes. I saw the killer in his.

His bloodied left hand hung limp, but probably not useless. He didn't seem to have her gun; had it fallen into the fire? At least that afforded me the safety of distance—I would have liked to put plenty of distance between us.

"I won't hurt you," he lied. "Stop, Jenny, you've got to help me!" He wasn't in as good physical shape as I'd thought—already he was breathing hard. I felt a sudden fondness for those foul French cigarettes he smoked.

He started toward me again. I knew I'd never be able to escape him in the light. I was paralyzed; I didn't know what to do, though falling to the floor and weeping appealed to me a great deal.

The problem was solved for me by the fire. It reached the fuse box and the central wiring. The corridor shut down to black once more. As I took off running again, I wasn't entirely grateful for my reprieve, however, for in shutting off the electricity the fire had also disarmed every single alarm in the museum.

I took the steps to the first floor and then to the second floor two at a time. All the rooms on the second floor opened into each other, so there were no dead ends where I could get boxed. There we could play endless cat and mouse until I guessed wrong or he guessed right. As for the squeaky old floor beneath us, we shared its hazards equally; at any given moment it might betray him to me, or it might whisper to Simon, "Psst, she's over here."

The upper floors of the museum were dark as the inside of a temple on a moonless night. The original windows of Martha Paul's house had been boarded up to provide more wall space for the display of paintings. In my stocking feet, I fled by memory into the cold gallery that was second on my right. Oriental sculpture. I prayed to all the Occidental and Oriental gods I could think of to help me remember the locations of all the sculptures that might teeter and topple if I crashed into them, of every bench that might trip me, of the red velvet ropes that were meant to cordon off visitors, but which might catch me at the waist and throw me violently to the floor.

From that gallery, I passed silently into the Persian Gallery and crouched down beside a wood and glass display case to listen.

I didn't hear a sound from Simon.

I did hear sirens! And then shouting. What the alarms and I had failed to do, the neighbors had accomplished. I blessed them for having looked out their windows and seen the smoke or fire. I almost relaxed, thinking that with the arrival of the police and firemen, I'd be safe.

The wooden floor creaked.

I knew that creak. It told me Simon was in the Sculpture Gallery near the entrance to the Persian Gallery where I crouched. Fool, I called myself, idiot. If my situation had momentarily looked more hopeful with the coming of help, Simon's looked more desperate. He'd find me now because he had to. Somehow, he had to kill me and get my body into the fire before anyone knew we were there. Only then could he escape from the building. Once out, he could run up with the rest of the crowd and no one would question his presence. Of course he was there, they'd say, he was the museum director.

I stood up.

The floor did not creak, but unfortunately my knees did.

"Jenny, love."

I ran for the outer door and didn't give a damn how much noise I made. In fact, I began screaming. With people arriving downstairs, it seemed the sensible thing to do.

For a few desperate minutes, we wound in and out of the labyrinth of galleries like art devotees gone mad—past the knowing eyes of Buddha and Rama Krishna, through the reconstructed Shinto Shrine, back and forth, racing through thousands of years of culture like broken time machines.

I stopped screaming. I didn't have the breath for it any longer. Outside, the sirens were louder and closer; unintelligible yelling mingled with the wails. They'd never be able to distinguish my screams from all the others anyway, so I gave it up as a lost cause and crossed silently in my stocking feet into the Chinese Furniture Gallery.

Trembling, exhausted, I decided to crawl up onto the Testered Bed With an Alcove to hide. Once on the bed, I closed the thin silk curtains that surrounded me and it on all four sides. The bed itself, that fine old piece of furniture, centuries old, did not creak. They don't, I thought wildly, make them like they used to. I almost laughed hysterically, out loud.

I clamped my hands across my nose and mouth to stifle the noise of my breathing. I heard Simon follow me into the gallery. Then I heard nothing at all.

I waited.

He waited.

And then he walked over to the bed so quietly that I would not have been able to hear him if I hadn't been absolutely still myself. I tensed my exhausted muscles, ready to roll through the curtains and off the bed if he reached for me.

He stepped up on the platform.

He stepped into the little alcove that was attached to the bed, the alcove where a Chinese aristocrat might have entertained a friend with tea and conversation.

He sat down on one of the two facing benches in the alcove, just a thin silk curtain and about four feet away from me. Obviously, he didn't know I was there. Now I could hear the breathing *he* was trying to quiet—harsh gasps dredged up from deep in his unhealthy, equally exhausted lungs. I knew he'd never be able to hear my small movements over the noise of his own breathing in his ears. For a crazy moment, I wanted to speak up suddenly and say, *"Now* aren't you sorry you didn't stop smoking?" It was momentarily hard to remember that the man in the alcove was not my old friend Simon but my deadly enemy who had already killed two people and tried to kill a third.

With that chilling reminder, my moment of hysterical craziness passed, leaving in its place a cold clear fear that focused my mind wonderfully on one object —the question of how to disable Simon so I could escape.

I crouched silently on my haunches on the bed and wondered what in hell I was going to do next. My right foot went abruptly to sleep. Wonderful, I thought. If I made a rolling dive, I'd fall down again the minute I stood up. My left nostril started to run; I'd have given anything to blow my nose or sniff. The middle of my back ached, as did the inside of one ear. I didn't dare swallow for fear he'd hear me. And, naturally, I felt a tickle in my throat that made me desperately want to cough.

I had two choices: I could think about my misery or

think about getting out of there. I forgot the various bodily complaints. I stopped listening to the sirens and shouting because they were not likely to be of any help to me. It was a case of help thyself, or never need help again.

A weapon. I would have killed for a weapon. More to the point, I would have killed *with* a weapon. Did Simon have Allison's little gun? Like the wolf in Little Red Riding Hood, he certainly had bigger legs with which to trip me and stronger arms with which to grab me and more massive hands with which to strangle me. I had only a penknife tucked away in a pocket of my purse in Simon's office. And a winter scarf, draped helpfully across the back of the chair in his office.

There was nothing at hand with which to knock him out, nothing with which to stab him. I couldn't tackle him with my bare hands because he was at least eighty pounds heavier than I and not so terribly out of shape that he couldn't throw me about as he pleased.

What I needed was to catch him off balance and somehow restrain him just long enough for me to drag my painfully tingling feet to the exit. And from there tumble if I had to down the stairs to the first floor where there were windows I could crash open and shout out of.

My legs reported to my brain that they didn't like being bent for so long in so awkward a position. My brain told them to shut up and cooperate or we'd all be in trouble.

He was still breathing noisily and trying to cover the sound. Any minute now he might lunge out of the alcove to search for me again. Did he think I'd already escaped down the steps? Maybe I should continue to crouch on the bed until he left it; maybe he wouldn't detect my presence once he got the sound of his gasping under control.

Maybe the moon is blue, too. I didn't like those ideas; they depended too heavily on luck and this was a day on which luck hadn't shown any particular propensity to favor me. It was far more likely that any moment he *would* sense me kneeling so close to him. I had to act fast, before he did.

I peered at the old silk curtains, wondering if they'd do as a weapon to strangle him with. But no, by the time I tore them down he'd have heard me and lunged at me.

And then suddenly, I knew exactly what weapon to use and where to find it. I had it on me.

Slowly, I reached up to unfasten the top four buttons of my blouse. Soft as the old silk was, it still made a faint swishing noise which very nearly gave me a heart attack which would have rendered the whole exercise unnecessary. I stopped my hands in mid-air, paralyzed. When he didn't react, I knew he hadn't heard. I moved faster, but it was harder because now my fingers were really trembling.

I got the buttons undone.

Then I unfastened the buttons at each wrist.

I put my fingers between my breasts and touched the plastic clasp of my brassiere. Thank God I wore a front-opening variety. Pressing my fingers very tight against both sides of the clasp so my flesh would muffle the sound of the snap, I unhooked it.

With my right hand, I reached inside my now-loose blouse and slowly, slowly pushed my brassiere strap down to the middle of my upper arm. With the same hand, I then reached up inside my blouse from the wrist and pulled the strap down. It caught at my elbow. My heart missed a few beats while I straightened my arm so I could slide the strap past the obstacle, over my wrist and then over my fist until the half inch width of tough white elastic hung loose below the waistband of my skirt.

I would have breathed deeply if I dared.

I performed the same gymnastics with the other arm and the other strap. And still, the rasp of his breathing deafened his ears to my small sounds. When both straps were draped at my waist, I held my breath and tugged the whole bra down, then slid it around me until it pulled out from under my blouse and lay free in my hands on my lap.

Every woman knows the lazy way to remove her bra without having to take off her blouse and then go to the trouble of putting it back on again.

I slid my shaking hands through the armholes and wrapped the straps tightly in my fingers. I held the bra stretched out in front of me and it glowed white in the complete darkness: a weapon for a woman. Or a transvestite.

Well, Simon love, I thought, you've always wanted to get me out of my clothes and into a bed . . .

I lunged through the silk curtains toward his head. My aching legs failed me so that I fell upon him rather than tackling him. But his reflexes were a second too slow. I threw the bra over his head, wrapped it around his throat and pulled backward with all my strength.

The gun went off, a late reflexive shot like Allison's, answering my question as to whether he'd taken it from her.

Then I heard it drop on the floor and he threw both hands up to fight me off. By then I'd twisted the cotton and elastic several times behind his neck. I'd managed to knock him off balance so his upper body slammed painfully against the edge of the bed; his lower body twisted against the seat and floor of the alcove.

I half stepped, half fell off the edge of the bed, dragging his big head and body with me until I had him where I wanted him. The blows he beat on me were bruising and they hurt like hell.

I drew the straps around opposite sides of the thin post that supported the bed's canopy and tied the tightest knots I could. He fought and twisted so hard I worried the bed might come down on both of us. I prayed my knots and the ancient wood would hold long enough for me to run away.

I started to pull back from him.

One of his flailing arms knocked me back toward him and with his other hand he grabbed blindly for my hair, catching an agonizing handful of it and then using it to pull me down across his face. I bit his cheek as hard as I could and tasted blood. In that instant of his pain and shock, his grip loosened and I pushed myself away.

I rolled off him and the bed, missing the last vicious and desperate kick he aimed at me. I stumbled across the gallery floor while he thrashed like a beached and wounded whale.

Instinctively, almost unconsciously, I fumbled with my buttons, managing to fasten them again. God only knows what ridiculous and inbred sense of modesty prevailed. I was just tucking in the last edge of the tail of my blouse when the outer door slammed and several people with flashlights came pouring into the gallery.

The sudden light hurt my eyes so I put my forearm protectively over them.

"Jenny!"

I couldn't see him, but I threw myself toward the sound of his voice. Immediately, I was in Geof's arms and it was impossible to tell which of us was shaking more.

From that safe haven, I watched Ailey Mason and two firemen weave their flashlights around the gallery. All three beams came to rest at once on Simon, illuminating his desperate, bug-eyed, purple face and the white fabric that choked him.

Mason held a gun on him while the firemen cautiously untied him. Simon sank to the floor of the alcove, gasping painfully.

One of the firemen held up the weapon I had used. It dangled absurdly from his fingers. Mason flashed his light on it, then on Simon, then on me. And finally, the hysterical laughter bubbled out of my throat.

It must have seemed like a classic locked-room mystery to Ailey Mason: a man with a brassiere wrapped murderously around his throat, and the only woman in the room has her blouse neatly buttoned and tucked into her skirt.

The expressions on the faces of the men were so funny I began to cry.

Chapter 35

We sprawled—Geof and I and a weary cohort of neighbors, firemen and police—on chairs and floor of the Port Frederick Community Center. It had been opened to the scores of people who'd poured out of their warm houses on this frigid night to help rescue the treasures in the Martha Paul.

We drank gallons of coffee and munched dozens of doughnuts. We smiled companionably and virtuously at one another, sharing a communal pat on the back for our successful efforts. Some people closed their eyes briefly, but most of us couldn't sleep for the rushes of adrenaline surging through us.

We'd just performed a Herculean task in miserable weather and dangerous conditions. We were proud of ourselves. And exhausted.

By midnight, the old museum/house looked like an ice palace because as the firemen extinguished the blazes, they coated the mansion in ice. If the fire hadn't ruined it, the weight of the ice surely would—not to mention the water damage when all that ice melted, or the smoke damage.

While the firemen sprayed and hacked in the lower south end of the museum where the fire started, we volunteers formed a human chain to remove the art to relative safety. It was hard, heavy work, and God only knows how many nicks we knocked in costly picture frames, but we got the job done. Everything was laid on huge tarps spread on the snowy ground, then covered by other tarps. Now, armed police from neighboring towns guarded the several centuries of beauty and genius that lay on the lawns and in the parking lot of the museum. "Hell of a time of year for an outdoor art show," one volunteer was heard to crack.

We wouldn't know until morning—or even later—about smoke damage to our treasures. At least none was destroyed by fire. Well, almost none. We did lose several paintings in the storeroom, but they were there in the first place because they were examples of the occasional lapses of good artistic judgment on the part of certain curators. Nobody, especially those curators, would miss them. And we could use the insurance money from them to purchase more worthwhile works of art. Thank you so much, Allison Parker.

They thought they'd found her and the old guard among the icy ashes, but the fire had burned so hot and long at its source that identification of human remains was hard to make. Of Allison and the guard, only one was mourned.

Simon was taken first to a hospital to repair the damage I'd inflicted on his throat, and then to jail. I hoped his throat was sore as hell. I hoped it hurt so bad he could hardly swallow, much less talk. I hoped he was painfully bruised from his battering against the bedpost.

I was not in a forgiving mood. My head hurt where he'd yanked my hair and I had a few blue bruises of my own to nurse. I would have liked to have seen my teeth marks on his cheek; I hoped it got infected.

Geof's head hung off the back of the straight-backed chair where he had finally, wearily, slumped to a well-deserved rest. His arms hung limp at his sides and his eyes were closed. Without opening them, he said, "Your sister called the station to see if you are okay."

"My sister?"

He turned his head on the rim of the chair back and watched me ponder that surprise.

"I think I'll think about that tomorrow," I said.

He smiled and said, "Good idea, Scarlett. I'm told we got another call, too. Long distance. Gunnison, Colorado. Inquiry about the state of your health."

"Michael?" I said, yet again surprised. "So *that's* where he is. Wasn't that sweet of him to call?"

"Um," he said sardonically, "sweet."

"How in the world did he hear so soon?"

"You're big news, kiddoo," Geof informed me. "This story's already on the twenty-four hour cable news networks." He imitated an anchorman: "In Port Frederick, Massachusetts, tonight, a mass murderer turns out to be a mass of murderers!"

"Don't know that I'd call two a mass," I said and had a moment of déjà vu. Where had I said something like that before? I was too tired to try to remember; everything seemed long ago and far away.

I turned my head and looked at a volunteer who was sunk in a heap on the floor about a yard away from me.

"How you doin'?" I said gently to Ginger Culverson. She'd been one of the first volunteers to respond to the plea over the local radio. Even Franklin and Marvalene had come out to help—they huddled now in a corner of the room, audibly telling each other how wonderfully altruistic they were.

"I ache," she said and smiled sadly back at me. "Bodywise and heartwise."

"You aren't the only one who misjudged him," I told her, as if that could help. "You'll have to get in line behind me, for instance."

"I liked him a little differently than you did, Jenny."

"I know. I'm sorry."

"We'll get our new museum now, won't we?" she said, and even managed to sound as if she cared.

"Either that," I said, "or we'll have to set up shop permanently in the parking lot."

"Guess the insurance will build it," she said.

"I hope," I said.

"But you could probably use some financial assistance to make the new museum bigger and better," Ginger mused.

"Undoubtedly," I said carefully.

"Well, here I am," she said brightly, just as her eyes filled with tears. "Simon's dream come true."

We exchanged teary, ironic smiles before she buried her head in her arms. Her father, I thought, would have liked her so much.

Ailey Mason trotted in the front door of the center. I watched him search the crowd for Geof. Once he spotted us, he slowed down to a weary trudge and made his way through the volunteers to stand in front of us.

"Mr. Mason," I said formally, "you don't happen to have a certain article of clothing for me, do you?"

He actually grinned and looked his age.

"Evidence," he said sternly. "We have to hold it as evidence."

"Oh dear," I muttered while I imagined a lot of cops getting a lot of good laughs. I turned my head to plead for special dispensation: "Geof?"

"I'll get it back for you," he promised and leveled Mason with a cold look generally reserved for suspects. Mason swallowed his laughter and turned on his heel to search out the more sympathetic and good-humored comforts of hot coffee and doughnuts.

I had closed my eyes and was nearly napping when I heard Geof say my name softly.

"You called?" I said and smiled at him.

"When this is over," he said, "I'll have to get a move on moving, so to speak, out of my house."

"I suppose you will," I said neutrally.

"I just wondered . . ." He hesitated. "Do you have any architectural preferences? Contemporary? Cape Cod? Federalist? Tudor?"

"Actually," I said, "my architectural preferences are more along the lines of Cheap. Easy To Clean. Comfortable."

He laughed and I said innocently, "Why, pray, do you ask, good sir?"

"Well." He seemed to have developed a hesitation in his speech that I hadn't noticed before. "I've been thinking how I need a new place to live . . . and how

313

you don't want to live in your parents' house now . . . and . . ."

"Geof," I said, "I don't know how I feel about being number three of anything."

"I know." He was humility itself. "I don't blame you."

"I'd like to think this over," I said gently, "and give us some more time to see what develops."

"Sure," he said quickly, "I can see that, sure." But he sounded disappointed nevertheless.

I rolled my head over the rim of my chair and smiled at him again. "Geof, have you ever lived with anybody without benefit of marriage?"

"No," he said, "actually, I never have."

"That would be a first, then."

He was beginning to grin back at me.

"Yes," he said, "that would be numero uno."

"Good," I said and leaned back again and closed my eyes. "I like to be number one."